# Best Gay Stories 2017

# Best Gay Stories 2017

edited by JOE OKONKWO

**Lethe Press**
**Maple Shade, New Jersey**

# Contents

# Introduction

We hear a lot about the "gay experience." It is often evoked in a generic way, as if that experience was identical for every man attracted to another man everywhere. In that evocation, the gay experience is monotonal—it sings in one voice.

This is totally incorrect. I know men of different hues, different shapes, different ages, backgrounds, and vision. In actuality, gay experience sings in a variety of voices, a true chorus rather than single tone. In our current national climate, where truth and facts are often denigrated or outright dismissed and where years of painstaking political and social justice progress is in real danger of being rolled back, our voices, the truth of our experience, and getting that truth out into the world are more critical than ever. Listen to the many voices.

I read many, many stories for this anthology. The ones I bonded with and chose to reprint were the ones I found that turned preconceived notions of the gay experience upside-down; that shattered or undermined my expectations; that showed me that there are elements of gay life in places (sometimes otherworldly) where I had not thought they would/could be. In short, these stories represent a vivid cross-section of gay experience and the voices with which they are told are unpredictable and, at times, dangerous.

This anthology celebrates our eclectic voices. In this volume, you'll hear voices urban and rural; voices sex-inflected and soulful; meth-induced and melancholy; humorous and dramatic; ghostly and complex. Each and every one is rich in timbre.

I hope you enjoy *Best Gay Stories 2017*. Its many voices ring out loud and clear.

# JOE OKONKWO
Spring 2017

# How to Survive Overwhelming Loss and Loneliness in 5 Easy Steps

DAVID JAMES PARR

---

Furnish your new apartment with a homely wooden chair you find abandoned on the sidewalk. It's like the last puppy left at the pound, the last Christmas tree left in the lot, the last person to stagger out of a singles bar: look at it the wrong way and it will collapse.

Buy a shower curtain adorned with big red apples but don't hang it. You're not sure about the apples. Maybe you should have bought the one with the school of goldfish swimming across it. Which are more cheerful: apples or goldfish? You can't decide.

Hit your head on the bare curtain rings every time you get into the shower. Listen to them rattle behind you like gossipy party guests.

Sit in your new old chair. It creaks and wobbles but you trust it not to give in completely.

At the suggestion of your mom, who has been through three divorces, buy a ficus tree and put it near the front window. "Something green and alive," she says. Remind her that frogs are green and alive, and that she is terrified of them.

At a flea market, get an ashtray with a picture of Niagara Falls painted inside. You've never been there. You don't smoke.

Within a week the ficus tree starts crumpling, its once green leaves littering the floor as if scrambling desperately for another plant to populate. When your mom asks, "Didn't you talk to it?" say, "Yes, Mom, that's probably why it killed itself."

---

Buy a pack of cigarettes and practice inhaling. Buy a mirror and watch yourself practicing. Use your Niagara Falls ashtray. Pose in your new old chair and pretend to be an aloof character in a French film who doesn't care about *l'amour*.

Ask your mom: "Apples or goldfish?"

"Are you still taking sleeping pills?" she replies.

Lie and tell her, "No." Lie and tell her you'll call her back.

Browse the Self-Help section at the bookstore. Study the lengthy titles skating furiously down the spines of the books: *He's Just Not Interested In You, Okay?* and *Are You Crazy? Dump the Jerk!* and *How To Survive Overwhelming Loss and Loneliness in 5 Easy Steps*.

## Step 1: BUY THIS BOOK!

Browse the other customers in the Self-Help section of the bookstore. Notice how much you don't resemble them: their nervous stares, their drab clothing, their palpable desperation. Feel sorry for them. Make sure they don't see you taking a copy of the book to the cash register. Tell the nosy clerk, "It's for my sister," then add a trio of gruesome crime novels featuring serial killers. Say, "Those are for me," and wink creepily.

Price mattresses but don't buy any, even though your back aches from sleeping on a pile of blankets on the floor. You don't know whether to buy a Single or Full. You feel somewhere in between.

Call Paul. Don't leave a message, but do leave a solid twenty-six seconds of definitive silence before hanging up.

Identify more with the serial killers in the novels than the FBI agents. Study how they mess up. Plan how you would do it better: what weapon you would choose, how you could get away with it, where you would flee. Mexico, Copenhagen, Nova Scotia.

Start hanging out at the coffee shop down the street from your new apartment, the one that is open until midnight and sells fancy coffee for too much money. Do crossword puzzles. Jam letters into the tiny squares, sometimes two at a time, the curves of the letters smashing into one another like ill-fated lovers.

When Paul comes into the coffee shop one night, pretend not to see him. Pretend that he doesn't see you sitting alone in the back. Pretend not to notice the cute man in the blue turtleneck at the front table whom he meets.

And kisses.

Even though your bladder aches and feels full as a water balloon, don't move from your dark spot. Drink from your empty latte mug. Pretend to read your book.

Wish Paul was dead.

Wish the cute man in the blue turtleneck was dead.

Wish you were dead.

Buy a new set of kitchen knives. Buy a baseball bat. Buy travel guides to Mexico, Copenhagen, Nova Scotia. Pull out your copy of *How To Survive Overwhelming Loss and Loneliness in 5 Easy Steps* but read it only in fits and starts: on the subway in the morning, behind your office building at lunchtime, in your bathtub while letting the water around you slip from hot to cold.

## Step 2: GET YOURSELF BACK OUT THERE!

In bars, introduce yourself as Trevor, Nikolai, Hans—all names you wish were yours. Adopt a vaguely European accent and tell people you are visiting for the weekend. When they ask you what you like in bed, tell them: clean sheets.

Buy a goldfish. Fill the wide square vase that used to hold weekly gladiolas from Paul with water and put the goldfish in it. Name her Gladdie.

Work late, but don't do much work. When you turn out the light in your office, stare into the darkness around you. Worry that Gladdie may be lonely.

From the corner of the coffee shop, watch intellectuals play word games. When they leave, open the Scrabble box and steal a couple of the tiles, the ones loaded with points. *Q* and *X*. When you get home, flush them down the toilet. Now nobody will be able to score.

Put on a tight ribbed undershirt, blue jeans frayed in the crotch and a spritz of designer cologne. Brush your teeth and then squirt breath freshener into your mouth. Say, "Hello" to yourself in the mirror in as many different languages as you can.

At the bar, tell the tall Mexican bartender, "Hola!" and order a vodka y tonic. Leave a two-dollar tip. Drink it fast.

Order another one. The second is stronger than the first. Leave a three-dollar tip, then go out onto the dance floor which is not yet crowded. The songs all sound the same. You are not sure when one ends and another begins, much like your past relationships. The lights swirl around you in different colors. Smoke is piped in with long, heavy gasps, as if from a train engine's spout. It sprays over the crowd, soaking you all in one musty scent.

Dance closely to the guy nearest you. Meet his eyes briefly, then turn casually. Brush against him. Turn again, to make sure he is still looking. Stop dancing at a lull in the music, as if you are too hot, and wipe sweat from your forehead. Avoid eye contact and head back to the bar. Order another vodka and tonic.

The third drink is stronger than the second. Forget to tip.

Lean against the bar. Pretend once again that you are an aloof character in a French film who doesn't care about *l'amour*.

Notice that the man leaning next to you is drinking something that glows green. "It's called Kryptonite," he tells you. Make a mental note of this, for the next time you go out. When he asks you your name, tell him, "Christophe."

Finish the vodka and tonic and head back onto the dance floor. Weave your way through. Find the most attractive man and then dance near him.

Smile.

When he offers to buy you a drink, accept it. Ask him, "Apples or goldfish?"

"Around the corner," he answers, licking his lips as if he's just said something dirty. Excuse yourself to the men's room, then quickly exit the bar. Hail a cab, jump in the back, try to remember how many vodka and tonics you drank. Try to remember where you live.

### Step 3: DESTROY *ALL* REMINDERS & MEMENTOS!

With your hole punch stolen from the office, erase Paul's face from certain photos in which you think he looks happy. At work, flirt with the hunky mail delivery man whom Angie from the next cubicle has told you is married with three daughters. Make him visibly uncomfortable with comments about his big biceps. Later, tell Angie about it in the break room and make her visibly uncomfortable.

Don't be sad when Gladdie dies abruptly. You've had shorter relationships. Whisper a prayer: the serenity prayer, the only one for which you can remember the words. "God grant me the serenity to accept the things I cannot change," then screw up. Say, "The wisdom to change the things I can and the, and the—" Don't finish. Flush Gladdie down the toilet.

At a high volume, listen to music by angry female singers who have been discarded, left, dumped—everything that is also done to garbage.

Leave Gladdie's vase full of water. Steal the letters *R*, *I*, and *P* from the Scrabble game at the coffee shop, drop them into the water and let them rise to the surface as a floating eulogy.

When Paul next comes into the coffee shop wearing a shirt you bought him for Christmas years ago, go over and say, "Hi." When he says, "Hi?" like a question, answer him with, "No, I ran out of pot weeks ago."

When he doesn't laugh, tell him, "Don't lose your sense of humor, buddy. It was your best quality."

Make sure to say "was" like he's dead. Make sure to say "buddy" like you're friends. Make sure to say "Nice shirt," before knocking his coffee into his lap. Storm out like an angry female singer with a song to write.

While exiting, try not to picture him standing outside of your apartment building after three years asking you, "Don't you feel like things have gotten strange between us?"

Try not to picture him standing outside of your apartment building after three years telling you, "I'm sorry, I just don't think I'm attracted to you anymore."

Try not to picture yourself standing outside of your apartment building after three beers begging him to not break up with you.

Don't turn around to see if he's watching you leave. Don't cry until you are three blocks away, and then only behind some hedges, and then only inaudibly. Tell a concerned stranger who stops that you have severe allergies. Wonder if it's possible that you are going crazy.

Go back to the same bar as before and order some Kryptonite. Pretend it tastes good. Ask the bartender, "What is in this anyway?" When he explains, act like it's the most interesting thing you've ever heard. Act like he's explaining NASA, ASCAP, DNA.

Meet a man drinking the same green drink. Introduce yourself as "Gustav." Accept when he offers to buy another round.

Go home with this man. Share a taxi and watch as blocks and blocks whir by you like running water, all blurred into the same color of burnt orange. Hope that there will be a cab somewhere near when you leave. Hope that you will have cab fare when you leave.

Don't notice how drunk he is as he fumbles for his wallet. Don't notice how drunk you are while you are watching him fumble for his wallet. When you both stumble on the way up his stairwell, say: "Well I guess neither one of us is Superman."

Don't ask for his name. Don't give him your real one. When he calls you "Brian," while undressing you, say nothing. When he slurs, "I miss you so much, Brian," put your tongue in his mouth so he can't say anything else.

Notice over his shoulder a framed photograph of him kissing another man who looks vaguely like you. Same color of hair, similar chins, identical noses. When he says, "I love you, Brian. I love you so much," don't interrupt him. Tell him, "Me too." Tell him only, "Me too."

### Step 4: RECONNECT WITH OLD FRIENDS!

Ignore Dan E. when he asks why you have an empty vase with Scrabble letters. Ignore Dan E. when he asks why there are piles of dead leaves around your apartment. "Leave me alone," you say, then giggle. Dan E. stares at you blankly. "It's a pun," you say. "It's a double entendre." You figure Dan E. would appreciate this, since his own name is a homonym. You are talking in a shrill, too-loud voice. "Get it: leaves. *Leaves!*" Since Paul, your voice seems to have gone up an octave and is stuck there like a radio with a busted knob.

This is how you mark time now: *Since Paul.*

Dan E. reads the back of your Self-Help book and suggests, "Maybe you should try a two-step class rather than the five."

Say: "Two doesn't seem like enough."

"I meant dancing," he says.

Snap, "I know what you meant," in a tone meaner than you intend. Apologize. Promise him you'll go off of the sleeping pills. Promise him you'll hang a shower curtain. Convince him that you are your Old Self and A New Me at the same time.

Commit to a Single but don't buy sheets. The sheets you have are Full and were Paul's and don't fit your new mattress at all. You take this as a sign.

When Dan E. phones later, ask him, "Apples or goldfish?"

"Seriously, get off the pills," he says.

Buy a new ficus tree and ask for instructions on how to keep it alive. Buy two goldfish so that neither will ever be lonely.

On your way out of the store, run into Paul by chance as he comes out of the drugstore next door. Realize how frighteningly small big cities can be. He's wearing a coat you bought for him on his last birthday, brown corduroy with elbow patches that would look silly on anyone else. Thoughts of his body snake their way into your brain: the dent in the center of his collarbone, the camber of his earlobes, the spongy curve of his penis. He approaches you like a freight train, all hips and zipper. There's nothing you can do except brace yourself.

Wonder if you shaved this morning. Try to remember if you put on deodorant. Wish you had just popped a breath mint.

"Hey," he says, smiling, but it's an exaggerated version of his normal smile. Possibly he's bleached his teeth. He opens his arms and hugs you firmly but awkwardly. Hug back as if this is an easy thing to do. "So how are you?" he asks, breaking the embrace. He's eyeing your new fish, suspended in a large plastic baggie full of water.

"Good, you?" is all you can manage.

"Just picking up necessities."

Try not to notice that condoms are among the necessities. Try not to imagine him fucking another boy who isn't you.

"How's life?" he asks. "Anything interesting going on?"

"Lots of things interesting," you say, your mouth dry enough that it comes out as, "Loss of things interesting."

Paul nods, then smiles the too-big smile again. "Well, nice to see you. Talk to you later," and he pivots and turns with the grace of a ballet dancer. Try to turn around. Fail. Watch him walk away. Watch him turn his head slightly to see if you are watching him walk away.

Once home, open your new set of kitchen knives and take out the shortest of the bunch. It still looks grotesquely large when placed against your slender wrist. The idea suddenly seems absurd.

Decide on sleeping pills instead. Take one, then three, then nine, chased by water from the faucet. Get into bed.

Your travel books sit in a polite stack beside your mattress. Think of how you'll never go to Mexico, Copenhagen, Nova Scotia. Think of how the only thing to your east is a large, dark ocean where the *Titanic* sank. Arrange yourself on your mattress in the position in which you'd like to be discovered.

Don't dream of Paul, but when you do, remember that it will be the dream you have forever.

Don't wake up.

Wake up with jelly beans caught in your throat. Vomit them onto the floor beside your bed.

Don't wake up.

Wake up with egg yolk in your mouth.

Wake up with the mattress pressing up against your body rather than your body pressing down on the mattress. Get up for a glass of water, knocking over the stack of travel books. Glance at the clock and notice that it is two days later. Realize that your new goldfish remain trapped in their plastic baggie, and that their plastic baggie is sitting lopsided on your kitchen counter precariously next to the sink. But somehow you are all still alive.

### Step 5: ENJOY BEING YOU AGAIN!

Buy tickets to a romantic comedy but keep your arms folded across your chest in a protective manner while you sit in the theater and endure it. Every time someone says a line you find sappy, cluck your tongue, roll your eyes, glare at the couple sitting beside you.

Notice that your ficus tree has three remaining branches, two reaching for the ceiling and one thumbing for a ride. All of them are bare. It resembles the hand shape which means "I Love You" in sign language.

"It blends the *I*, the *L* and the *Y*," Paul explained on your first date.

You took this as a sign.

When Angie from the next cubicle asks you to lunch, accept. When at lunch she asks casually, "How come your sweetie Paul never swings by for lunch anymore?" try not to collapse into heaving sobs. Don't stutter, blubber or sputter. Instead, calmly finish chewing your BLT sandwich.

"It blends the *B*, the *L* and the *T*," you jokingly explained to Paul on your first date, inventing a hand shape. It was the first time you made him laugh.

"He broke up with you?" Angie asks incredulously after you tell her, her eyes going wide, a bit of mustard trapped at the corner of her mouth. "I would have thought it would be the other way around."

Don't stutter, blubber or sputter. Instead say, "We should have lunch more often, Ang," and wipe the mustard from her lip with the corner of your napkin.

When Paul next comes into the coffee shop, look at him momentarily but don't stare. Take your empty mug up to the counter. Flirt with the cashier. Make sure Paul sees you looking, taking, flirting— but leave without saying anything, like an aloof character in a French film who doesn't care about *le Paul*.

Accidentally leave your Self-Help book behind on the coffee shop counter, but tell yourself it is deliberate. Consider it **STEP 6**. Wonder if it's possible that you are going sane.

Go back to your new apartment where your bare Single awaits you, floating in the middle of the room like a lifeboat. Don't turn on a light. Lie down on the mattress and shut your eyes. Decide you'll get rid of your new old chair. Decide you won't do as much sitting.

Promise the ceiling that you will sign up for Two-Step lessons. Promise the ceiling that you will study another language: maybe Japanese. Promise the ceiling that you'll get rid of the sleeping pills, and not in the way that you've already tried getting rid of the sleeping pills.

Remind yourself of the enormity of the universe and how small Paul really is in context. Convince yourself that three years is really not such a long time. Remember that the average life span for a fruit fly is thirty days.

Consider getting a tattoo, piercing your navel, doing crunches—all things that once seemed painful but now seem entirely possible. Dream of sumptuous meals, bucolic forests, sexy movie stars. Dream of having a sumptuous meal in a bucolic forest with a sexy movie star.

Rethink your life in anecdotal form, as funny and poignant short stories you can tell and retell later at dinner parties. Try to come up with better endings. Try to come up with a punch line.

Look at your two goldfish swimming in their tiny bowl and hope that they fall in love. Somehow you are all still alive.

Think: *goldfish*. Definitely goldfish.

# Black Sheep Boy

## MARTIN POUSSON

L ike a morgue, no matter the blistering pavement or the bulb-red temperature outside, the classroom remained a cold chamber. Windows frosted inside with tiny stalagmites of ice rising around the edges. Books stiffened like frozen meat and made slapping sounds when the covers shut. And chairs all stuck in place, screwed down by the alabaster man in front of the room.

"Morphodites and Bedlamites," our junior-year English teacher shouted over the heads of the class, while a cloud of white smoke billowed out of his mouth.

Mr. Hedgehog, as we called him, was a prickly short-limbed monster who wore a frock coat no matter the weather and wielded a baton like the conductor of a manic orchestra. He brought the baton down on our essays as if they were hideous scores of sheet music. He beat on the covers of books as if they were hidebound drums. More than once, he beat on the back of a pupil's hand. Then, lightning quick, he'd snap out the words: "Just a love tap!" His tongue practically hissed against his teeth.

Before we were born, he often told us, before we were "dirty thoughts in our dirty parents' minds," our city had been the site of famous riots, with fire hoses, street bombs, and bloodhounds. At the start of one long hot summer, "the Blacks just rose up," he said, "and the South fell down."

He taught English but rewrote history with every book we read. His baton slapped my desk and sometimes slapped my hand too when I corrected a fact or a date. About the riots, he had the year right, but the city and state were wrong—and there was something else wrong too. He spoke the word "Black" as if it was the sound you made at the first bite of a wretched meal.

During exams, he paced the aisles with his baton, bringing it down on the head of the student who reached for an eraser or a bottle of whiteout. He saw any answer but the first as evidence of cheating and any stray ink on the page as evidence of guessing, more vile than cheating. He saw closed eyes as the work of moles and crossed-out words as the mark of worms. He saw errors in us all and even foresaw our end, as he put it, "scratching out the days like birds on a shrinking shore." What exactly he meant, we couldn't figure out, except that it sounded like the last line of a novel. Maybe one he wrote? Like a lot of our teachers, he hated teaching, hated especially teaching his subject and dropped reminders of his once promising writing career before the Great Sacrifice he made for us all. He trusted no book and told us how every author got it all wrong except one. Dizzy with opium and teenage girls, with salty air and sailors, with jazz and martinis, with gunpowder and arms, every American writer wrote a pack of lies, he said, except the one who came on like a liar—with a fake name and the full costume of a fake Southern gentleman. When we read the *Only* Great American Novel, our teacher fondled the ribbon tie he wore and, at each dramatic plot twist, brought one of the tips into his mouth for punctuation.

"Can't depend on nobody but your slave," he told us when we reached the sidewinder ending. "That, *mes enfants*, is the moral."

When I raised my hand with a correction, he delivered a sharp love tap to my knuckles with his baton and said, "Not this time, smartypants. This time you let it stand or dance those prissy feet right back to the counselor's office!"

No else said a word, frozen in their seats, frozen in time, so I let my hand fall. In the next row, another student sat stiff but angled his head around to look me dead in the eye. Boogie, the sole senior in our class, almost never looked up from his desk and never raised a hand. Yet on the field, his wide hands tore through the air to catch pass after pass and run play after play. "Best Offensive Player in Acadiana" the papers said, "Best Running Back in Louisiana." He had another title on campus too: "Best

All-Around Black." Black and white students sat in the same class but on different student councils and for different award ceremonies, long after that long hot summer and long long after Reconstruction. To most, that was just a fact, no question. So when Boogie wouldn't pose with his Best All-Around Black trophy, the other students chalked it up to vanity.

"Too big a star for us already, Boogie," they teased, but our teacher put it another way.

"Maybe he's holding out for valedictorian," Mr. Hedgehog said. "Now that'd be a plot twist!" Then he clapped the air in applause.

Boogie was barely passing English, barely passing all his classes, even though, rumor had it, his college test scores set a campus record. Teachers constantly found him dozing in his seat—when he showed—or drawing odd shapes instead of writing answers for fill-in-the-blank exams. For multiple choice or true/false, Boogie placed an X in every box, and for essays, he wrote with backward letters in a cursive hand that caused our English teacher to wrinkle his nose.

"Give a jock a pen," Mr. Hedgehog said, "and he uses it like a ripsaw."

When he taught Civics, his other subject, he called us "miscreants and reprobates" and pronounced "civilization" like it was a congenitally contracted disease. Close contact with Mr. Hedgehog, we were sure, would be worse than any STD. He'd leave you bloody with quills.

We were riding across the Atchafalaya Basin, Boogie and me, down one of the longest bridges in the world, eighteen miles of concrete rising over muddy swamp. The water below looked nearly black, but it was covered in patches with a green overgrowth that looked like the hide of some prehistoric creature. Through the patches, tall gray trees rose up, bald and spiny, the skeletons of a day when cypress was cut down like reeds. They looked like old debutantes, those trees, with their branches spread out for a waltz and their trunks arranged in billowing rows of pleats. The whole picture was frozen in time, except for the quivering nose of the car and the quick tongue of the running back next to me. For that moment, I had no idea where we were headed and little idea of where we'd been. As if the swamp itself gave us permission, we lifted right out of the car, right out of high school and the roles we played: the football star and the quiz kid, the stag and the fag.

Nearly dizzy from the night heat, I struggled to remember how Boogie ended up in my car. Already painted a Jenny Woman at school, I'd openly set my sights on studying the cheerleader stunts. During the game, I couldn't tell a route from a sweep, but I knew every step of an arabesque. All season, I followed our football team to away games, this time to a school in Assumption Parish in a town called Confederate. I secretly hoped to join the cheerleaders, to sit on the bus next to the players and their broad backs and wide grins. In the locker room, I might've been taunted for the direction of my eye, but in the bleachers I could stare openly at the boys in padded shoulders and tight lace-up pants. And when they lifted each other off the ground or delivered slaps to backs and rear ends, I could throw my hands together with the cheerleaders and yell each player's name out loud.

After the game in Confederate, I'd sat at a red light, yards behind the school bus, while tumbles and twirls ran through my head and a circle of players huddled before my eyes. Without warning, the passenger door opened and Boogie sat down beside me. He said not a word. He just looked straight ahead until the light turned green.

On the long drive back, he pumped me with questions, and to each one, I lied. Yes, I drank every lewd shot he could name. Yes, I smoked this, snorted that. Yes, I yanked it in the lockers, in the bleachers. Yes, I'd nailed a girl, nailed her good, nailed her again and again. I hadn't done any of it, not yet, but I knew the signs of a test, and I knew how to score an A. Still, I didn't know where the test would end. Suddenly, Boogie looked me in the eye and asked, "Ever stick it in a guy?"

I stammered and pretended to look at traffic, not ready to switch on the truth.

"A guy ever stick it in you?"

My eyes stared at the school bus ahead, and my tongue thickened.

"Ain't any different," he said. "A hole is a hole."

The words hit the windshield and burst like fruit. No one had ever talked to me like Boogie, like I was another player on the field. His talk made my ears burn and my head throb, but his voice wasn't the only one I heard.

All around, I heard the furious sound of pent-up laughter. The laughs slipped out of the cracked windows of the school bus ahead, crammed with the rest of the football team, the pep squad, and the cheerleaders. The players rose and fell in shadows against the window with pantomime movements and quick jerking arms. The cheerleaders beat time with their gloved hands, and the pep squad opened their mouths in unison. They looked like they were cheering Boogie and me from the back of the bus, but I knew they weren't. Already the rumors were starting, already the talk was hitting the air like splinters of glass, clear and piercing. What was Boogie doing with that fag?

I opened my mouth and laughed, a tinny nervous laugh. Boogie laughed along, his eyes shining like copper pennies in a fire. Did either of us know what the hell we were doing together?

To avoid any more of his questions, I started asking Boogie some of my own. Why didn't he talk in class? I'd seen him write down an answer when Mr. Hedgehog called a question, but Boogie never spoke it out loud. Why?

"Don't play by the rules," he said, "when the game is rigged."

"But what about your grade?" I asked.

"Got that in the bag."

"How?"

For a moment, Boogie fell silent, his face set in concentration. Whether from the stadium bleachers or the seat next to him, his sturdy body looked built for the game, built for running, catching, and tackling men on a wide field. Yet up close his face looked delicate, like a guy about to play a cornet, with a shadow around his eyes and a worry on his lips. Did he have the breath ready? The notes right?

"Oh, I'll pass," he said, almost in a whisper. "Wanna see my study guide?"

I gripped the steering wheel and nodded yes. What would he show me?

The bar was named after one of its lewd shots: Between the Sheets. Only everybody called it Sheets. "Don't skid the Sheets," I heard one guy say to a burst of laughter—before a cloud of silence moved overhead. Once Boogie passed through the door, a hand went up in my direction, palm forward. Then a string of eyes lit up, feet spread, and nostrils flared. No one said a word, but I heard them clearly. What is it you want? Drinks rattled in glasses, and a funk song throttled the floor. What is it you want, white boy?

Suddenly, I wasn't just the fag. I wasn't just the queer quiz kid. Here, I was white before all. Even with the red flashes of Sabine skin, even with the wild bush of hair, I wasn't black. At Sheets, there were only two options, no choice, the same as Boogie's award at school. Other people may have argued about prairie Cajuns and swamp Cajuns. Other people may have argued about pure French and Sabine French, Creole and mulatto, quadroon and octoroon. Here, there was no argument. Everything was clear as black and white, and I was the pink-eyed opossum in the room.

In the static of the moment, a hand on my shoulder jolted me into a chest-exploding gasp. When Boogie shouted "Boo" into my ear, and I jumped, the rest of the crowd laughed then turned back to pound the bar for more shots. "Slippery Nipple!" "Screaming Orgasm!" "Cocksucking Cowboy!" they hollered, and the names echoed in my head. Down at the end of the bar, Boogie introduced me as "little bro" and told everyone I was there to help with his studies. The guys in jerseys scoffed but looked at me as if a quiz kid might have some use after all. First time at Sheets, first time as little bro, I thought. What was next?

Most of the guys towered over me, and their hair rose even higher in geometric shapes, flat tops, blunt sides, sharp tips, sometimes with angular lines cut through the hair and to the scalp. Or else, their hair fell in a sheen of loose curls. The cloud of pomade filled my nose like musk, and I would've played little bro to any guy in the room. None of them laid a hand on me, though. None grabbed my shoulder. Instead, they barked at the girls in shiny spandex and chunky gold necklaces and grabbed at the air left in their path.

Just past the bar, the dance floor filled with couples jerking hips to songs about freak-a-zoids, robots, and neutron bombs falling from the sky. The whole place shook when a growling singer commanded them to "tear the roof off the sucker" and hands testified when a voice shouted about a black First Lady, but the dance floor really turned to riot with a song about an atomic dog. All at once, everyone shouted "dogcatcher" and bared teeth at the mirror ball as if it was the moon. The glistening bodies and surging beats drove the heat way up until bottles exploded and the guys in jerseys rained forty-ounces of beer over Boogie's head, and I suddenly remembered they won, our team won, and Boogie's name would splash all over the papers again. With fiery eyes, he schooled everybody on his moves and boasted of going pro faster than any rookie in history. His voice roared in a way it never did in class, and his hands looked wider than ever as they arced the air. Right then, I wanted to be the hips jerking next to him, the knees dropping to the floor and the feet twisting into the ground. I wanted to be his freak-a-zoid little bro.

Instead, I was the hands on the wheel leaving the bar, taking directions from Boogie as the car wound through a neighborhood nearly as crooked as the bayou next to it. Lights from another car blazed in the rearview mirror, then vanished before blazing again. Houses leaned in and out of view, most with a steep pitched roof and long galley porch. Then Boogie pointed his finger at the only Victorian house I'd seen in Lafayette, with millwork like tattered lace and a small domed doorway. On the steps, he grinned at me, and I grinned back. What would he show me now? At Boogie's first knock, a voice shouted "Entrez" and he pushed the door open with one hand. The night was hot and damp, but the house was cold and dry, with vents blowing from the floor. A single light clicked on at the end of the hall. Boogie walked straight ahead with sure steps, but I held back and eyed the street. When I heard the hum of a car engine, I slipped inside the house, feeling for the wall and blinking at the dark until my hands tipped over a coat rack. As I set it back, I could barely see the outline of a frock coat. I froze. Now I knew Boogie's study guide. It wasn't any spandex girl at Sheets and it wasn't ever to be me.

Down the hall, Boogie's hands flagged me toward an open door. His face beamed like a fugitive with a free boat and a way out. On the bed, a man's bare ass rose in the air, while a white silk nightshirt pooled around his face. Could he see me? I worried. Could he see anything? A chill had me rubbing my arms until Boogie laid his hand on my shoulder.

"You first," he said.

My hands dug deep into my pockets, and I shrank into my shoes, then shook my head. So Boogie dropped his pants and jumped right onto the bed and right into Mr. Hedgehog, thrusting his haunches back and forth with his teeth bared and his head aimed at the ceiling. Outside, the moon shone like a disc of ice, white and cool and quiet. Yet inside, a grunting sound came from the bed, and it wasn't Boogie. The sheets were twisting and a set of hands were shaking and Mr. Hedgehog started to scream. A shrill sound tore out of his throat and rang overhead. In the window, a face eclipsed the moon. First one, then half a dozen guys in jerseys stared straight at the bed, straight at Boogie riding Mr. Hedgehog. They'd tailed us here, the football players, and now they crowded the window with flared eyes. Boogie didn't stop, though. He didn't see them, so he kept thrusting into our teacher while his teammates kept moving their mouths until a loud word rose up, then two: "Dog! Gay dog!"

At that, Boogie's head whipped down and caught sight of the players in the window. Suddenly, he was the dead-eyed guy in class again, wordless and blank. He slipped out of Mr. Hedgehog, slipped off the sheets and onto the floor. Mr. Hedgehog fell too, clawing at the air and gnashing his teeth. He tore a chunk off Boogie's shoulder and anointed his own skin with the blood. Then he curled into a ball and started moaning about headlines and reputation and a wrecked career.

Boogie's eyes flickered back to life, and he bolted down the hall, out the back door and hit the ground running. The players howled into the air, shaking the houses awake, then revved their car and left a hot streak on the road. I should've busted through the window and emptied my chest to the night. I should've torn the roof off the house and chased the players with a mad fury. I should've run after Boogie and hollered his name to the moon. Instead, I dropped to the floor and tucked tail, lower than any dog and stiffer than any opossum.

Yet when the cops showed, I found my feet and a story, however wrong or full of lies. I told them Mr. Hedgehog had lured me to his place with the promise of an A and a shot at a trophy. I told them he had pounced on me in his nightshirt and had shoved my face into a pillow. I told them he had a seizure in bed and had fallen to the floor. The teacher stayed silent as a corpse in a morgue. What could he say? That the promise went to a black boy? What could he do? Point his baton at the truth? No, he kept his thin lips shut while I told the cops my sidewinder of a story and Boogie ran free, with his long legs and his strong back leaving not a trace on the ground or a scent in the air.

Behind closed eyes, I followed his moves. He ran all the way down the street, to the end of the bayou and right out of this city, right out of this state, right out of history, as far away as his feet could take him. Come winter, he wore a second hide, wrapped himself in a cloak of wool and slept under the northern lights. No one's dog, he studied the sky and re-drew the constellations. No shepherd to heed, no flock to fold, he cut a crisscross path in the snow like a guide for the outlaw and the wayward, the outcast and the misfit. When I finally reached him, he shaded me in the sun, warmed me in the moon. Under his cloak, we lay together, and no one could tell the black sheep from the white or the field of stars from the dome of night.

# Dancing in the Dark

## EDGAR GOMEZ

The headlight fell off again. It's a little sooner than expected, but I'm not altogether surprised. When it rains, water creeps under the packing tape securing it to my car, gradually weakening the adhesive so that over a few days it peels off completely, leaving me driving ten MPH under the speed limit and dragging my front left headlight down the road by its cord like a stubborn dog that's got its own ideas about where we need to go, which currently is the nearest CVS and quick.

I've been making excuses for not fixing it for the past six months, since I lost control of my steering wheel at a Pollo Tropical and careened into the white picket fence bordering the restaurant's friendly front doors, bulldozing a family of shrubs along the way. Seated in the wreck, I counted down the seconds wondering when someone would emerge from the building to ask me if I was okay, or at least scold me for driving with headphones on, but no one seemed bothered. Unsure of a proper course of action to take and growing more annoyed that no one had as much as pointed and laughed at me, I stepped out of my car and tip-toed toward the fence to survey the damage. No harm done. The shrub had simply been pushed to a lean, like it had clocked out for its smoke break and would be back to work in a minute. Except for the fallen headlight, my car, too, seemed blithely unfazed by the accident, so with no one to answer to, I went on with my day, driving to work savoring my stale Get-Out-Of-Jail-For-Crashing-Into-a-Global-Conglomerate card.

Ever since, it's been all "You'll fix it with your next paycheck" and "It's not like the light doesn't work. At least now it has character." Even more dumbfounding, my stepfather is a former mechanic and I have a close friend who recently repaired my taillights who would be delighted to help with the headlight problem, yet I don't ask either of them for help. Part of me believes I deserve this headache, as if by getting away with crashing into the Pollo Tropical, I owe it to the universe as cosmic penance to be burdened with this slight inconvenience.

It's not just the Pollo Tropical. Three years earlier my legacy of driving into things that are not roads began when my right front tire collided with a curb on a side street outside of Pulse, the Orlando gay bar with the least accessible parking, almost all next-to-impossible parallel spaces. Inspecting the damage with my fingertips and feeling the rubber only barely dip where it had scraped the concrete, I thought, "Idiot. You are such a lucky idiot." Add to my cosmic debt the time I almost drowned in the community pool in my uncle's apartment complex when I was ten. When I got a flat driving home from school and my car skidded down a six-lane road and glided neatly into a ditch. Being rushed to the emergency room after donating blood and fainting just steps outside of the Big Red Bus in full sight of a team of nurses. And being gay, because—despite the rush of revolt I get when I put on my patent-leather boots and silk floral blouses in the morning—I am often confronted with the irrational idea that I've survived being gay. Irrational because surviving being gay seems like such an antiquated notion. My generation doesn't survive being gay. This is 2016. My mother watches *Ellen*. Ellen watches *Modern Family*. A drag queen has a single on the Billboard dance charts. Even so, when I got the call from my best friend that a man had walked into Pulse, our Pulse, and used his gun to do what guns do, I was again thrust into acknowledging the harsh truth that I have survived being gay.

I don't want to ask myself what I would have done had I been inside of Pulse between 2:02 and 5:15 a.m., yet I still do. "Would you have made it?" I find myself wondering while doing the dishes, surrendering to my pesky ego. "Would he have looked at you and seen something worth sparing?" In these moments of selfishness, I am the universe's incontinent pet and it is shoving my face into a puddle of my urine, trying to house-train me by asking, "Why do this? What are you going to learn from this mess?"

A coworker, a classmate, a woman at a garage sale noncommittally perusing through a copy of *Atlas Shrugged*, all are interested: "Did any of your friends die?" Each time, my face is pressed back down to the floor. "Why do you ask?" I want to know. "Do you really think this is going to get us anywhere?" Each time, I could say no, thank you for asking, and maybe attribute my apparent sudden weakness to something else, perhaps a potassium deficiency, anything that would give me a valid reason to grieve when none of my best friends are dead at Pulse.

In the chaos of the first few days after the shooting, when there are still phones inside of Pulse ringing, a nagging pang in the back of my head follows me wherever I go, questioning my certainty that everyone I know is safe. In describing this doubt to a friend, I tell him that I feel like Catherine O'Hara in *Home Alone*. I am at the airport running towards my gate, already late for my flight, when suddenly it hits me: Kevin. The people I love the most are accounted for. My best friends are safe, I believe, but what about Kevin? Am I forgetting Kevin?

I remember a night at Pulse several years ago—the same night I rammed into the curb. It's the week of my twenty-first birthday and I'm electrified by the power of gay spaces, partly because I can finally legally order a drink at Pulse. I rush home after the club to write in my diary, still buzzing from too many well cocktails and schmaltzy after some of my first public flirting with being a gay man. I recall a vow I made with myself that I would only drink one beer so that if my tire was deflated by the time I got back to it at the end of the night, at least I would be sober, and how I promptly broke that promise when I ran into my ex-boyfriend inside the club. Given the choice between being drunk on the phone with Triple A or lucid at Karaoke night with the guy that broke up with me over text message, I opt for an all-you-can-drink wristband and fall in love with the first cute guy I see. He's a blur with a blond Mohawk and he's punching at the air a few feet away from me on the dance floor. Even in the dark I can make out how white his skin is, as if all the lights in the room have conspired to make him someone important. I'm not even beside him, but I'm already imagining us reading back to back in our country home in Connecticut and laying my head on his chest. I don't introduce myself but I do Charleston a few times in his general vicinity which is just as good anyway as long as my goal is to drive home alone on a bad tire. I never get his name. All of my best friends are safe, but three years later, I worry about Kevin.

I could stretch the truth. Yes. To those who are wondering whether anyone I loved was there, I could describe the night I met one of the victims, not exactly a friend, but someone that I used to know. I could catalog the drinks it took me to grow the balls to walk up to him that night at Savoy, the less popular gay bar across town famous for its aging go-go boys and three-dollar beers, the bar with the shotgun behind the counter that one of the bartenders once told a friend of mine is always kept loaded "just in case." I could feign wonder at how despite not quite being drunk, I still found myself serendipitously falling into him, pretending to catch myself on his pleasantly toned arm that barely seemed to register the new weight of me. I could admit that the mixture of a recent breakup, liquor, and a tough pop song about life after love had me diving wholeheartedly into my own private rom com. I could say that when I kissed him, silhouetted against the lurid neon lights spotlighting our half-empty glasses of booze, wrapping my body in his like this is what my arms were always meant to do, I thought, "Finally! So here is why it's all been worth it." I could recall his mouth, soft and sticky with cocktail syrup, so that when I took a step back to get a better look at him, late twenties, with an impish grin that made him seem like he was keeping a good secret, I could still taste the lingering sweetness of him on my lips. I could tell them he had a boyfriend back then, watch their faces closely to see if that changes what they think about him now that they know he's not perfect—this is a real man who is now gone. It wouldn't matter, really. Either way, they would just be glad that I'm safe, that it wasn't me, that I survived being gay.

The curious woman at the garage sale who wants to know if any of my friends has died asks me for help piling her secondhand loot into the back of her car. "I'm so proud of your generation," she says, handing me a trash can designed to look like an antique apothecary jar to stow in her trunk. She looks at me warmly, adopting me in the way true parental spirits take in all stray children, and drives off satisfied, convinced that she has nothing to worry about. I would have never been there, not her sweet, chaste, not-that-*kind*-of-gay son. It's almost like it never happened at all. But her story is wrong. She is too eager to get back to her daytime soaps, and her picture of me, of us, is not complete. It has been sanitized like the tools of the apothecary that inspired her fun new trash can.

Friends of mine have joked about how the catch-all slogan of late—Orlando Strong—sounds like a 5K marathon, disguising the unquestionable homophobia motivating the shooting with a baffling motto that sounds like a quote from *The Incredible Hulk.* "Orlando Strong!" The Hulk would bellow, tearing his lab coat to smithereens before growing three times his size and pounding on the bad guys. Erased is the queerness essential to the LGBTQ lives lost, replaced with generic calls to action to be McOrlando McUnited as if acknowledging our varying sexualities, genders, or authentic stories would make our lives any less worthy of reverence. Of representation, civil rights activist and author Audre Lorde wrote, "The visibility which makes us most vulnerable is that which also is the source of our greatest strength." I want to make myself visible. I need to be strong, not just #OrlandoStrong.

When I am fourteen, I wade into the full potential of my power when I tell my mother I am gay at a Saks Fifth Avenue. Even so, I prepare for this moment like a breakup, doing it in public in the hopes that she won't make a scene. When I am sixteen, my history professor asks me to prove my worth, instructing our class to debate whether gay adoption should be legal, a debate in which I am the only student who believes I am not inherently a bad role model. At twenty-two, my best friend is sexually assaulted at another gay bar in Orlando. I am almost handcuffed for "disturbing the peace" after screaming at the officers called to the scene to stop laughing. For years, that is what being gay has felt like: disturbing everyone's peace.

I have stripped off my mesh tank top to dance in midnight foam parties, undressed in cars tucked deep into parking garages with strange men I met on the internet, had my first kiss with a boy folded inside the lush red velvet curtain in sophomore drama rehearsal, a kiss so new and strained it felt like banging cutlery. Alongside all of this, I have survived being gay. Never tragically—always magnificently, absolutely fabulously. Still, I would be lying if I said I've gotten away with it unscathed. My queerness has, in fact, had its toll on me, a price of admission I can only imagine many closeted LGBTQ youth are skeptical of paying in the wake of so much hate. Even when it doesn't get you, death snags you, tearing off your outer layer like in a horror movie where the virgin outruns the masked villain, leaving him behind clutching her crumpled cardigan, knowing they are destined to meet again in Act 3. But the real world isn't a horror movie. In the real world villains have Sig Sauer MCX assault-style rifles and their stories are echoed in today's pop hits, cleverly concealed in the lyrics to Foster the People's deceitfully mellow "Pumped Up Kicks" blaring out of the stereo system at the Gap. They doff their corny masks to reveal centuries of support backing their hate: doctors declaring us mentally ill, legislation banning my friends from donating our tainted blood, preventing us from holding jobs, turning partners away from visiting each other in hospitals, expelling our transgender brothers and sisters from bathrooms, conveniently forgetting to hold our killers accountable in countless, nuanced ways.

Days after the shooting, gun sales in Florida double—people thinking that if they had weapons of their very own, they would have made a difference, or else worried that this will be the last straw, the deadliest mass shooting since Virginia Tech and Sandy Hook. A Florida congressional candidate announces a contest on Facebook to give away an AR-15 rifle. Now that we've seen the worst of it, surely gun legislation will tighten. Better stock up while we can.

However, this fight is not entirely unfair. We, too, are more powerful in disaster. Even when we are killed, we cannot die. We are like the mythological beast Hydra—cut off one of our heads and three will rise in its place. Stop our Pulse and our hearts will beat three times as strong. We are faeries, they tell us, and I believe them because we are nothing short of magic. I have witnessed our enormous political and social power firsthand. The morning after the shooting, lines at blood drives wrapped around blocks—our indomitable, mighty dragon's tail. At vigils, swarms of us gathered so tightly in grief that in the rooftop images splattered across every major news outlet we resemble the shadow of a fantastic beast hovering just out of sight. More than all of this, though, I am most overwhelmed by our power over death at every Orlando gay bar the week of the shooting, packed with the fiercest of activists bouncing along to our favorite queer anthems, my comrades in revolution singing along to three different versions of "Born This Way."

Three years ago at Pulse, I am in trouble. My best friend has ditched me for a one-night stand and my ex-boyfriend has teamed up with a drag queen to openly debate whether I qualify as being short, yet a moment on the dance floor redeems it all. That night, I write in overly romantic prose, hoping to trap the moment like a lightning bug in a jar: *I'm finally 21 and I'm alone on the dance floor flailing around to the tune of "MMMbop," alone and engulfed in a swarm of gay guys. They are anything but apologetic. They have a few drinks in them and are at their most honest. They push when they are intruded on and shout when they have something to shout. You'll never see a gay man so political as when he's dancing to Hanson.*

Looking back at that night, it's easy to imagine that I'm still in that crowd on the dance floor, singing along to the nonsensical words of a cheesy '90s song, alone yet part of a tribe more powerful than any dynasty I've ever heard of. It's hard not to laugh at myself for ever feeling bad about a drag queen calling me short when all along the only thing that truly matters about that night and every night since is that there was a drag queen at all, that I got to be at Pulse in the first place, just as it doesn't matter that there aren't really words to "MMMbop" as long as in my memories there will always be music to dance to and a gay space to lose myself completely in. I can't help but think of anyone who has ever been to Pulse or any other gay club as my friend, my clan, in the truest, most authentic sense: Who else will you allow yourself to unapologetically sing along to Hanson with? Where else could I have ever learned to take my first steps toward love? As last call pulled everyone away from the dance floor, I remember feeling my best friend grab my hand. He did not leave with his one-night stand after all. Together, we make our way to my car a block away from Pulse. Lo and behold, the tire did not deflate. It's looking a little rough and is featuring a brand new gnarly war wound, but it will be fine.

Back in the CVS parking lot, again I find myself patching up my car. I reinforce the headlight with a fresh layer of packing tape, securing it into place and testing it to make sure the light works. It does. Despite falling off and being dragged through two hundred feet of pavement, it's still burning bright. I know it's dangerous, if not altogether stupid, to not get it professionally fixed, but I can't help but dismissing it as yet another thing I'll get to eventually. Right now, I have to get to work and there is so much work yet to be done. It's only for a little while longer, anyway, I tell myself. It's a rough bandage, but in a bind, I can trust it to help me see where I'm going.

# One More Day

## GEORGE SEATON

---

Earl Day stepped out of his house, carried three metal bowls stacked one atop another, stood on the porch, and whistled for his dogs to come. They did come—three long-legged, lean, brown-with-swaths-of-black-colored dogs of indeterminate lineage. They sat in the dirt at the bottom of the porch steps, their eyes meeting his, drool dripping from their mouths. He'd taught them this politeness among other things when they were young and now it was routine. Here you go, he said. Set their bowls down on the porch—dry kibble with some raw pronghorn mixed in. The two younger ones leapt to the porch, while the older one took his time navigating the steps. Earl looked at the expanse of the land beyond the porch, his herd huddled in clumps here and there, a few cows with calves off by themselves. Buffalo Head Mesa bordered the southern edge of his land, which he again affirmed looked more like the head of a poodle just washed and blow-dried. He'd woken too late to witness the hard orange dawn, a sky afire boding possibilities he did not believe were within his reach. Didn't feel like smiling this morning, but he did. Couldn't help it. Glanced at the dogs, shook his head, sighed, stepped back into the house, grabbed the .38 caliber handgun and a half-full bottle of Uncle Jack from the coffee table where he'd set them the night before. Walked through the parlor and into the kitchen, placed the weapon and the bottle on the table, pulled out one of two chairs, sat and stared at the revolver. If he hadn't been able to do it last night when he was skunk drunk, he sure as hell couldn't do it now. Scratched at the stubble on his cheek. Maybe tomorrow, he thought. *Maybe tomorrow.* Knew he had to keep moving, though, or he'd lose another day to his dark thoughts and the whiskey, both of which had yet to provide the courage for him to finally do what he'd determined was the only thing that made sense anymore. He stood and grabbed the pistol. Walked into the parlor, put it in the side-table drawer. Snatched his keys off the table, then his ball cap from the hook by the door. Turned to view the parlor where his mama used to sit on the sofa by the window, wearing a brightly colored bandana to cover her bald head. Sent him into Cheyenne to buy the bandanas after she'd cut off her hair. Told him to buy the primary colors. Just get the bright ones, she'd said, her palms atop her head as if ashamed for him to see her. She'd sit the day through studying the wall covered with pictures of those who'd slept under the same roof for generations. She'd smiled now and then, crying when she thought he couldn't see her. Told him several times she regretted she'd not had more children, siblings who could help him keep the old place up.

Bill used to lie on that couch too, his boots shucked off, his intent to watch the tube, but his eyes soon closing with the fatigue the day had gifted him.

Earl shook his head, sighed, and walked back outside.

Three days of graying black stubble, same clothes worn for four days, Earl slowed his green pickup off the highway onto the apron. Pulled into Kearn's Farm and Ranch Supply parking lot where remnants of yellow lines provided witness there was once an intent that customers should park appropriately though Earl never had and he didn't today. Kearn was outside gabbing with a young man wearing jeans faded to gray, a white t-shirt, and a red ball cap.

Mister Kearn waved before Earl cut his engine, and the young man smiled Earl's way and stuck his hands in his pockets. Earl got out, said, "Hey," as he passed them. Walked into the hardware store where Missus Kearn stood behind the register.

"Earl, we ain't seen you in an age." She beamed a smile, large lollipop-shaped glasses pooched up with the rise of fleshy cheeks. "'Bout to send a search party to find you." Giggled like a schoolgirl. Reached under her blouse and picked at the uncomfortable squeeze of her bra against her breast. Tweaked her bangs. Appearance was an important component of customer service.

Earl walked down an aisle toward the display of fence wire, nails, and staples. "Didn't know I was missed."

"Lookin' for more a' that wire you like?" She pushed up on her tiptoes. A short woman with horizontal mass, she watched the back of Earl's head as he walked down the aisle.

Earl didn't answer. Maybelle asked too many questions. She'd always done that and most ignored her except those inclined to the inane as she was.

"How's it goin', Earl?" Mister Kearn stepped into the store, walked down the aisle. His gut filling out the front of his gray Sears overalls. Like Maybelle's, his face scrunched up in a smile. "Lookin' for more a' that wire you like?"

Earl walked past the wire he liked. "Need some a' them two-inch U-nails."

"Staples? Sure, I got a whole ten-pound tub. Right there on the floor." Nodded toward the tub, stuck his thumbs behind the overall straps at his chest, satisfied he'd anticipated the needs of a customer. The science of needful inventory his forte.

Earl looked at the tub on the floor, eased down to his haunches, lifted the plastic lid and peered inside. "What I need." He put the lid back on, stood, and picked up the tub.

Kearn followed Earl to the register. "You gonna start fencin' then?"

Earl hefted the tub onto the counter. "Yeah. Thought I would."

"You need any help?"

"No."

Kearn sidled up to Earl. Put his palms on top of the counter, leaned toward him, lowered his voice, and jabbed his thumb toward the window. "That boy out there is lookin' for work. Just come in from Cheyenne, and he's lookin' for work."

Earl smelled lilac. Imagined Kearn at his morning libations, patting his cheeks with scented water. Looked out the window, saw the young man still standing there, now touching flame to a cigarette.

"He seems like a good kid, Earl. Down on his luck and all, and he needs work."

"*You* hire him," Earl said, pulling out his wallet as Maybelle rang up the purchase.

"Don't need any help right now." Kearn took off his glasses, held them up to the light from the window. "Been a long time since you had any help out there." Pulled a red hankie from his back pocket, huffed a breath on the lenses, wiped them with the hankie. Held them back up to the light.

Shaking his head, Earl handed Maybelle two twenties, waited for her to give him the change. When she did, he stuffed the paper in his wallet, put the coins in his pocket. "You take care," he said.

"Come back and see us soon." Maybelle smiled again as Kearn put on his glasses.

Earl grabbed the tub from the counter and walked outside. Looked at the young man's pretty face. Young man looked back at him and nodded, then lowered his eyes and bowed his head. Earl walked to his truck, opened the door, set the tub on the seat and shoved it over to the passenger side. Sat down, closed his door and started the engine. Stepped on the brake and pulled the lever to R. Looked again at the young man who had raised his head, and nodded at him. "You lookin' for work?"

The young man tossed his smoke on the ground, stepped on the butt. Walked to Earl's window. "Yessir, I am."

"You ever fix fence?"

"Yessir. More times than I can recall."

A nod to the right. "Get in then." Pulled the bucket of U-nails to the middle of the seat.

The young man got in, closed the door, and reached his hand out to Earl. "I'm Tom."

Earl squeezed his hand, then grabbed the steering wheel. "I'm Earl." He backed the truck up, pulled the lever into D, and gave the old girl gas.

Driving Colorado State Highway 85, north from Pierce and passing through the roadside town of Nunn, Earl said not a word to Tom, who appeared happy to be on the road, the cool springtime forever wind finding his open window, his ball cap pushed up on his forehead. Earl glanced at him two or three times as the highway dissected the dismal burg.

Broad flatlands, rolling hills, errant mesas spread nearby from both sides of the highway. The longer western view bordered by the Front Range of the Rocky Mountains, blue to purple peaks, sawtooth juts, some summits wearing a white crown of snow that had yet to succumb to the season. A vast prairie farther east. Grasses already green, hay and alfalfa too, some sprouts of corn, black baldies and Herefords with calves, bands of antelope, ten thousand miles of prickly wire, metal and wood posts, homesteads sitting back on land effusing whispered hopes for good harvests, fat cows, dead coyotes, early rainfall, late frosts, bankers with consciences, the Lord's mercy.

Four miles from the Wyoming border, Earl slowed and turned onto a dirt- and pebble-topped county road. The forever wind caught the cloud of fine dust that rose behind the truck and blew it out to nothingness.

Three miles in, Earl slowed again. Turned onto an unmarked road, a clapboard house and a cluster of outbuildings in the distance appearing to have been set down on the land by the hand of one without a sense of order or symmetry. Three skinny, long-legged dogs rushed from nowhere and howled at their approach. Earl stopped the truck twenty yards from the house, killed the engine, and grabbed the bucket of U-nails.

"Dogs are fine once they get to know you." Earl opened his door, walked toward the house.

Tom stepped out of the truck. The dogs danced around him as he held out his hands, patted them on their heads, rubbed their sides. "You're good ol' dogs for sure," he said looking toward the house. Earl opened the screen door and stepped in. Tom watched the dogs rush off to some other excitement. Walked to the porch, glanced inside. Shoved his hands into his pockets.

"C'mon in," Earl hollered.

Tom opened the screen door, stepped in, stood in the small parlor, the center of the house, the core of so many memories, joys, hurts, pains, happy times, sad times—all fused into an amalgam of dust and dimness. He didn't sense what lingered there except for the hoary odors that defied categorization.

"I'm in the kitchen," Earl said.

Tom walked to the kitchen. Stopped in the doorway. The tub of nails sat on the table. Earl reached into the refrigerator.

"Got a nice place," Tom said.

"Want a beer?" Earl closed the refrigerator's door, turned with two long-necks clamped between his fingers. "Have a seat."

Tom sat at the table as Earl pried off the cap of one beer on the opener attached to the side of the table. Caught the lid in his other hand, handed the bottle to Tom.

"Thank you," Tom said.

Earl opened the other beer, tipped it to his lips. Sat and fiddled with the two caps he held in his palm. "Kearn said you come in from Cheyenne."

"Yes, I did." Tom sipped, wiped his lips with the back of his hand. His face still set in boyhood, blue eyes too large to be real, hint of facial hair yet to bristle.

"That your home?"

"Grew up there."

Still fiddling with the caps, Earl asked, "You about…what? Nineteen? Twenty?"

"Just turned twenty-one."

"From a ranch family?"

"Yessir. Cows and hay and alfalfa grass."

Earl nodded. "Why you on the road?"

Tom didn't answer for a moment. "Guess you could say me and my daddy don't get along."

Earl tossed the bottle caps into a waste can at the side of the table. "How come?"

"We just don't."

"Okay. You didn't get very far. Cheyenne ain't that far away."

"Left kinda quick. Didn't have time to think it all through. Was waitin' for another ride when Mister Kearn started talkin' me up."

Earl sipped. "Yeah. Kearn is a talker for sure." Motioned with his beer in his hand toward the front of the house. "This was my daddy's place and his daddy's before him. Now it's mine. I got some cows, but buy my grass. I don't usually want or need any help, but…hell, I was feelin' old today."

Tom nodded. "I'll be happy to help with whatever you got goin'. Fixin' fence, you said?"

"Uh-huh. Let it go too long. Couple heifers got out on the road the other day through a hole that shouldn't'a been there."

"They'll do that. Can I ask you a question?"

"You can."

"You married?"

Earl smiled. "If you only get one question, would that be the one?"

Tom looked at Earl's smile. Smiled himself. "I guess."

"Never wanted to marry. Are you?"

"So far, I haven't wanted to either."

"So far? Let's see," Earl looked at the ceiling, then back at Tom. "Since I was your age I got about seventeen years of *so fars* and still don't see it happenin'. A thirty-eight-year-old man without a wife is an oddity for sure. You're young yet. Might change your mind someday." He stood, finished his beer, and tossed the bottle into the waste can where it clinked against others. "If we can get goin' on that fence, we might get it done before dark."

"**D**addy fought in Vietnam, come home, married my mama, I got born, and then my daddy shot himself in the head in the barn when I was thirteen." Earl cranked the fence stretcher and Tom pulled the loose end taut, wrapped it around the wooden pole, then lapped the wire two times around itself, and then wrapped the loose end around the pole again.

"Wow." Tom bent down, grabbed two U-nails and a hammer. "Why'd your daddy do that?"

"The war fucked him up."

"What'd your mama do?"

Earl took the hammer and the U-nails, waited for Tom to brace himself against the post. "She took up the slack. Raised me and kept the ranch goin'. She lasted till about, oh, ten years ago." He pounded the U-nail into the wood, and then another one.

"So just you and your mama out here all those years?" Tom stepped back from the pole as Earl eased the pressure on the wire.

Earl plucked the wire. Satisfied with its tautness, he carried the stretcher to the next post and positioned it. "Yeah, just us and the critters. 'Course we had a couple Mexicans to help out with the calves. An uncle, my mother's brother, showed up after my daddy died and stayed around till I came back from the Army, and then one mornin' I woke up, and he was gone. Cancer got my mama. Started in her breast, then moved to her belly. You got brothers or sisters?"

"Got an older brother." Tom grabbed the loose end of the wire. "Joined the Marines and he's in Afghanistan for the third time."

"So, only you at home to help your daddy?"

"He hires a couple Mex every spring. But, yeah, just me and him to get on each other's nerves through the winter."

"Pull that a little tighter."

Tom unwrapped the wire he'd just wrapped around the pole and did it again. "That good?"

"Believe it is. You're done with ranchin' then?"

"No. Just done with my daddy."

Earl studied Tom's face for a moment. "Don't know what you got till it's lost." Smiled when Tom raised his ball cap off his head, letting the breeze cool his brow.

"If you mean my family, yeah, I know it." Tom put his cap back on. "Thing is… Well, my daddy don't understand me, or, I guess, me him."

"Uh-huh." Earl again plucked the wire, saw the sagging wire below it. Sat to his haunches. "Let's get this one."

"How come you still got wood posts? I see that other line is metal."

"A few years ago I had some help. Put in the metal on my neighbor's side, but that's as far as we got."

"Who helped you?"

Earl hooked the stretcher on the wire and cranked it taut. "Doesn't matter. He left."

Earl cooked bacon and eggs for supper, the dirty dishes left in the sink, and he and Tom took two beers each to the front porch. They sat in aluminum chairs wrapped with frayed multi-colored fiberglass strips, the light from the kitchen a dim presence at their backs. The dogs reposed in the dirt at the foot of the porch.

"Made some headway today," Earl finally said after they'd sat for ten minutes without a word spoken.

"Yes, we did." Tom crossed his legs, stuck his bottle between his thighs, pulled his smokes from his t-shirt pocket, tapped the pack, and reached it out to Earl.

Earl took a cigarette. Leaned over when Tom offered his lighter. "Thank you," he said, inhaled deeply, leaned his head back and exhaled. "Only smoke when somebody gives me one."

"I oughta quit. You still got the rest of that section along the road?"

"Yeah, that and my other neighbor's line."

"I suppose I could stay over to help get that done." Tom grabbed his beer, sipped, and then again stuck it between his thighs.

"Had somethin' else in mind for tomorrow." Earl placed his empty on the porch, picked up the full one.

"Oh, okay. I prob'ly ought to get goin' then. I know I can get a ride from somebody on the highway."

Earl closed his eyes, saw irrevocable consequences. Whispered, "But who would feed the critters?"

"You say somethin'?"

"I was just..." Earl opened his eyes, dropped his smoke into the empty bottle. "I believe what I was gonna do tomorrow can wait one more day. I can put you up in my mama's room."

"Good deal."

"Okay then." Earl looked at his dogs, looked for his cows but night had fallen upon them.

*One more day.*

Earl and Tom rose with the sun, ate bacon and eggs for breakfast, emptied two cups of black coffee each that Earl had poured from a tin pot.

"Gotta feed the cows, then I figure we'll finish the road fence this morning, and get started on the neighbor's line." Earl took the plates from the table and put them in the sink with the ones from the night before.

"Sounds good." Tom stood up, grabbed the cups. Set them on the counter and looked out the little window above the sink. "Why don't you grow hay out there?"

"Used to. Don't anymore." Earl rinsed out the black iron frying pan.

"You could have a good crop."

"Yeah." Earl unplugged the percolator. "I could."

"Gotta use the bathroom," Tom said.

"Okay. I'll feed the dogs, then load up some hay."

"I'll be right out."

Earl backed the truck up to a wooden canopy that stretched for thirty-five yards, the now grayed pine sagging in places. Several holes in the roof allowed shards of sunshine through to the stacked hay grass underneath. Got out of the truck and waited for Tom to walk over from the house.

"We need twelve bales," Earl said.

"Bet I could get fifteen in there."

"Sure you could. Only need twelve, though. Still lotsa grass out there."

"Okay. You want me to hand them up to you?"

"You get in the bed. I'll toss them up."

Tom climbed into the truck's bed. Earl grabbed the hay hook and hefted a bale onto the tailgate.

"This problem you got with your daddy?" Earl said, pulling the hook from a bale. "What's that about?"

"Oh." Tom shoved the bale across the bed. "We just been on each other for a while. Just thought I might get away from all that."

Earl put another bale on the tailgate. "What's your mama think about that?"

"Mama is in the middle. She don't say much." Tom positioned the bale next to the other one.

They were silent then. Continued to load bales.

"My daddy thinks I oughta settle down." Tom grunted as he placed the last bale on the stack. He jumped down from the bed. "Daddy's been on me to…"

"What?" Earl walked toward the cab.

"Get married."

Earl waited for Tom to get in the truck. "If that's what you want to do." Started the engine, gave the truck gas. Steered for the pasture gate.

"Yeah. Well…I ain't ready for that."

Earl glanced at Tom. "No argument here."

Tom smiled. "A day without an argument. I like that."

"You know how to spread hay, I suppose."

"Does a bear shit?"

"Okay." Earl pointed to the dashboard. "Take them wire cutters there. You spread it and I'll drive."

Earl let up on the gas, and Tom opened his door. Leapt out of the pickup and opened the pasture gate. Waited for Earl to drive through, then closed the gate, sat on the tailgate as Earl drove farther into the pasture, cows already gathering ahead.

Earl drove to the county road, stopped where they'd left off yesterday, cut the engine and stepped out. Tom got out too. They both walked to the truck's rear, gathered up the wire stretcher, U-nails, and tools they'd put back in there after earlier sweeping the hay leavings from the bed.

They set to work, both falling into the rhythm they'd established the day before. The morning's cool breeze picked up warmth and energy with the ever rising sun and soon the breeze became the constant wind. Toward noon, Earl paused, pulled his handkerchief from his back pocket, and wiped his forehead. Walked back to the truck and grabbed the two bottles of water he'd put in there earlier. Sat down on the tailgate.

"Let's take a break," Earl said.

Tom bent down, slipped under the top wire of the fence. Took the bottle Earl held out to him, drank half the water, and then screwed the cap back on. "What I needed."

"I never eat lunch. You want some?"

"I guess I could wait for supper."

Earl looked at Tom and smiled. "I take that as a yes."

Tom nodded. "Yeah, I am hungry. You could take it out of my wages."

"We never talked about wages."

"Oh." Tom glanced at Earl. "Room and board is okay with me. I didn't mean… I was only…"

Earl patted Tom's back with his hand. "It's okay. How about fifty bucks a day? And, room and board?"

"Sure. That's…okay. Yeah."

Earl slid off the tailgate. "I got some lunch meat, and I think the bread is still okay." Got into the cab, started the engine, and waited for Tom to join him.

"I appreciate this," Tom said closing the door.

"What?"

"Well, lunch and… Everything."

Earl turned the truck around, headed back to the house. "Young man has got to eat." Glanced at Tom who was looking at him. Thought his eyes were the color of the morning sky.

**"I** got a package of towels I never opened," Earl said as he and Tom sat at the kitchen table.

They'd finished the road line fence as the day began to fade, ate a supper of hamburgers without buns. Had chips and beer, as well. As Earl set two more beers on the table, he looked at the grime on his hands, the smudges on Tom's face. "You can take a shower."

"Good deal."

"Since you're travelin' light, I got some clean clothes you can put on after. We're about the same size."

Tom nodded. "Yeah, I think we are. Like I said, I left in a hurry. I must smell like a horse."

"Didn't notice. I oughta shower too. Livin' alone, you neglect those kinds of things."

"Yeah." Tom smiled. "My mama always reminded me how long it'd been since I last cleaned myself up. Like she kept a ledger or somethin.'"

"You miss them?"

"My parents?"

"Yes."

"No. I…I'm lookin' for something different, Earl. Don't feel like I belong at home anymore. I need—I guess I need to figure myself out."

"Figured my own self out a long time ago." Earl sipped on his beer.

"What'd you figure out?"

Earl waited a moment to respond, turned his head, looked away from Tom's eyes and then lightly slapped the table top. "That I wanted somethin' I couldn't have." He stood, picked up his bottle and drank what remained of it. "I'll find those towels."

Tom remained at the table until Earl returned from his bedroom with a plastic-encased set of two blue bath towels. Earl opened the package's flap, reached into the bag and pulled one out.

"Got these a while ago and never opened 'em up." Earl held a towel out to Tom. "You go ahead and take your shower, and I'll clean up these dishes."

Tom took the towel, downed his beer, and stood up. "If you want, I'll do the dishes."

"Nah. Go ahead. Didn't hire you wash dishes."

"I don't mind."

"S'okay. Put a new well pump in a couple years ago." Earl moved the dirty dishes from the table to the sink. "Believe the water pressure will stay up with us both usin' it. Gimme a holler if it doesn't."

Tom walked down the hallway, then turned: "What did you want that you couldn't have?"

Earl placed his palms on the edge of the sink, lowered his head. "Nothin'. Go on. Take that shower."

Tom turned, walked down the hallway. Earl raised his head, looked out the window above the sink. Saw his reflection backdropped by the dark of night. Studied his mama's collection of green, red, purple, blue porcelain pigs and cows on the sill and shelves that bordered the window. Looked again at his reflection. "Love," he whispered to his own faint image. "Just love."

Earl set out a clean pair of jeans, a shirt, and underwear on his mama's bed where Tom had slept the previous night. Listened to the shower water continue to fall in the bathroom. It'd been almost ten minutes since Tom had turned it on. Didn't matter. He could clean up tomorrow if the hot water crapped out. Imagined Tom lathering up his body, the water cascading down his back, soon turning his face into the flow. He jerked his head toward the sound of a frantic chorus of barks and howls from the front yard.

Earl ran through the house, flipped on the outside lights. Grabbed a flashlight from the side table near the front door. Stepped out onto the front porch just in time to see two of his three dogs leap over the fence into the pasture. Quickly stepped back in the house and hollered to Tom, "Somethin' goin' on with the cows. Maybe coyotes." Grabbed the .22 rifle he kept just inside the door. Rushed back outside, down the steps and ran toward the pasture gate. Pulled up the wire loop that held the gate shut and ran toward the ruckus. Waved the flashlight in front of him, saw the tunnel of light illuminate only snippets of pasture, deep shadows to the side. The dogs' cries became frantic. He continued to run and abruptly stopped, focusing the light on what he'd just glimpsed—his dogs standing over a calf on its side, both dogs hopping up and down on their front legs as they kept barking at something he could not see. Shined his light on the calf and saw a bloody leg. Walked farther, hushed his dogs, and pointed the flashlight into the distance. Saw nothing, not even the telltale reflection from green eyes set close together. The calf was alive and calling for its mama who stepped in from Earl's right. She nudged her baby with her nose.

"Coyotes?" Tom's voice came from behind Earl.

"Believe so." Earl turned his light on Tom, who stood there with only the blue towel tied around his waist. "Can you stay here while I go get the truck? Got a calf down."

"Sure." Tom walked to the calf and lowered to his haunches. "She don't look bad."

"Prob'ly not. Here." Earl gave Tom the rifle and flashlight. "Dogs'll let you know if they come back."

The injured calf bawled for its mama as Earl and Tom hovered over it in the barn.

"Hand me that sulfa powder on the shelf over there." Earl pointed to the wall. "Looks like they just got her down and nothin' more. No deep wounds."

Tom grabbed the container. Handed it to Earl. "Got some good dogs, Earl. Ours back home would a chased those sonsabitches till next Thursday."

"Trained 'em as puppies not to do that, to just stay by the cows." Earl shook out some powder on the wound. Glanced at Tom. "You got cow shit all over your feet."

"Yeah. Stepped on some burrs, too."

They both rose up at the same time. Earl took a step back. Looked at Tom. "I laid out some clothes on the bed for you."

"Didn't have time to dress."

Earl nodded. "Thanks for the help." He turned and put the sulfa powder back on the shelf.

"Maybe I oughta just wear blue towels from now on."

Earl looked at Tom, smiled. "Your choice."

"Earl," Tom said as Earl started to walk out of the barn. When Earl turned back to him, he said, "Me and my daddy's problem..."

"Yeah?"

"I got arrested a while back."

Earl waited for Tom to continue. Looked at the full spread of Tom's body, naked except for the blue towel.

"I got arrested for what they called public indecency."

Earl nodded. "Almost got arrested for that myself years ago."

"Yeah. But..." Tom took a couple steps toward Earl. "It was with another guy. In a park in Cheyenne."

Earl glared at Tom for a moment, then lowered his head. When he raised it, he nodded at Tom. "Okay. Why'd you tell me that?"

"Thought you ought to know."

"All right. You keep that calf here while I go get its mama. She'll be bawlin' all night."

As Earl stepped out of the barn he heard Tom say, "But..." He didn't stop. Walked down to the pasture gate where the calf's mama stood calling out to her calf. When he opened the gate, the cow lumbered toward the barn and he followed.

"Why don't you go in the house and clean yourself up." Earl prodded the cow into the barn. "I'm gonna get some hay in here."

Tom didn't say anything as he walked past Earl. Earl watched him gingerly make his way to the house. Saw the movement of Tom's ass against the damp blue cotton as an unexpected gift.

When Earl walked into the house, Tom sat at the kitchen table dressed in the clothes he'd laid out for him.

"Get yourself a beer." Earl grabbed the rifle and flashlight, both on the table, and took them to the parlor, put the .22 next to the door and set the flashlight back on the side table. Walked back to the kitchen, stopped in the doorway and saw Tom's expression. "That long face is gonna freeze like that. I'm gonna take a shower."

"I used the other towel. Sorry."

"S'okay. Got some more hangin' up in there."

Earl stood before the medicine cabinet mirror, looked at his face, and brushed his hand against the stubble. Turned on the water, splashed his face. Grabbed the bar of soap on the sink's edge, lathered his cheeks, chin, picked up his razor on the other side of the sink and shaved off the five-day growth. Turned on the shower water, took off his clothes, left them in a pile at his feet and stepped behind the curtain. He turned his back to the flow and felt the soothing patter against his skin. Thought about what Tom had told him and knew the conversation wasn't over. What could he tell Tom about himself? After all these years, could he tell that young man his own secrets? He didn't know. Lathering his body with soap, the thought struck him that Tom had twice tonight touched himself with what he now held in his hand. Raised the bar of soap and studied it as if there were some epiphany he could glean from it, but none came. Smiling, he shook his head, and put the soap back on the edge of the tub.

Dressed in clean clothes, Earl found Tom still sitting at the kitchen table where he'd left him. Tom hadn't opened a beer and still had a glum expression on his face. Earl opened a cupboard, pulled two glasses from the shelf. Grabbed the bottle of whiskey on the counter. "Let's go out on the porch."

As they sat down in the aluminum chairs, the dog that had not leapt the pasture fence slowly came up the stairs and lay down at Earl's side. Earl set the bottle and the glasses on the porch. "This is Badger, Badge for short." He reached down and scratched the dog's ears.

"He's got some gray on his nose."

"Yeah. He's gettin' old. He's Sadie's and Jake's daddy."

"That's the other two? Where are they?"

"Yeah. They'll stay out there with the herd prob'ly till mornin'." Earl leaned down to the other side of his chair and poured the whiskey into the two glasses. Picked the glasses up and held one out to Tom.

Tom took the glass. "You get him as a puppy?"

"Got him when he was three. Me and Bill…a friend and I got him from a neighbor down the road. Been almost ten years now."

"Bill?"

Earl sipped the whiskey. "You got any more cigarettes?"

"Sure." Tom pulled the pack from his shirt pocket, tapped two out and offered one to Earl.

"Thank you." Earl took the cigarette as Tom held the lighter out to him. Put the cigarette between his lips, leaned toward Tom, and touched the tip to the flame. "I guess you want to talk about that arrest you were tellin' me about?" Raised his head and puffed smoke from his nose and mouth.

Tom shook his head. "I shoulda never told you. I'll leave in the mornin'." He turned his head away from Earl and stared into the black distance.

"Guess your daddy ain't as concerned about you gettin' married as he is about what you were doin' in the park." Earl glanced at Tom's profile. When Tom didn't say anything, he said, "I met Bill after my mama died. I'd gone to Denver for the National Western. You know, just to try to get over the hurt and to be with people for a while." Smiled as Tom turned toward him. "Drink some a' that." He nodded at the glass Tom held in his left hand.

Tom appeared as though he'd forgotten he was holding the glass, looked at it, raised it up, and took a sip.

Earl took another sip. "Bill had come in from Lamar for the calf-roping competition. Handsome young man. A real cowboy." Paused and sucked on his cigarette. "Anyway, we saw each other at the saddle displays—he was lookin' to buy and I was just lookin'. We smiled at each other and we both saw…" He shifted in his chair and stared at Tom. "There's somethin' in men's eyes, don't you think? Bill and I saw it in a quick minute. There's a reason I ain't married, Tom."

"You're?" Tom returned Earl's stare.

Earl saw Tom working on a smile. "Yeah," he nodded. "I am." When Tom's face finally bloomed a full smile, Earl smiled too. "Small world, huh?"

"Well, goddamn," Tom said. "I don't believe it. I mean…" Shook his head, slapped his thigh. "I'm goddamned speechless here, Earl."

Earl picked up the bottle. "Here." He held the bottle out. "Let's…oh, I don't know. Celebrate, I guess."

"Yessir." Tom held his glass under the bottle's lip as Earl poured. "We can celebrate this thing."

Pouring a little more whiskey into his own glass, Earl held it up and out between their chairs. "To us. A couple of queers who don't give a good goddamn right now about anything in particular, except the two of us. Right here. Right now."

"I will drink to that." Tom clinked his glass against Earl's.

They downed their shots. Badger rose to his feet and carefully walked down the porch steps to the dirt below.

"He ain't used to celebrations," Earl said, setting the bottle back on the porch. "You got another cigarette I can have?"

"Yes, I do." Tom pulled his pack out. "Can you tell me about Bill?" He again held his lighter out to Earl.

"Sure." Earl leaned in to catch the flame, deeply inhaled. As he exhaled he smiled. "Bill come home with me. This was ten years ago, you know." He looked at Tom.

"After your mama died."

"Yes, it was. Guess I told you that." Inhaling, he crossed his legs. "Bill was a pretty good calf roper, but not *that* good. He'd never get in on the big money. Tried bronc ridin' a few times and all he managed to do with that enterprise was break his leg in two places. Told me he concluded that bronc ridin' was a short man's disease anyway, and he shouldn't have done it in the first place. His daddy had sold their ranch down in Lamar before Bill decided to come up to Denver for the rodeo and… Well, he had nothin' to go back to. Besides that, he was lookin' to find a boyfriend. Lived all of his twenty-two years wonderin' what it would be like to finally realize his desires and figured Denver would be the place to do that."

"And he did?"

"Yes, he did." Earl paused a moment. Took another puff on his cigarette, sighed as he let go of the smoke. "I'd had a few…lovers over the years. Told my mama I was goin' into Cheyenne or Fort Collins for the night, and she'd smile and tell me to have a good time. Expect she thought I was lookin' for a woman that I would eventually bring home and introduce as my girlfriend, and maybe later on marry. She was always hopeful, you know?" Glanced at Tom and saw him nod. "After a while, though, I think she prob'ly knew I wouldn't be doin' that anytime soon—fallin' in love with a woman, that is."

"Did she know you were…gay?"

"Yeah. I think she did. Mothers know their sons that way. Expect your mama knows."

Tom nodded. "Expect you're right."

"Well…" Earl looked at his cigarette and tapped the ash onto the porch. "After Bill and me spent the night in a rundown motel in Denver, I asked him if he wanted to come home with me. Told him I had a little cow operation near Cheyenne, and he took about two seconds to say, 'Okay. I think I'd like that.' Can't tell you, Tom…" He paused, looked at Tom and smiled. "I can't tell you how much I prayed he'd say yes to that question and he did."

"So he moved in?"

"Yes, he did. Hell, we grew hay, enlarged the herd, bought a new tractor, dug a new well, started replacin' the wood posts with metal for the fences. We did it all." He poured more whiskey into their glasses, then set the bottle down. "For seven years we did it all. Loved on each other like teenagers discovering the complete joy of such a thing for the first time. Seven years. Even got us a couple horses."

When Earl didn't continue the story, Tom said, "What happened to him?"

Earl downed his whiskey, leaned over and rolled the shot glass between his palms. "Bill took one a them horses out early one mornin'. Both horses were green as could be, but Bill was workin' with 'em every day. Thought the mare was ready to take a saddle and Bill took her out to the pasture. Only the second time he'd put one on her, but damned if he didn't take her out there. Hell, he'd been ridin' since he was a kid, and the calf ropin' and all. I had no thoughts at all about him gettin' in a fix with that mare." He stood up, motioned toward the black expanse beyond the porch. "Just him and the mare out there by themselves. I was workin' in the barn. We ate breakfast together earlier." Turned toward Tom and leaned against the porch rail behind him. "We talked about what we were gonna do that day, and Bill said he'd be back in an hour, that he was gonna teach that sassy lady—that's what he'd named her, Sassy—to behave under bridle and rein. So, he did that and I got to workin' in the barn. About an hour later I came out from the barn and there was Sassy outside, diggin' into a hay bale, still saddled, the reins hangin' down from the bridle. But Bill wasn't there."

"Wow."

"Get yourself some more whiskey."

"That's okay. I had enough."

"Okay." Earl sat back down in the chair. "Well, I hollered for Bill and Badger come a runnin' from the pasture with Sadie and Jake right behind him. Badge let out a yip and started runnin' back to the pasture. I followed him and after about two-hundred yards I saw Bill layin' in the hay stubble, his head cocked at an odd angle. Not movin'. Badge was whinin', and the other two were sniffin' at Bill like they'd never seen anything like that. And they hadn't. Bill was dead. His neck was broken."

"Earl." Tom leaned toward him, put his hand on Earl's thigh. "I'm sorry."

"Yeah. So am I. That was three years ago. Sold the horses and quite a few cows after that. Let the weeds have the hay. Been takin' one day at a time since then." He faced Tom. "You asked me about me wanting something I couldn't have?"

"Yes."

"I wanted love, Tom. Hell, after Bill died somethin' told me that I couldn't have that. Love was just somethin' that wasn't meant for me to have."

"But you had Bill." Tom's voice was near to breaking.

"Not for that long, I didn't." Earl grabbed the bottle, stood up. Looked down at Tom, into those morning-blue eyes. "I've not told another soul about that. Folks around here thought Bill and me was just a couple a bachelors poolin' resources. Thought I'd die with my secret my own."

Tom stood up, hesitated a moment, then put his arms around Earl and hugged him. "Thank you for telling me." His voice did break.

Earl patted Tom's back. "You're welcome. You find your own love, Tom. Hold onto it."

Tom let go of Earl and wiped his eyes. "Maybe I could stay here for a while? Give me some time to figure things out."

"I guess." Earl pulled his handkerchief from his back pocket, held it out to Tom. "Maybe one more day. Maybe more."

Tom wiped his eyes as Badger roused himself from the dirt, shakily climbed the stairs. Nudged his nose against Earl's leg.

"C'mon then." Earl opened the screen door to let Badger pass into the house. "You go on to bed, Tom." Put his palm on Tom's back and ushered him across the threshold.

Earl closed the screen door, then stepped back out onto the porch. Stared into the darkness, saw all those stars. Remembered things he'd been trying to forget. Wondered about Sadie and Jake out there doing what he'd taught them to do. They'd be fine. As he turned to go into the house, he smiled and shook his head. Badger hadn't even tried to go inside the house since the day Bill died.

Earl sat on the couch. The meager amber illumination from the kitchen seeped unwelcome into the parlor. He wanted the blessing of darkness, but decided not to get up and turn off the light. Listened to Tom finish up in the bathroom, then cross the hall and close the bedroom door behind him. Badger, who'd managed to climb up on the couch, rested his head on Earl's lap. "Good ol' Badge," Earl whispered, his fingers working on the dog's ears, his head, then brushed his hand down the old boy's back. Imagined Tom crawling into his mama's bed, his head on the pillow. Didn't know exactly why, but the image brought a smile with it.

His mama once told him that smiles were the only way the little bits of rainbows we capture with our eyes could get free to rise again another day. His mama told him a lot of things. Good things mostly. The childish things, though, like the rainbow story was one of the best. She said if people didn't smile enough there'd be no rainbows at all.

Earl leaned his head against the couch's back, closed his eyes. Kept his palm on Badger's back. Felt the rise and fall of the old boy's still vibrant but slowing down life. Thought about things that had once mattered.

# In Our Cars

## MARK WILLIAM LINDBERG

---

In her car, after we dropped him off at his house.

"So, I have to tell you something."

I expect her to say they hooked up finally because that's what we've both been hoping for and pushing him towards.

"Turns out there is indeed a reason he hasn't hooked up with me yet."

Oh no. I feel it already. Cassandra-like, I see it all coming. I have one final delicious moment where I get to be naïve, oblivious, young.

"What is it?"

"He's gay."

Now all of that is over. She doesn't know it yet. But I do. It's all over now.

"I'm the first person he's ever told. I told him to talk to you. You'll talk to him, right? He was really scared to tell me."

"Of course."

I'll talk to him. I know I will. I know everything that will happen.

In his car, after he picked me up to just go somewhere and talk.

"So she told me."

"Yeah."

"Do you wanna talk about it? I don't know, ask me questions or anything?"

"Not really."

"Oh."

"I've known for a long time, just never told anyone."

"Oh."

Did he know she had fallen for him? Did he know she thought he was into her? Did he know she and I had been planning their wedding already?

"But I just told my sister, and it went fine, and she thinks my parents will actually be okay with it."

"Wow. That's great."

I was supposed to give him advice, now I feel like I should be asking him for some.

"I'll probably tell them soon, I don't know, maybe tonight!"

"Really? That's so…fast."

"I just feel so good telling people! It's really freeing!"

He's so damn cute.

"Well if you're on a roll, go for it!"

He puts his hand on my hand.

"And since I'm feeling in the mood to tell people things…"

Cassandra prepares herself.

"Yeah?"

I should look in his eyes, not at his hand on my hand.

"I like you."

There it is. I honestly had no idea. I honestly had no idea about any of this. But now I know everything.

"I like you, too."

In her car, later that night, after I got out of his car, after we made out and never actually went anywhere to talk and I called her and told her we should go for a drive.

"He told his sister already."

I can't say the real news.

"Wow, that's great!"

"And he thinks he's gonna tell his parents tonight."

I can't say the real news.

"Oh my god! That's so…fast."

"Right?"

I can't say the real news.

"What else did you talk about?"

I can't. I have to.

"He...told me he likes me."

"I thought so."

What?

"You did?"

"Yeah, I mean, as soon as he told me, I figured it must have been you and not me that he liked."

"I had no idea."

"Really?"

She had no idea either. Did she?

"We kissed."

That just came out.

"Nice."

"Is that okay? Is this weird? If it doesn't feel okay to you, I can stop, I don't have to."

Can I stop? Don't I have to?

"It's okay. I'm okay with it."

"Okay."

"You two will be super cute together."

Cassandra shouts at me, but I can't hear her.

In his car. The back seat. Slightly later in the summer.

"I don't know what love is supposed to feel like, and I feel like this is too fast, but I can't imagine feeling more strongly for someone."

"What are you saying?"

I know exactly what he's saying, but I want him to say it.

"I love you. I think I love you."

"I think I love you, too, and I also don't know how or if it's right or too soon or—"

I've been stopped with a kiss. I've been stopped with a kiss and with hands and with a body on top of me.

In her car, the next night, driving toward the ocean.

"I'm not okay with it."

"What do you mean?"

I know what she means, but I want her to say it.

"I'm not okay with you seeing him."

"Why?"

She won't want to say why.

"I'm just not. And I don't think it's right, he's too new, you know, he's too, like, young."

"He's two years younger than me."

"I don't mean age."

"He is not that young. He's more mature about it than I am."

"I think you should stop seeing him, okay?"

"But.... No."

Her car pulls over and stops.

"Look, it's really uncomfortable for me. It's kind of a big deal to me."

"That we're together?"

"Yeah."

"But...."

"You said you would stop if it was weird for me."

"Yeah."

I said that what feels like a lifetime ago.

"So you'll stop?"

I'll try to. For her.

"Okay."

In his car.

"How's she doing?"

I can't even try to.

"She's fine."

In her car.

"I just don't understand. I know you're in a terrible situation, but, like... this is me, I thought...."

"I know, I just...I'm like...."

I'm like not saying that I love him.

"It's not that hard."

She thinks it's just fooling around. I can't even speak up for myself. Not to her. Not to her, who has spoken up for me in my life more than anyone. Not to her who I literally owe my life to after my own traumatic coming out process.

"It is hard. But…."

But why can't I have both? I shove my anger into the closet. She starts to cry.

"It's me. I thought we were together in everything."

I can't blame her for her feelings. She's losing two friends.

In his car.

"She doesn't want me to keep seeing you."

"That's none of her business, right?"

"We've been through a lot together."

"I love you."

His anger is out and marching. Again, I sit in awe and feel like he's the veteran here. I adore him.

In my own car, alone, parked at the ocean, I cry and cry.

In her car, parked in my driveway, after a lot of silence.

"How will you make it work when you go back to school and he's across the country?"

It's a good question.

"I don't know."

I'm so damn confused.

"Well, I wish you the best."

"Don't say that."

"It's okay. I do. I hope you can make it work, you both deserve to be happy."

I can't let her go. So she's letting me go. I get out of the car.

In his car, parked in my driveway, after a lot of silence.

"I'm sorry."

"I just don't understand."

"I know, I just…. It's how it has to be."

How can I be saying this?

"Okay."

I get out of the car.

In my car, driving back to school, I roll down the window and breathe as deeply as I can while sobbing. Cassandra sits in the passenger seat and takes my hand. She tells me what will happen. It will take a few years, but friendship will win out. It will never be what it was, but my best friend and I will ride in cars together again. We will forgive. We will move on. In three years, I'll ride in a car with him one more time. I'll apologize because after some distance and perspective I'll realize that he was the one who really lost out here, who got caught up in the existing drama between her and me, in stuff we were already trying to work out between us. I'll throw myself at him pathetically one last time, and he'll politely refuse because he'll already have someone. I'll know I never could have held on to him anyway. He'd have been too free, evolving too fast for me to keep up. There were signs if I had known to look for them. If I could have seen anything at the time.

In my car, driving back to school, breathing as deeply as we can, Cassandra and I look ahead. And I ask her, just for the rest of this car ride, to stop speaking.

# Usefulness

## VAL PROZOROVA

---

The first time he had done this, Alistair had been made to. He had spit and he had cursed, and he had been told that should he wish to stay in this arrangement, he would obey and he would thank his master for it. Alone was something Alistair had never been able to be. He lost his mind when he was alone, pacing and fretting, like a caged animal. Too much energy and nowhere to go.

No.

He could not be alone.

So he had sucked it up and obeyed. He had gotten down on all fours on the floor, and held up the weight of his master's feet where they rested crossed on his back. One hour, another, Alistair had lost count by the end of it. All he knew was that when he was released, his arms were trembling, his legs were like water, and he felt entirely fulfilled.

After that, he did not have to be made. After that, he would crawl beneath his master's feet himself, every night, and hold them up as long as his master saw fit.

In truth, humiliation had never been one of Alistair's desires, even back when he wasn't part of the scene, he never got off on being called names or disgraced in public. He enjoyed sex as he supposed sex should be enjoyed: often and with a capable partner. He had gotten lucky, frequency was never a problem when it came to sex for him, there were many willing, and he was easy enough to please. And yet, it was rare that he would leave his partner feeling entirely satisfied. Sore, often, sated, frequently, but satisfied...there was always an itch, something just beneath his skin, that no one could ever quite reach.

And then he had been reduced to a footstool and had found himself wanting for little else.

There was no demand, there was no possibility of dissatisfaction for either party. It would be hard to mess up a task as simple as *stay still*, and it was always easy to be used. Once his master had learned that Alistair needed that release from control and responsibility, needed that subjugation and gentle push, his trysts as a human footstool became Alistair's reward for being good.

And he was good.

Infrequent, now, were the outbursts and backtalk, when the threat against it was for Alistair to spend his night sitting on the sofa instead of kneeling before it. It was rare, too, that Alistair would not complete his chores, that he would not take up new ones in hopes of another reward alongside. A hand through his hair, perhaps, whispered words of praise. Those he would get daily, murmured against his skin and into his hair as he lay sprawled warm beside his master in the wide bed, but being told throughout, being touched while he was a thing, not a person, was something that would drive Alistair's mind and body to reckless abandon every time.

It had been a hard week, work had kept him late, and with the mutual understanding between them that Alistair's exhaustion would not benefit either of them, his master did not force chores on his boy, and thus there was no reward for having done them. Seven days, and Alistair's old panic was back, he would fret and pace, squirm in bed until a soft hand was laid against his forehead to soothe him. He couldn't rest. He could do nothing but think of what he was no longer being given, what he was no longer earning, because a life outside of their arrangement, outside of their control, was infiltrating the intimacy of his comfort.

He would not have asked—he had never asked, playing petulant and stubborn despite both men knowing better—had the itch beneath his skin not grown to a burning pain. He would not have asked had he been allowed, just once, to kneel and take his master's feet against himself during the week. But it had, and he had not, and the desperation in his tone, the twitching scrub of one hand against the other drew his master's attention.

Regarding his boy, the man merely beckoned and Alistair had gone, following him through the wide rooms of their shared home, hoping that he would soon be allowed the relief of pressing his knees to the floor, settling his balance and holding his posture.

They had gone not to the sitting room, with its plush carpet and wide fireplace, but to the bedroom, and when his master had climbed into bed to sit atop the covers, Alistair had near-sobbed his displeasure. But again, he was beckoned, and again, Alistair had gone. Slow steps to reach the side of the bed, a curious tilt of his head when he was told to undress, to fold his clothes neatly away and set them to the chair by the closet. Once bared, Alistair climbed onto mattress as well, knees on one side of his master, hands on the other—bent over his lap like a personal worktable.

The balance was different, the bed soft beneath Alistair's knees and hands, and there was nothing on his back to press him into place, nothing to arch his back and make him lift his chin, nothing to draw beautiful curves over his body and make him useful. Here, he was nothing more than a frame, pretty but unneeded. Not as he was needed before the couch, on the floor, holding up his master's feet after a long and hard day at work. Here, he was useless.

He found his protest silenced not by words or gestures, but a tickling sensation of a page of paper laid atop his back. His muscles tensed, his entire body shivering from the novelty of this, brows furrowing in confusion. But as silently as the page had been laid down upon him, so lightly, too, was the pen set upon the page.

What his master wrote, Alistair could not be sure, and he would never ask, but every scratch of the pen against the paper, every curl of his master's cursive hand brought new tension to Alistair that he had never experienced before. His nerves were alive, then, with every tickle and touch of the nib, his mind filtered through confusion to displeasure to reluctant satisfaction without his express permission and Alistair could feel himself warm to the sensation as he had so quickly to the pleasure of being nothing more than a stool for his master's feet.

He held his place and held his posture, and every scraping line of the pen brought forth in him a delight he had never before felt. He was a proxy, a living, breathing thing that was bringing these unknown words to life. Without him, as without the pen and without the page, these words would not exist. Never again in any time in any place and any moment in history would such words be made in such a way and he, Alistair, had been granted the opportunity to be here and facilitate this as it happened.

He could weep for the mercy of it, could weep for his master's fore-thought and understanding. A week without his usual release and sud-denly this: an entirely new experience, and entirely earned and worthy gift.

His master wrote, and Alistair stayed.

As his hands shook and his legs ached, Alistair stayed.

As he lost sensation in his back from the working of the pen, Alistair stayed.

Moment after moment, what felt like hour after hour, he did not move, and his master did not stop writing. Empty pages replaced filled ones, and slowly, Alistair's master began to touch him. A caress across his trembling thighs, a skim of knuckles up his spine to straighten Alistair when he had begun to slouch, fingertips tracing the delicate skin of his ear until Alistair turned into the touch and a palm spread across his cheek instead.

This was euphoria. This was release.

Nothing mattered but the hands against him and the pen carving prais-es into his back. Nothing mattered that had happened at work or the train to get there, nothing mattered what was said or misunderstood between his colleagues, nothing mattered at all beyond the small sphere of freedom that Alistair had been granted.

He swayed by the time he was released, elbows weak and sore from staying straight, spine stuck in an arch Alistair was sure he would never be able to unbend. Warm hands against his back, then, to soothe the ten-sion of his muscles, warm hands down his arms to bend them and to let Alistair lie flat across the bed, across his master's lap, as he was massaged and touched, feeling returned to his exhausted limbs and heat to his ex-posed skin.

Alistair alternatively stretched out and curled against his master, unfurling like a sleepy kitten when hands ran through his hair and fingers traced his lips. He was in heaven. He was shapeless and formless and entirely alive. He was praised and touched and gentled. He was told he had made his master proud. He was reminded of his usefulness.

# Off the Hudson

## MIKE DRESSEL

---

It was Colton's proposition to leave the city for the summer and since I loved him I agreed to it.

I wasn't enthusiastic just for Colton's sake. I do enjoy adventure. This, though, had the whiff of something—maybe the pull of inevitability for us as a type of couple—that I had to stop myself from balking at.

We had taken the train up the Hudson for a day trip to a little hamlet in the process of rediscovery and refurbishment by exurbanites, those who wanted space to do their art installations or pursue their dream of selling artisanal shaved ice. The trace elements of a township that had hit the rocks some time ago were still present, but coated over, patched, not unlike like a wobbly, pocked wooden floor disguised with a bright, festive new rug (woven of cruelty-free yak, here, presumably). Now the extant derelict storefronts alternated with the refashioned, those that entreated weekenders to buy their handblown glass dildos or dine on locally-sourced vegan comfort food. Dreamcatchers abounded. There would be kale.

Colton was wearing his mint-green J. Crew shorts and New Balance sneakers that afternoon, and I loved how he looked in those shorts, how they hugged his crotch, and during our ride back to the city, with our thighs pressed together and my head resting on his shoulder I drowsed as he monologued about the possibilities of spending a month or two out of town.

Sebastian, he said, we could probably find an affordable place equal to what we'd pay for like a week in the Pines or P-town. I could use the time and space to work on my film. We'd be close enough to the city that I'd go back on weekends if need be. We'll get Marci to water the plants.

Though it was not even late May it was already wiltingly hot in Manhattan and if this weather was a harbinger of the summer to come, then the sooner we left the better. I nodded as he went on. I can cover most of the cost, he said. His proposed generosity made me feel like a grateful hostage to his largess, even though it wasn't that large. He was funded by a grant to finish his documentary, and had some money stashed away from a steady run of editing work. I hadn't planned to take the summer off necessarily, though I had done little to nothing to procure any employment. Still, this semester I'd taught two online classes for a somewhat shady educational property, on top of my adjunct position, and I had set enough cash aside to hopefully float me until the fall if need be.

So by the second week of June we were once again on our way up the Hudson Valley with our luggage, set to occupy a "homey" apartment built over a former soda shop. The building stood a bit outside the main part of town, offering more privacy but less of the glamor—if one could call it that—of being centrally located.

Colton had handled the rental details while I spent my time Wikipedia-ing the town and investigating the Chamber of Commerce's website: History, population, economic upticks and downturns. I clicked on articles in the *Times* about the area's hipster renaissance and felt a mild sense of foreboding, including a piece about a former frazzled rock star now residing there in blissful repose, leading Reiki classes and music workshops for parents and tots. She claimed the town had given her back her soul. Oh.

I tried to temper a pang of disappointment as I sniffed at our lodgings, opening windows to chase the dust clinging to the surfaces and trying to banish the cloying scent of its rightful occupant. Colton was oblivious, instantly stowing his belongings and adapting his tall, lithe frame to the space. The apartment would grace no spread in a glossy shelter magazine or merit a feature on a design blog, but it would be inhabitable. It wasn't quite what I imagined, but then it wasn't overstuffed with embarrassing tchotchkes and crocheted samplers either. The owner, a forthright, middle-aged lesbian, was down in Florida tending to an elderly relative and happy to have us as seasonal tenants.

After unpacking, Colton lay down to nap. That is one thing that I envy about him, his ability to sleep anyplace, anytime. He pulled me down on the bed next to him, his long grasshopper legs tucked together. Stay with me, he murmured, already drowsy. I lay next to him, trying to settle, but I felt squirmy. Sensitive to my movements, he said, sleepily, or you could go for a run. I had quit smoking and taken up running approximately one year, four months, and three days ago. Colton was someone who could still manage to smoke occasionally, at a party say, or outside a bar, and then the need would not grip him again past the moment he discarded the cigarette butt. I was not built that way, so now I run.

I scooted myself close and began to dart my hand into the waistband of his shorts, but Colton was already near-asleep so I retreated, resting my palm on his flat stomach and inhaling the scent of his hair. He kept it longish; it was a honey-blond color and it always smelled earthy and herby like a small patch of fertile garden and, sometimes at home when I found myself missing the scent of it and if he'd gone to work before me, I would press my nose deep into his pillow. I could not, however, drift off. So I took his suggestion, as I usually did, and set out for a run. It would give me a chance to see the town again.

When should I disclose that Colton hit me? Only once. And I forgave him. It did not, in that instance and contrary to the song, feel anything like a kiss. In the interest of full disclosure, it was because he thought I had been cheating. I hadn't. Not technically. He forgave me. But that's something each couple must parse for themselves, right, what constitutes fidelity; where do boundaries of propriety lie?

It had been a misunderstanding on both our parts. We had been in a nasty fight in our kitchen, late one evening this past winter, shortly after we first began living together. It escalated rapidly from a light shove to the actual moment, the crack across my cheek and the reverberation of that sound, knuckles connecting with flesh, followed by tears and then we were a tangle of groping limbs on the linoleum which progressed to a tangle of limbs in the bedroom. The thing is, Colton is not at all violent and I'm not one to stray, at least in the way we both present ourselves, so I can't entirely justify it but to say the season had been exceptionally cold and who does not go a little crazy by mid-February?

Why the incident came back to me as I made my loop around the town I couldn't say, other than we were about to negotiate our "us-ness" in a new setting. My path took me once more near the river, then the irregular slope of green park, past a rushing water mill and up a small incline. I tried to stick to the back roads and side streets, to get a better sense of how the town was put together, how the pieces fit and where the seams showed through, removed from the scrim of a blissful weekend visit. I ran over disused train tracks and passed still-abandoned factories: one had a Banksy-esque mural on the wall, while most of the other façades were tagged with the amateur graffiti scrawl of disaffected youth. A college friend of mine currently lives in Frankfurt, Germany, and when I went to visit her, and she was guiding me around the town, she told me of a game played with the different buildings: Bombed Not-Bombed. It was the way of distinguishing any construction from the edifices that had survived from WWII. I thought of that as I turned down a back road near the South end of Main Street, behind the diner. From behind me roared a large 4x4 truck, coated in a Rorschach blot of dried mud. It came to an abrupt stop near a dumpster. A man, youngish and loud, who I felt appeared casually menacing, hopped out. He was tan, his dark hair kept trimmed close to his scalp. He spat on the ground after swinging himself out of the truck. I had paused to stretch and he now caught me looking at him. He appraised me coolly for a second before entering a screen door of one of the buildings facing the parking lot.

Colton was awake and staring at his laptop by the time I returned from my run. There was a little desk by the window, painted robin's-egg blue, that he had already commandeered, a yellow legal pad scrawled with notes and other important detritus from his current project spread out. He gestured to the Formica table in the cramped, L-shaped kitchen where several white cartons sat, ready to be opened.

Chinese takeout? Really?

Um, you're welcome. I mean, unless you wanted to buy groceries and cook? He returned his attention to his laptop.

I didn't particularly. Pulling off my running clothes, I tossed an air kiss towards him before muttering something about the one single Chinese restaurant in town and then ducking into the shower.

We went down to a small wine bar on Main Street, after putting away the leftovers, to toast the beginning of our little summer idyll. We killed a bottle of Sancerre and discussed how we'd spend our time. Colton had already amassed a collection of maps, marking the trailheads to hikes he thought we should take. We listed certain nearby galleries to visit, ones that we'd overlooked on our first trip, and omigod maybe we can score some shrooms for fun, Colton said. We briefly considered but nixed signing up for weekly transcendental meditation classes. There is only so far one can go native. As we were waiting for the check I brought up the guy I'd seen in the parking lot.

Cruising for town trade already, Colton joked, but with an edge to his voice.

It was the way he looked at me.

Seriously?

Not in *that* way. It was like he was taking note. Of my arrival.

Oh sure. Maybe he's with the welcome wagon and will show up at our doorstep with a *big* basket.

Ha. No, but. I can't quite explain but I thought. I mean, I sensed.

You're drunk. Or paranoid.

Fine. Let's drop it.

We sat in silence until our change arrived, and then I followed a pace behind Colton as we walked back to our little rental.

We should have fucked that night, to christen the new space. I started to initiate something but Colton blamed the wine and the greasy food as he shifted away from me.

The yarn we'd spun for ourselves, the one of green market weekends and leisurely strolls, had not exactly come to fruition. I barely made a dent in my ambitious summer reading list—now's the time to tackle Proust, I told myself—and Colton dug deep into his film, a piece centered around Frank O'Hara as flâneur. So I would attempt to read, take runs, shop, and Colton would be in front of his laptop, researching, logging interview footage and emailing and texting with his producing partner. Trying to get the narrative to coalesce. It was all very much like our life in the city, only with more fresh air and isolation, and seemingly more togetherness, but only because we occupied the same space more hours of the day.

I started to get creative in a manic happy-homemaker way, experimenting with meals that were beyond my capacity to cook well, and devising a series of intricate cocktails based on the imported spirits at the one liquor store in town that provided such a stock—Aperol Negronis, or something with Lillet. Which is how we managed to fall into a routine within our break from routine. Colton would usually turn to me in the early evening, as I, apron-clad, was banging around and muttering to myself in the kitchen, trying to manage a recipe with ramps or sorrel, or whatever, kohlrabi, and ask something along the lines of what's farm to table tonight, Sebby? And I'd reply smartly, and then I'd say something like, Colty, would you like your evening cocktail and he'd reply, ooh yes, and I'd serve him that day's specialty and we'd toast and drink, then he would return to his screen and I would go back to the kitchen to bang and mutter some more.

The cutesy "y" we appended to our names, that had begun shortly after we had started dating. I think it was Colton who initiated it, but we were in such a cocoon of bliss and single-mindedness early on I'm not certain where his thoughts ended and mine began.

I started watching Colton in bed at night—I found it hard to sleep minus the white noise of the city, the insistent thrum—marking the easy rise and fall of his breath. He would drift off to sleep and I would softly pad back into the kitchen, repeating my cocktail recipe or more often just pouring whatever liquor was at hand straight into a glass, and then, finishing that nightcap, fumble my way back under the sheets. I thought about the amount of time I had spent looking at him, how I knew the planes of his body, his dimples, the way he absentmindedly flexed his calves when sitting on the subway, the manner in which he scrunched up his face and tilted his head when I was imparting some bad news or unfortunate story to him, his pale lunar ass. What features of mine, I wondered, what attributes, did he know, notice, catalog?

Then, sometime around the end of the first month, Colton returned to the city.

I finally secured an interview I've been desperate for, he said, the morning he left. It could only be shot during a very small window, he said, meaning tomorrow. Oh, okay, great, go, I told him, having a hard time masking my disappointment. You could come back too, Sebby, he said, but I'm only going for like thirty-six hours so it doesn't seem worth it. Stuffing clothes into his green overnight bag, he was preoccupied. No, no, I said, I shall remain here, and swanned off into the kitchen to rinse and dry dishes.

Colton gave me a perfunctory kiss as I stood at the sink and promised to text upon his safe arrival. The moment the door clicked shut I fell into a mood. The thing is, I don't mind being alone. I just dislike being *left* alone. The distinction is important.

I stood on the small woven rug unable to make a choice as to what to do with myself and the day. This was part of the arrangement after all, the idea he might shuttle back and forth, so why did it irk me? We had fought, a few days prior, over money. He made a comment about my wanting to purchase something useless and extravagant, and I should have let it pass but I didn't. We were both sensitive and touchy for the remainder of the afternoon. It was our second fight of the summer about money.

When Colton contacted me, it was to say that the interview had been pushed back, and he'd be staying in the city for at least another day, maybe two. Fine, whatever, I replied. Don't be mad, he responded, and asked if there were anything from the apartment I wanted him to bring back. Nope!!!, I wrote, hoping he'd read into my breezy response my intended sense of irritation.

Though it was only early in the afternoon I fixed myself a drink—an Old Fashioned—and began to obsess over Colton's imagined movements through the city.

I awoke around eight that night groping at the bed next to me but finding it empty. I checked my phone and, not seeing any more messages, stifled my impulse to write to him. Instead I reheated leftovers, fixed myself a Manhattan, neat. I went to a bar, that first night without him, and then every subsequent one he was gone, which turned out to be four. It took some searching to find the right place. The place I settled on was not one of the newer drinking establishments but an old, grizzled thing nestled off a side street—a dive. A true, proper dive, not some designer's approximation of one, not some cute simulacrum fashioned to lure young, trendy cocktail enthusiasts. This bar was the repository of the tears, sweat and fistfights of an untold number of blue-collar boozers. Long, and faintly mildewy smelling, with a blinky neon sign out front. The only nod to cheer was the strand of Christmas lights strung up behind the bar, and even those were coated in a film of filth and dust. A fly strip hung from the ceiling. I likely would not have had the courage to come in had I not been fortified with my pre-outing cocktail. In contrast to the space, the bartender was shockingly young. We chatted for a bit: Her name was Rosie, she was Irish, and had moved to the town with her carpenter boyfriend. She was polite but adequately disengaged, as the bar seemed to require, and after she gave me those brief details of her life she returned to rinsing pint glasses.

The second night there I recognized the boy from the parking lot, the one with the mud-spattered truck. He had a beer and a shot in front of him, arm curved protectively around his drinks, head lolling from side to side. Something emanated from him, something prickly and caged-animal tense. Or the alcohol was just making me anxious. He lurched up from his seat and tottered towards me and I immediately began fumbling with my napkin, then stirrer, anything to look busy, but as he passed I realized he was only going to the toilet. Still, following that I finished my drink in one swallow and left.

The third night, after having communicated obliquely with Colton, and he had adamantly stated his return the next afternoon was definite, I still went to the bar. It had become the thing I did to occupy my nights without him, and it made sense (at least to me), my inhabiting this lost-in-time, unkempt space. Rosie acknowledged my presence with a half-smile, but then carried on with the task that occupied her attention this evening: slicing wedges of lime.

Colton was distant when he returned, there was a haze over his responses, a fuzzy nimbus obscuring his usual demeanor. I could have chalked it up to his being busy, or the difficulty with the interview, how the project was not quite coalescing, but I was not feeling overly generous.

He scrabbled through his bag, then flipped through his notebook, then grabbed his laptop and toggled through the multiple tabs in his browser after flopping onto the bed. We did not know how, here in this space, to negotiate each other's temperaments. I began to tidy up—I'd let things become dismally cluttered in his brief absence.

I guessed he had seen Max, though he didn't say it. Max had been on the fringes of the whole documentary since its conception. Max was also Colton's ex-boyfriend. He and Max were now, he assured me, fervidly platonic. I found it hard to dislike Max, and I also found it hard to not. Colton was, well is, a serial monogamist. I was the first and only person he began seeing after he and Max parted ways. I was, prior to meeting Colton, the opposite, not quite so ready to nest. Which is why it surprised me when I did with him, the ease with which we came together. I had met Max only a handful of times, as he and Colton kept a cordial distance from each other's social circles. Colton has a way of containing the different portions of his life, hermetically sealing off the different portions.

Since I've admitted several unpleasant truths already, I suppose I can admit that I felt superior to Colton, during those first giddy months, when I was falling for him and him for me. All right, after too. Which is ridiculous. We generally read the same books, received roughly the same liberal arts education. Yet there it was. Maybe it was the way he downplayed his intelligence, or how he let his enthusiasm overtake him in moments, something I had difficulty doing. The fact that he was a terrific artist but wasn't invested in his own success. Maybe we're too similarly wired, and I needed some wedge—imagined, but there—to pry between us.

In bed that night I did the things—Colty, I whispered, would you like and shall I, and then before he could answer—to which his body responded, I knew the locations and methods, tongue in places. When he submitted, it was just that…a surrender. Hadn't I always been the one, of late, to initiate things?

Do you think this was a mistake? he said the next morning, without inflection, over bacon.

I clutched the handle of my coffee mug tighter. The faraway aspect I had noticed had taken root. I knew he was obsessing over his film. In that moment I wanted him to go back to the city, and the instant I had the thought I regretted it, because I knew that was exactly what he was going to do. So naturally I suggested it to him.

It was with this second departure I began to think that this whole thing was a set-up, that he'd brought me up here to gaslight me. That this was an elaborately constructed ploy to break up with me (or get me to break up with him). I vowed I would not act like some nervous heroine, left to shred tissues and fret and take to bed in the afternoon, nervous and overcome. I was not faithful in my vow. What happened was, I did take to my bed. The bed, the rented one, in the rented apartment. When we texted the responses I sent were curt, tart. I wrote to mutual friends, however, how much I was enjoying my time away: how refreshing it was, how revitalizing. I was intent on muddying the signal.

From afar neither of us addressed the things that needed to be said. He ramped up his enthusiasm. I really needed to be back in the city. I want you to stay and enjoy the place. Enjoy it for both of us. Are you sure you're okay? I mean, it's paid for. So. Be back soon. This weekend. Next week. See you soon. Soon.

I entrenched myself, invested in my solitude. I began to move in similar patterns to the locals, locating the ebbs and avoiding the swells of day-trippers. I learned new routes and took shortcuts and side streets, I clung to the outskirts. I ran. I sunbathed in the park. I took a flyer for the meditation class. I still did not read Proust. I vamped, I marked time, I dawdled. I continued making elaborate recipes for dinner, and trying out new cocktails, despite my dwindling bank account, the balance I loathed to check. Evenings I generally found myself at the bar, the dive, which I'd taken to calling Doldrums. I appreciated that Rosie was pleasantly disaffected, and that there was a group of elderly men that played darts in the back often.

I returned from the restroom to find, seated on the bar stool next to mine, the boy with the truck. I had not seen him in some time, though I had seen the truck often on my runs, midnight black and mud-caked always, generally parked near the alley where I first encountered it, and him. He was concentrating on something. I saw it was a game on his phone. His squinting made him look I thought like a confused old man. His head jerked up when I sat down, then his focus went back to the shiny, staccato plinking. He gestured to Rosie for another drink, just two fingers thrust into the air, not breaking his woozy attention to his device, and after she'd brought him another bottle of beer I signaled for another round as well. I pretended to read a day old copy of the *Times* that someone had left at the bar but my attention was drawn to this guy, for no other reason than I wanted a distraction. I wanted something different than Colton: raw, un-polished, inconsiderate, callused. He might damage me, I thought, and the idea held a sick appeal. When he got up to go outside, I followed, first placing a napkin over my drink, to reserve my place and it, even though this was not Manhattan and the bar so occupied that to leave your stool was ceding hardwon territory.

He was standing under a lamp in a pool of yellow light and the whole set-up, it occurred to me, felt too cinematically porny to be dangerous. He had a cigarette clutched tightly between his thumb and index finger.

I bum one of those? I said. Or slurred. And there it was. How quickly when the chips are down we gravitate back to the comfort of our vices. He fished a pack of Winstons out of his pocket and when he offered it to me I noticed a constellation of freckles on his right hand. I took one, and he then offered me a light.

Thanks. Sebastian, I said, and already my named sounded too faggy coming out of my mouth. I should have made something up, Brock or Jake or Flint, something with one syllable, less precious and lilting.

Huh?

He'd misheard, and now I was forced to repeat my name, and my em-barrassment quickened.

Sebastian, I was introducing myself.

Oh, uh-huh. Andy, he said, and hissed out a stream of smoke from be-tween his front teeth, which I noticed now were large and square, like two marble tombstones side by side in a graveyard.

Thanks, I said, waving the cigarette towards him, trying to keep the con-versation going for whatever reason, I quit but, yeah. And I let the sen-tence trail off. The burst of nicotine had made me woozy, and I wondered if I'd puke.

He did not seem to want a dollar for the cigarette, nor was he interested in engaging in the requisite small talk that seems to accompany these ex-changes, the social currency I'd known at home. We stood in amiable si-lence. I nodded to myself, as if I were in some reverie of thought. He was fit, though more from actual labor I guessed than a gym membership. He flicked the spent butt of his cigarette into the night in a furious arc, like a dying comet. He was halfway back inside before I managed to sputter out thanks again, and spent the next second contemplating the burning end of the cigarette I should not have bummed and had not wanted to finish, before trailing back inside.

So this would be a reprieve, a vacation of indulgence, a return to vice and bad behavior. A walkabout, free of Colton and our stagnating roles. There was a time when the quickest way for me to get over someone was to have them profess their affection. I had assumed this flight behavior stopped when we began dating.

When I got back inside Andy was in conversation with a boozy Asian man of indeterminate age, a rotten front tooth prominent in his raw-looking mouth. I tried to psychically signal my return to Andy, but he was engrossed; his body language, his attention to this clearly sodden individual—a neighbor, a co-worker—could have also read as a hustler vibe? Or maybe he was just a good listener? Remaining attuned to his conversation, I had another drink. Then another. Heady from the cigarette and the thrill of embracing something, or jettisoning something, or both. In the back of my mind I knew I was running out of money, and would have to limp back to the city, broke and shamed, but I did not want to acknowledge that fully, not yet.

I must have "rested my eyes," or whatever euphemism is appropriate, but I came to when Rosie was tapping on my forearm with her black lacquered nail. I smiled, composed myself, and lurched off the stool, steadying myself for a second before heading out the door. There was some weather pattern rolling in, and the night had grown muggy, thick. I was orienting myself towards the apartment when I saw Andy opening the cab of his truck. Overeager, I called out to him, Hey hey, and when he turned back I stopped, halfway between the door to the bar and his vehicle. I just…can I bum another cigarette?

He patted the pockets of his jeans as I moved closer.

This, I'm sure you're thinking, is where the trouble starts. You'd be wrong. The violence we expect is seldom the violence we receive.

Here, finish these, he said, tossing a soft pack containing the two remaining Winstons. I watched his taillights weave down the road. I stuck a cigarette in my mouth, then remembered I was without a light.

I woke up late the next morning, well, early afternoon if we're being honest, my mouth feeling gummy and foul, remembering I had forgotten to charge my phone. I plugged it in while I made toast, and when I looked over it there were a stream of texts from Colton, an escalating barrage of entreaties. Need to talk; Project fucked; Saw Max; Miss you; Need your guidance; Coming up this Sunday; Sebby? Sebby!!! My finger hovered over the keypad as I waited for the coffee to percolate. I wanted to know how far we could hurt each other so we would never go that far again. I set my phone back down and poured a cup.

I showed up at the bar that night with a fresh pack of cigarettes and the will to see Andy again. I was up against a timetable, an inevitable reckoning, and I didn't like being cornered. So, I ordered a whiskey neat and waited. And waited. And was ultimately rewarded when Andy did show up, sawdust-covered and tense-seeming; ready to unwind. He settled in and the bartender, not Rosie tonight, but instead a sour and puffy Greek man, pushed a bottle of beer towards him and collected the requisite bills. I let him collect himself before offering a gentle wave of recognition. He signaled back, a head nod, an affirmation. We sipped our drinks, and then another round, and then, when I caught his eye, I signaled with my pack of smokes. Would you care to, the meaning. He gave me a thumbs up.

We convened outside, under the yellow lamp, and this time I, the generous one, supplied him with cigarette and fire.

Stephen, right, he said.

Er, Sebastian.

Yeah, sorry. He messed around with his phone for a minute, his thick fingers mashing out a text message.

You like to play poker? he asked.

Is that an attempt at euphemism, I said.

He responded with a blank look. Perhaps even blinking.

Never mind. Sure, I mean, why?

Got a game set up.

Then why not?

Come on. Let's finish our drinks and go.

My feet rested on take-out bags and balled-up paper towels and who knows what else as we rode the few short blocks to the apartment. We walked up a flight of steps outside the main structure and he rapped his knuckles on the weathered red door, which was opened by a witchy, blowsy woman, grey hair kinky and disheveled, wearing a loose black smock and thick jangly bracelets. Come on in, took you long enough, she said. Introductions were made, and while she busied herself in the kitchen, fishing out bottles of beer from the fridge, I scanned the room, which contained a few worn leather couches and some framed art prints. The only real light, aside from a few flickering votive candles on the mantle, came from the fish tank, where a collection of saltwater creatures sluggishly glided around. A door, from down the hall, banged open.

Kostya's just leaving, she said. Right, kiddo?

Kostya, thin but jagged, all sharp angles, conveying a weariness with life beyond his age, dug his fists into his thin jacket and eyed me before he scooted out the door. Roommate? Relative? Boarder? The arrangement was unclear. I took a bottle of lager and was ushered onto the back porch, where on a forest-green plastic table the game was arrayed. I met the other players, sort of: two guys in their mid-twenties to early thirties, if I had to guess, thick and hard and inscrutable—Joseph and Gil. Andy took a seat to my left, Callie, whose house we were at, to my right.

I know nothing about poker. Texas Hold 'Em was what we were playing, and, being tipsy and intimidated, my strategy was just to wait until I came across a pair of cards. Otherwise I bluffed. This, as it turned out, was not a terrible strategy. The buy-in was twenty bucks, I won more hands than not, and by about three in the morning I was up two hundred dollars. Gil had left by this point, frustrated, and Callie was yawning, Andy teasing her about her advancing age. I'm calling it, she said, and began to clean up the table. Andy shrugged and started to help, emptying ashtrays and scooping up bottle caps, and I pocketed my money. I'll just, I can walk home, I said, feeling vaguely confident I could do just that. Andy was disappearing down the hallway, and said, See ya, and I said, Thanks again, Callie, and was out the door.

Someone waved to me from the base of the staircase. When I reached the bottom to address the figure there were suddenly other shapes, bodies, limbs, hands groping and I was enveloped, caressed in a near-clinical fashion, then released, spat back, minus, of course, my winnings and my phone and my credit cards, the encounter punctuated by one final sharp blow.

I jogged after the figures for a few paces before tripping over my own feet. The fall knocked the wind out of me. Rolling over onto my back I lay staring up at the sky, dotted with stars. So plainly visible. I hadn't bothered to notice the stars since I arrived here. Through the swelling slit of my left eye I was convinced I saw a UFO. It wasn't a shooting star, or comet. This object, shimmery and in flux, remained, in my (albeit limited) field of vision for several minutes, moving not only left and right but up and down. It seemed intent on observing, commenting. It hovered like a poem. Colton was my immediate thought, I should tell him about this, he'd want to record it, and reached instinctively for my stolen phone.

# blue

## DAVID BARCLAY MOORE

The sharp outline of Juju's dark body flashed across Blue's eyes. It spun majestically in space, arms punching up into air. Matte black muscles twitched together.

Blue swallowed.

Reese, his own arms waving uselessly, could only stand beneath Juju.

(catapulted ball arched into net)

And watch.

"Nah, nigga, three points!" cried Juju, his smiling bald head bobbing up and down. He glanced in Blue's direction.

Sitting on the concrete side court, Blue diverted his eyes and began inspecting ash around his black knuckles. "Ju wins," he said, smirking, "again."

"You don't think I can count?" Reese asked Blue and spat into the bushes. "Best out of nine, Ju."

"I ain't got all day to shoot bricks with your ass," said Juju.

"You scared of getting beat," said Reese.

"Uh, I whooped your ass four times today," said Juju.

Reese's brow wrinkled. His mustard-colored face, topped with oily curls and sweat, started turning red. The ball shot from his hand and bounced off the fence behind the pole supporting the hoop. Chest heaving, he turned toward Blue.

"You play, man?" asked Reese.

"It's getting kind of late," replied Blue. His large round eyes blinked in a nervous way. Blue grabbed his backpack. He wobbled to his feet and dusted the seat of his jeans.

Reese gave Blue a quick once-over while bending to scoop up the ball. "Faggot-ass can't hoop," he mumbled under his breath.

"Naw, he don't *want* to play," Juju spurted. "That's all. Me and Blue got to step."

"A'ight, then," said Reese. "I'll get up with you later."

The young men slapped hands.

"**H**ow come you ain't hoop with us, Blue?" asked Juju.

"Didn't want to. Felt like watching."

"That's cool."

Juju's rough black fingers slid over his faultless baldy. Letting the palm rest on his forehead, the teenager paused, squinting with almond-shaped eyes at Blue.

"If you can't play, I'll teach you," said Juju.

The two young men ambled up the footpath in D.C.'s Rock Creek Park, Juju absently dribbling his ball. There was quiet as they stretched their necks to the changing trees. The various oranges and reds of autumn were in full effect. Brilliant leaves fanned out above and lay beneath.

"Hey, you see me dunk on that boy Reese?" yelled Juju.

"I was there, man."

"I'm cold ain't I? Huh? Ain't I? I *slammed* on that brotha!"

Blue looked at him like Juju was mad.

"Ka-whoomp!" Juju laughed, sticking out his tongue, Jordan-style, as he faked a right past Blue's head.

Blue grinned. "You *silly*."

Approaching them on the path, two men strode holding hands. They were both Black and thirtyish. One wore a red and purple warm-up suit, the other blue jogging tights and a gray sweatshirt. They chatted quietly, chuckling at each other's comments. When their eyes met they smiled self-consciously.

Clasped hands parted briefly as they passed Blue and Juju. The older men nodded to them in acknowledgment. No expression marked the teenagers' faces. Juju stared straight ahead. Blue glanced back over his shoulder to see the men's hand hold resume as they disappeared around the leafy bend.

Juju shook his head. "My father live around the way from one of them *places*," he said, "over in Southeast. Where them fags be going."

"For real? They got a *place*?"

"Yep."

"You been?"

"Fuck naw. What I want to go for? I ain't no punk."

Juju started off the trail, up a wooded hill.

"Come on," he said.

"What?"

"Come on. I want to show you something."

Just on the hill's other side, he led him down a small shaded valley, closer to Connecticut Avenue. It was darker here than on the footpath. The cool dampness of the air raised jet-black goose pimples on Blue's skin.

Juju skipped across and hopped over rocks and fallen trees. Blue followed him deeper into the wood. The two descended the hill, kicking up leaves. The feeling of humidity grew.

(up ahead, sounds of rushing water)

Blue struggled to keep his balance as he crept across the log connecting two banks of a small stream. Legs dangling, Juju had straddled the log and was watching water pass beneath. Blue reached him and eased down beside Juju.

The wood around the stream was speckled with sunlight piercing the canopy. Blue's own reflection spied upward at the two. His round forehead and puckered lips resembled those of a baby. He breathed in deeply but stopped short when he noticed Juju's grasp on his reflection.

"This my private river," Juju said, holding the stare.

Blue gazed down at the stream carrying bits of debris elsewhere. The flow was smooth, gentle. He spat on a rock, protruding.

"I come here when I got something on my mind," Juju said.

Blue shifted slightly and examined how the light specks played on Juju's face. Above the stream's murmur, he heard the park animals chattering amongst themselves.

Jerking as if he had been shaken awake, Juju spat on the same rock. The stream licked at the foamy mixture. It began to break up.

The flow would wash everything away.

**A** hundred dark shadows grooved as one against a seamless black background. All together, they dipped shoulders to the left side, then popped right-sides toward the ceiling. A hundred knees froze.

(break of the record )

And jerked back to life when the needle hit the vinyl again.

Young backs caved while white teeth darted beneath dim basement light. A hundred kinky heads gasped backward for air.

And Blue thought they were drowning.

He and Juju leaned against a large washer in an empty corner. Juju turned up one of the forties that were on ice inside the washing machine. Through the brown glass, he watched the last of the liquor snake down the bottle. With bass shaking his whole body, Juju closed his eyes to fix on the alcohol rushing into his mouth.

"You going to sit against that washer all night?" a voice asked from the other side of Juju's eyelids. He opened them.

Karen pulled nervously on flat yellow braids, twisting one like a noose around her pinkie. Black eyebrows arched waiting for a response. Hazel eyes darted back and forth to Juju's.

"You heard?" Karen asked him.

"Nope," Juju chuckled. "Sho' ain't."

He stumbled forward, grabbing Karen around the waist. Juju's lips hung over her forehead. He belched a cloud of malt liquor in her face.

"Eyew, Juju! You are so nasty!"

Karen tried waving the smell away. Juju popped her ass as she ran off. The party people went out of control.

"My cousin like her," Blue said, laughing, "*sooo* much. He would do *any*thing to get with her."

"Oh, yeah?" Juju mugged Blue. "She broke my *dranking* groove." He waved his index finger in Blue's face. "Me no likey."

They both snickered.

Juju playfully knocked Blue's shoulder. A wave of warmth flowed over Blue. He grabbed Juju by the back of his neck. For a moment, they leaned against the washer like that, eye to eye. Juju anxiously glanced around the dark room, then pushed out of Blue's reach.

"Watch this, Blue." Juju reached down into the washer for another malt. "I was just fucking with her. She *a'ight*."

Juju pimp-walked over to Karen on the dance floor. At first she still looked pissed, but he leaned down to whisper in her ear. She stopped dancing. They stood frozen like that for several moments until Karen finally melted with a grin and a giggle.

The DJ threw on one of the jams.

As the two started to dance, again Juju lifted his bottle to his lips. He grinned across the room to Blue and waved for him to come over. Blue shook his head and glared the other way.

A pretty girl met Blue's eyes. She smiled at him. Her dark brown neck stretched back, letting him catch a glimpse of her.

"They got a place," Blue whispered to himself.

"I boned that bitch, uh, Karen," Juju repeated.

Blue stared at him blankly.

"You know her, man. Live around the way from your cousin Pooch and them," Juju said. He jerked toward a distant tire screech. "You know her, man."

The street was nearly empty. Blue's upside-down bicycle sat in the brittle yellow grass of Juju's tiny front yard. Juju's eyes never turned up from it. Hands blackened with oil, he tinkered with the chain, which was stuck between gears.

"From last night?" Blue's voice cracked.

Still not looking up from Blue's bicycle, Juju nodded. He started to grimace. The damned chain would not move.

Blue watched Juju's hands for a minute. Caked in oil. His hands were large. Blue felt their largeness whenever he shook one.

"Juju. I ain't happy like this."

(there was a snap)

Juju had yanked the oily bicycle chain free. "There it go." He laid it onto the gear track and spun the wheel around to test it. It ran smoothly.

"Ernest!" a woman's voice shouted from within Juju's row house.

"Ma'am?" Juju replied, then to Blue, "I'll get up with you, man. A'ight, then."

They started to slap mitts, but stopped. Juju's hands were stained with oil. Instead, they simply touched elbows. As Blue put on his backpack, Juju jogged up the steps, into his row house. The wooden screen door, peeling, shut with a splintering slap.

Blue mounted his bike and rode.

It was rush hour and his face ran hot and tight.

Blue had been racing against pavement for an hour, pedaling with the flow of automobiles. Metrobuses bullied their ways into the thick of things. Delivery vans halted suddenly in his path. Travelers were being channeled to destinations by a stream of taxis that poured around him.

Suddenly swerving his bike, he cut across traffic.

After having passed the sunny entrance several times, Blue finally ducked in. The black hole swallowed him.

The place smelled like a stew of beer and cigarette butts. Blue handed his ticket to a man in a cubbyhole, who tore it in half.

The man squinted. "Brotha, how old *are* you?"

"Twenty-one," Blue stuttered.

"Yeah, right." The man in the cubbyhole smiled slyly at him. "You expect me to believe you was born in '71? You gotta wear one of *these*." The man secured a plastic colored band around Blue's wrist. "All right, go on in, then." Other men kept filing in behind Blue from the outside.

As he neared the end of the dark corridor, the great room ahead glowed. The boom of music grew louder, jerking control of his heart. He lost his balance and fell against a wall.

Blue shook.

A man wearing a white polo shirt and khaki pants grabbed him. "Hey, baby, you all right?"

Blue tore his elbow away and glared.

Another man said to the first, "Leave his ass. He tripping."

They left Blue alone, leaning on the wall. Walking again, he was soon surrounded by a room full of men, all shades of brown.

On his left hand side was a long bar. These same men, all pressed into it, fought for the bartenders' attentions. Using his teeth, Blue tore at the plastic band around his wrist.

(it would not break)

A man painted in make-up and draped in silky ivory *pajamas* knocked into him. Blue hopped away, fists raised. The man continued speeding past Blue, dropping a faint "*Sorry*" in his wake.

The man in pajamas stopped at a group of tall lean men in dark business suits who clung around a shadowy corner table sipping beers. The pajama man kissed them all on their cheeks. One of the businessmen, the tallest, smiled at Blue as the man leaned forward to hug the pajama man.

Frowning, Blue curled the palm of his hand into a cone and easily slipped off the plastic band. It dropped to the floor. Blue kicked it away.

He stared back at the bar. One of the bartenders, a dark-skinned man with giant-sized muscles, mixed drinks, shirtless. Other than his physique, he looked like anybody else. Blue studied his hands as he tended bar.

The bartender waved for him to come over. Blue's stomach squelched. The bartender waved again, this time impatiently. Blue walked toward him slowly.

"What you standing over there, looking so mad at?" the bartender asked, flashing perfect white teeth.

"I ain't mad," said Blue, fixing an angry expression.

"Oh, really?" the bartender replied, smiling.

Blue was flushed.

"Homie, you better get that ugly look out your face." The bartender laughed, muscles twitching. "Cute little thing like you."

Blue glanced down at the carpet. He heard a bang on the bar and threw his eyes back up. There was a glass of something. He dove to his pockets for cash. The bartender waved him away.

"Go on now," he said. "You came here to have fun."

"Thanks," Blue managed. "I'm Blue."

They shook hands quickly. The bartender almost squeezed Blue's hand off. The teen flinched slightly, and bumped into a boyish female couple hugged-up next to him. One of them leaning against the bar, the other pressing her friend into it, they paused to look Blue up and down, before resuming a long kiss.

"I'm Marty," the bartender said. "Whenever you want some more *orange juice*, you come back here." Winking, Marty leaned over toward Blue. "Don't be so evil!"

Blue nodded, flickering a weak smile for the first time since he had entered the club. He held up his glass. "Thanks," he repeated.

"All right," Marty said, and then flew to the other end of the bar.

Blue walked back out into the crowd. Pausing near the dance floor, he sipped his drink and spat it back out. It *was* orange juice!

His eyes shot back to the bar across the room. Marty the bartender, now mixing a cocktail, was chatting it up with someone else. Blue frowned into his own glass.

"Something wrong with your drink?"

It was the tallest businessman who stood there, having left his corner of friends. The businessman grinned, waiting for a response to his question. Out of the corner of Blue's eye, he could see the rest of the businessmen watching closely.

Blue craned his neck upward. The businessman was tall, with a very light complexion, and about as old as Blue's father. Looking back to the dance floor, Blue resumed sipping his juice, wordlessly.

"Would you like another?" the man asked.

Blue shook his head. His attention was on two dancers competing in a vogue-down. On the dance floor, a large crowd had gathered around them.

"That stuff's tricky." The man chuckled. "You dance?"

Squinting his eyes, Blue leered at him.

"I'm John," the man said. "John Myricks." He handed Blue a business card. "I hope I'm not bugging you. I thought you were handsome."

Stone-faced, Blue continued to look straight ahead at the voguers.

"Give me a call. I'd like to get to know you. Maybe you'll let me take you out to dinner."

At this, Blue let a smile escape first, then a snicker. John's face emptied. Blue turned his own face away, snickering.

Then, "I'm sorry," Blue managed. "Thanks," and he escaped, giggling.

John stood there, face red. He pivoted back to his corner of buddies. They were all laughing too. He raised his eyebrows, shrugged his shoulders and rejoined them.

Blue had fled into the crowd, hysterical. A *man* had offered him a drink. A *man* had asked him to dance. A *man* had asked him to dinner. A *man* had asked him on a date.

What did he look like? What made *them* think he was like that? He knew he didn't look like he was *that* way.

Blue read the business card John had given him: JOHN H. MYRICKS, THERAPIST. The office address was downtown, near the Mall. Blue tucked the card into the back of his jeans.

"Who do I look like?" Blue mumbled to himself in disbelief.

He snickered again, unable to contain himself, unaccustomed to the everyday realities of this new world. Blue dissolved into the colorful, mixing crowds. They all looked so happy.

And it was suddenly so bright here.


As he snuck through the front door, the bluish hue of the TV lit up the hallway. Blue grimaced. Hoping to slip past the TV room unnoticed, he instinctively hunched his shoulders and stuck forward his toe. Maybe whoever was in there had fallen asleep.

Just then, his mother's shiny head of black curls popped into the hall. "Hey, Blue," she said smiling. "We was beginning to worry." Her head disappeared again. "Where you been?" her disembodied voice asked.

Blue winced. "Uh, *nowhere*," he said talking to the empty hall. Then, "I was on my bike." Laying his backpack on the hall floor, he quietly hung his jacket in the closet.

"Oh, okay!" Mama's voice yelled back, sounding distracted.

Blue sniffed his shirt. It smelled like beer and cigarettes.

"I told you that's where he was," another voice said softly, speaking to Blue's mother. Blue recognized Ray's voice, Mama's boyfriend. Ray acted like he thought he was Blue's dad.

"Shut up, Ray," Mama's voice said. "Blue, next time you call, hear? You make Mama worry about you!"

"Yes, ma'am!" Blue yelled.

"You never listen to me, *Angie*," Ray's voice scolded playfully.

"That's 'cuz you ain't never said nothing."

The sound of a slap echoed into the hall. Ray laughed deeply. Blue heard crackling. Like they were eating something crunchy.

Except for the TV, there was now silence. With a running start, Blue took this opportunity to race by the TV room door. He ran, heading toward the stairs and his second-floor bedroom.

"Blue!" Mama's voice stopped him.

"Yeah?" he called back.

"What you mean, 'yeah'?" she yelled. "Boy, come back here!"

Blue sighed and slunk back to the door. Inside, he saw the bowl of popcorn he had heard. Two bottles of beer and a glass of red Kool-Aid sat on the coffee table. Perched on the couch were Mama, Ray and, on one corner: Juju!

Blue jumped.

"Boy, what's got into you?" Mama asked.

"Nothin'," Blue said. "What's Juju doing here?"

"Ask *him*," Mama said, irritated.

"Hey, Blue," Ray said with a wide smile. "How you doing, partner?"

Blue raised his eyebrows to him and let his head float like it was bobbing on a lake.

"What's up, Blue," Juju mumbled. "I just came over."

"Yeah," Ray started, sounding exasperated, "that boy's been sitting here for hours and hours and hours—"

"I ain't been here that long!" Juju frowned and stood.

"Your narrow black ass's been sitting on this couch long enough!" Ray shouted after him. "Tossing back popcorn and Kool-Aid, ruining my *game*." Ray squeezed Mama's knee.

Mama slapped Ray's large thigh once more.

To Mama, "I got a long haul tomorrow, baby," Ray protested. "I won't see you no more till next month."

"Blue, why don't you all go upstairs," Mama said. "Me and Ray want to watch TV. You can watch TV up there."

Blue cast his eyes to the set. The Sunday Evening News was on. Footage from the Bush-Clinton debate flashed across the screen. An impish Governor Clinton smiled into the camera.

"Okay?" Mama repeated.

"Yes, ma'am," Blue said, returning his eyes to hers.

She glimmered. "You sure are getting grown. And handsome. You'll always be Mama's baby."

Blue rolled his eyes. He turned to Juju and waved him on. As the two climbed the stairs, they heard Mama giggle from within the TV room.

**B**lue locked his bedroom door and spun around. Juju plopped down on the bed, then stretched across the mattress to reach the remote control. He flicked on Blue's TV. Juju began watching it in silence; an old *M\*A\*S\*H* rerun was on.

Blue frowned at the TV and sat down on the far side of his bed.

"I can't *stand* this show," he said.

"Why?" Juju asked, keeping his eyes on the screen.

"'Cuz," Blue started, "it's depressing. It looks ugly. Why everybody got to wear that ugly green?"

"They in the *army*, nigga. It's a war."

Juju slid across the bed, closer to Blue.

"Yeah, but everybody they operate on dies. They never leave that, that camp, or whatever—"

"It's a hospital, a *military* hospital," said Juju.

Blue stared down at him. Juju placed his head so it was lightly touching Blue's knee. Juju's eyes were still glued to the TV. His large hands loosened around the remote.

Blue continued, "And they never got back home from the war. See? Even the music's depressing."

Rolling onto his back, Juju thought this over. His head turned on the mattress to stare up at Blue. "I think they do go home in the end."

"For real?" Blue asked.

"Yeah," he answered, breathless. "Everybody goes home, right?"

Juju coughed and wiped the corner of his mouth. All the air had been sucked from the room.

And with that, Blue leaned over and quietly kissed him. Their lips pressed together, Juju let out a whimper, the kind one makes when either pained, or relieved. Nervous, the two young men parted self-consciously and met eyes briefly.

Blue kissed Juju again.

Giddy laughter bubbled back and forth between their lips like oxygen.

# Bro

## DAVE WAKELY

---

*I* *shouldn't be seeing you like this.*

As I made the coffees, needing one to face you as much I guessed you would need one to face the day, Poppy had texted. "I guess he's with you?" it said. "Just checking. I don't want to talk to him."

A simple "Yes, he's here" was as far I ventured. I didn't feel up to knowing more. Certainly not to asking questions.

"Poor you," came the surprisingly quick reply. I left the phone on the table.

As I carry the mugs down the hallway, I'm wondering what the sympathy is for, beyond having to face you so early in the day. After all, I wasn't the one who went to bed with a bottle of Scotch. I tighten my dressing-gown belt and take a deep breath, and then a mouthful of my coffee, before I nudge open the door to the spare room.

*I really shouldn't be seeing you like this.*

The thought repeats like a self-help mantra as I look down at you, slumped half-dressed against the wall, knees drawn up to your chest. You were supposed to be—no, you always were—the Golden Boy, the one who made it all look effortless. The handsome athletic one with the walk of a panther, while I was the spindly antelope whose presence you tolerated while you kept one eye on the possibility of moments for unobserved torture. For all your lazy, loose-limbed loping, those haunches somehow always carried the promise—or the threat—of muscle.

You shouldn't be sitting here, so far past shame you don't even seem to care that your dirty T-shirt has ridden up over the baby paunch that last night's baggy sweater managed to hide. Against the whiteness of your sweating belly, its faded baby pink looks strangely colourful. "Ride Hard or Ride Home," it declares, the slogan stretched and skewed, its bike-wheel image stained with last night's spilled drink. You're not looking exactly saddle-ready.

And standards aren't the only thing that have slipped. Their presence no more invited than the rest of you, I can see your balls, as unshaven as your chin, fallen from the leg of your crumpled grey boxers.

*I shouldn't be seeing you like this…*

Old underwear at that. We were never alike. You've always mocked the way I groom and preen, as if you can sense the underbelly of anxiety. Do you still remember those teenage fights where you'd tell me how women judge on more than mere appearances—that you weren't just the handsome one? Luckier in love, you always boasted, even if that wasn't always the most accurate four-letter word for your liaisons.

Even bedhead hair used to look good on you, where you inherited Mum's sleek locks and I got Dad's unruly curls. So this is how you look when your luck runs out. I watch as you comb your fingers through your new-grown beard, its mannered Edwardian pomp out of tune with your carefully composed nonchalance, and realise I enjoy how much it disfigures you. It hides that cocksure chin that's always jutting slightly, like a man sneaking home in a photo-finish. That always seems to be saying "I could, if I wanted to." The exact verb has never mattered.

No wonder you never liked Paul. The only one who ever bested you, that time you shared the hall mirror, optimising yourselves before the dinner guests arrived. As Paul set to work with gels and brushes, taming the waves I adored and he detested, you couldn't resist. "Don't you ever wish you were naturally straight?" I heard you wisecrack. "So much easier." Smug, maybe, but not quick. Paul just eyed your reflection up and down and sighed. "Well, less of a handful, I'm told," he said, softly but firmly, his eyes lingering a precisely measured moment too long on your groin's reflection.

I squat down next to you, nursing the black coffee I've made you. Behind me, Trigger's claws clack gently as he pads down the hallway, curious as to why I'm in an unused room. His old-dog eyes squint in the sunshine streaming through the open curtains.

You almost make a matching pair, his ageing black fur turning brown in streaks just as the ends of your exuberant moustache glint with threads of orange. He stops in the doorway, rubbing his neck against the door frame, marking his territory as he eyes the intruder. Satisfied with his labours, he ambles forward, sniffing the air suspiciously. I watch you hold out a hand: palm up, the way I taught you. He pauses, nostrils flaring, and then starts to back away, lips curling.

"Here," I say, holding the coffee out to you. Your bloodshot eyes look up at me. "See if that brings you round."

There's no affection in my gesture, but before I can straighten up you've wrapped your arms around me and pulled me to your chest. Behind me, a low growl crawls out of Trigger's throat, his claws clicking against the bare wood floor as reflex extends them.

"Thanks, bro," you mutter into my hair, so self-pityingly it's almost believable. "I love you."

"And you stink," I protest as you crush me into your t-shirt's musky folds.

"Hey, that's not nice." You actually have the nerve to sound indignant. "I'm not one of your bloody primary school kids. And I thought you were pleased to see me?"

I let the question pass but the stench is unmissable, a sad bachelor's cocktail of whisky and wanking. Your inhibitions have always been highly soluble—two drinks and the satyr's out of its shirt and dancing. And blood may be thicker than water, but these walls are thin. Any flimsier and I might have even seen you, silhouetted by the bedside light. One hand wrapped round your glass and the other busy with wishful thinking. I hope you drew the curtains before you passed out.

*I shouldn't be seeing you like this.*

Understandable, I tell myself. Under the circumstances. Or your account of them, at least. Wandering back from your brother-in-law's pitch on a family camping trip to find a bare stretch of flattened grass. No tent, no car, no wife. Just a note tent-pegged to a tree, telling you she'd left you and not wasting many words to say it.

"Remember what Grandpa used to tell us," I say, prising myself free and standing over you. "He'd leave us in the living room, let us stay up to watch a late film." I can hear the schoolteacher in my voice now, but you've earned it. "Sleep well, boys, and I don't want to hear anyone rubbing Aladdin's lamp, you get me?"

You start to laugh before it's clear I won't be joining in, standing here blank-faced, one hand on hip and the other gesturing down toward you. It's a posture you would normally mock, but there's no comeback this morning.

"I'm loading the machine. Take it off and I'll wash it. It's not like you'll fit anything of mine."

I look away as you peel off your T-shirt, reaching over you to unlatch the window and push it ajar.

"There you are," I hear you say, holding up the ball of crumpled cotton for me to take, your face taking offence as I handle it cautiously between pinched fingertips. Trigger leans forward to sniff and then recoils, sneezing.

"Bro, behave. We share DNA."

"Not this directly we don't. Bro."

You fumble to your feet, either still drunk or fighting the aftereffects, and stand looking at your toes. Behind me, I hear Trigger backing away.

"I'll put the shower on. Leave the boxers here—I'll wash them too." You're already reaching for the waistband, about to shuck them off, and I turn to walk away. "There's a spare robe in the bathroom," I say over my shoulder. "Put it on, afterwards. I'll make breakfast."

This morning's lack of explanations hasn't come as a surprise. It took you two years to get round to introducing me to her, one messy Sunday pub lunch. "This is Poppy," you said. "Isn't she *intoxicating?*" As I reached out to shake her hand, she waved it away and kissed me, told me how lovely it was to meet me. I remember thinking you had the wrong plant metaphor. Not intoxicating but hardy. Upright and reliable, ready to root and propagate.

Sturdy too, from another moment I remember. You were trying to impress her brother with your globe-trotting piety, the whole Mr Cool social entrepreneur shtick I'd heard a hundred times. All those tales about how you charm "the locals", especially the ones you call "the females", as if anything that happens beyond Basingstoke is a wildlife documentary. "Sometimes I think my husband won't be happy till he's irrigated every canal south of Tripoli," Poppy said, and Ben laughed slightly too loudly. I remember thinking that, aside from the obvious, he seemed more your type than she did. Cocky, self-assured, never quite able to pass his reflection without pausing to admire it.

And then one day, Ben ditched the girlfriend and arrived with a man. Not unusual, Poppy said, for him. All those years of snide asides you'd made at a little brother you could torment, I thought, and now you'd have to deal with it with a friend.

I've always preferred Poppy, to be honest. When it was obvious that Paul and I were having troubles, she was the one who found quiet moments to take me aside, check that I was okay. You never asked.

Ben was worse. That dinner party after we'd finally split up, he wouldn't let it go, telling me drunkenly that it was a tragedy when lovers become brothers, that in a free world it should be the other way around. He didn't stop there. Under the table, his hand landed on my thigh and worked its way up to my crotch as I squirmed to get away. "Boundaries are for geography teachers," he whispered in my ear, though it felt more like a hiss.

All the while you sat opposite me, pissed and smiling, while my head flooded with memories. All those teenage years I avoided any sight of you less than fully dressed. Steered clear of the bathroom if you were in it, buried my head in a book when you changed on the beach. No matter how desirable you might have been if you'd had different blood in your veins, just the thought was enough to make me squirm. And you'd known too, never missing a chance to tease.

*I shouldn't be seeing you like this...*

It was Poppy who saved me, that evening, shouting at Ben to shut the fuck up till the pair of you slunk outside to kick a ball round the garden. "If he wasn't my brother," she'd said to me, putting an arm round my shoulder as we watched through the window, "sometimes I could fucking kill him." She turned and looked straight at me. "You probably know how that feels."

**A**s I sit as the kitchen table, Trigger at my feet, I can hear the roaring water and your groans as it starts to bring you round. You used to sing in the shower when we were kids. Rugby songs, or dirty versions of hits of the day. Anything to embarrass me as I sat on my bed, waiting my turn. This morning, you're silent.

My phone sits in front me, tempting as a tantalus, as I tell myself Poppy deserves a moment of concern.

"OK," I type, "what did he do?"

I put it back down, not expecting a response, and get up to load the washing machine. The sudden burst of jolly music startles me as her reply arrives.

"Not what, Bobby," it says, in its emotionless sans-serif font. "Who."

I sit staring at it, not sure what to feel, listening to you cursing in the bathroom. I smile at the thought of you washing shampoo from your eyes. The discomfort seems only right. And then it sings again, rattling on the table as it vibrates.

"Ben. He screwed Ben."

Before I can even pick it up, it serenades me again.

"I saw them. I guess you don't want to see the video?"

I'm not sure how long I sit staring, sipping my coffee and hoping it won't ring again. Long enough for you to finish your shower, wrap a towel round your waist and pad unheard into the kitchen on bare feet.

"Any tea going?"

Your voice startles me, and I splash my coffee over the photocopied lesson plans I'd left on the table. Outline maps of Europe soak up the spill, borders dissolving as the hot liquid reunites Czechoslovakia and blurs the boundaries of the Balkans.

I spin out of my chair to grab a cloth, scaring the dog, but you're blocking the way to the sink, water dripping from your beard. I'm too slow again, and your arms are back around me.

"More lovable now?" you say, pressing yourself against me, your nauseating confidence obviously starting to recover. As your wet moustache grazes my neck, I lean as much of my body away from you as I can, but you only push yourself forward more firmly.

I start to protest, voice muffled in your hair as I squirm. I try to wrestle free, smaller and less strong, and I can feel the towel slipping down between us, feel you more than I would ever wish, insistent now. And then the music comes again.

As your hand lets go of me to reach for the phone, the towel falls to the floor. "Shit," I hear you shout as you peer at the phone's screen, and I lose my footing on the towel as I try to swivel round. As my elbow hits the floor, I see Trigger jump, teeth bared.

For a second or two, there's a chaos of screams and growls, his jaws firmly attached to your naked backside. And then a sickening crunch before you collapse over the table and he runs howling from the room. Face down in the coffee-soaked maps, blood running down your thighs, I can hear you swearing over and over.

"Stay still," I say, as I grab the first aid kit from its cupboard. Flicking on the striplight, two things are obvious. The hairy arse leant over my kitchen table, bitten and bleeding, is recognisably the same as the one on the phone in your hand, albeit less mobile now. And sitting proud from its skin, a yellowing stump in the crease of your buttocks, is a dog's broken tooth.

As I put my hand on your hip, I feel you flinch. "Trust me," I say, as I watch your anus gasp like a landed fish. I grip the broken stump and yank it free, a fresh ooze of scarlet running down over your balls. Beyond a clench-jawed wince, there is no sound from you, although the phone is still broadcasting your energetic grunting.

*I really shouldn't be seeing you like this.*

"Phone," I say. An order, not a request. I snatch it from you and silence it, scrolling through my address book.

"Ambulance?" I hear you say, lifting your face from the table. Your beard is striped with different colours, my photocopying finally dissolving in a mixture of coffee and cold shower water.

"Vet."

"But he bit me!" you almost squawk, trying to lever yourself back upright.

"You'll live," I mutter, spilling the contents of the first-aid kit across the table to rummage through them. "And he's an old dog now."

"But he was being aggressive, vicious. He was being…"

As you realise I am about to rub stinging ointment into your buttocks, your words fade to silence.

"Loyal," I tell you. "He was being loyal."

I watch my hand slide past the antiseptic cream, fingers closing quietly round a pot of salt.

# Marsland

## CARLSON HEATH

---

**T**wice, during the months when the Dark Lord lived with us, we found him covered in blood. The second time was in our bedroom—there he stood panting by the nightstand, spraying the white wall with a fine red mist every time he shook. The first time was the day we found him. He was down in a road ditch, just his wagging tail visible over the top of the grass. We couldn't really see the blood until we got up close and even then the dead ewe he fed on distracted our attention. She was a black sheep—her neck torn open, a terrible red hole extending down between her forelegs exposing a bleeding anatomy lesson all the way to her udder.

The Dark Lord lifted his head, his teeth stained pink. He could have been a German shepherd mixed with a mastiff. Pétur said he looked like a Malinois. There was something wrong with his eyes. They were white—two white orbs inside a black mask.

Of course Pétur slid in between the dog and the carcass, cooing and putting his hands right under the beast's bloody mouth.

"Dammit, Pétur." I wanted to pull him away but was too chicken-shit to go down there.

"If the ranchers see him eating the sheeps they will shoot him," Pétur said.

He lifted the dog over his neck and carried him upon his shoulders. There was a tang on the dog's breath—a mixture of metal and dust. All the blood in the fur dripped down Pétur's white t-shirt, converging into a v-shaped stream toward the small of his back. I studied the two white eyes. They were a contradiction: somehow both vacant and knowing.

"He looks blind," I said. "How could a blind dog attack and kill a sheep?"

"I will take him do the vet, Sergio. We need do check for microchip."

"I don't think people out here microchip their dogs."

Only nine people lived in Marsland, Nebraska (according to the Internet). Since Pétur and I only recently moved in, we weren't sure if we were eight and nine or ten and eleven. That we were eighty miles from the nearest vet didn't matter to Pétur Dahlberg, who already made the 160-mile roundtrip to spay the tabby that came with our barn, and to euthanize his hen when she prolapsed her ovaries.

His Nazi-blond hair was magenta by the time we got home, where he peeled off his clothes and coiled his long figure into the bathtub with the animal. It was a Neoclassical painting—Nude with Hellhound. I leaned against the sink, clutching my phone while red suds dripped down the shower curtain. I had 911 pre-dialed, ready to hit "send" at the first growl.

"We should find his owner," I said.

"There were no houses out there. How would a blinded dog walk such far on his own?"

After taking him to the vet and learning he had progressive retinal atrophy and no microchip, Pétur became convinced the dog was abandoned.

"Just because he doesn't have a microchip," I said, "doesn't mean there isn't someone looking for him."

"There is no 'lost dog' signs anywhere."

"We need to find his owner."

Pétur had already gone to work setting up a space in his studio for the Dark Lord, while I fretted over how complicated our household was becoming. My boyfriend brought three pit bulls and two Belgian horses when we moved to our Nebraska farmhouse. I came with a spotted Great Dane, an off-the-track Thoroughbred, and an angry Siamese. Maintaining peace in the menagerie involved a precarious arrangement of pet gates, cat trees, and closed doors.

The Dark Lord spent his first night as our guest in Pétur's studio. The two pit bulls, Viskey and One-Fiddy, shared our bed while Puglilista and Mama-Bull got the living room.

At about two o'clock in the morning a terrible shriek woke us both.

"Holy hell!" I said.

It was similar to a coyote howl—high-pitched and wailing. As the yowling continued, loud and awful, it didn't sound like it was coming from outside, it sounded like it was in the bedroom with us, like the darkness itself had learned how to howl.

Pétur flew off the mattress and pulled his jeans over pajama pants. I rolled out from under the covers. The howling only got louder, seeming to double and echo.

"You don't have do wake up, Sergio," he said. He had to shout over the noise. "Is my dog. I will take care of it."

"It sounds like a pack of wolves," I said. "Like it's here, in the house."

Half-dressed, I followed him outside, my bare feet going numb as they crossed the frozen ground to his studio. Once inside, we found the Dark Lord pacing and howling—a howl so shrill and unreal, it flooded me with adrenaline.

"That's a good boy," Pétur said, creeping toward the dog. "Is oka-ay, is oka-ay…"

The Dark Lord smelled his hand, sidled up to his chest, and when Pétur slunk to the floor the dog curled up into his lap.

"It is very hard for him," he said. "Very hard because he cannot sees anything and misses his persons."

So, I moved Viskey and One-Fiddy to the spare bedroom, while the Dark Lord came to sleep with us.

In the morning Pétur got up early, putting a leash on our new guest.

"Where are you going?"

"I will take him on walk and ask de neighbors if they knows who he belong to."

"You can't go knocking on the neighbors' doors," I said. "You're going to scare everybody."

"Scare everybody?"

"You and that dog," I said. "They're going to think you're there to round up the Jews."

**B**ack when we first met, his accent was impenetrable—sharp V's where W's belonged, dull T's that caught in his throat and nearly muted the sound. His sentences were formed in a baritone that made everything he said seem grave and important; saying "Hallo" with such seriousness it sounded like it ought to be followed with "you may keep only one of your children."

I thought he must be German.

A client of mine had just moved her horse to a new barn—a show barn—and she wanted to know if I had time to take a look at her friend's draft, an older gelding that wouldn't stay sound. When my client's giant super-villain friend led his Belgian into the aisle way, the horse took short, tentative steps, and I found myself staring determinedly at those steps and not upward, not at the man's face. Even without looking, I knew he had an extraordinary face full of angles and intimidation.

"What do you use him for?" I asked the super-villain, who wore a track-suit and Nikes—unusual dress for a barn.

"Everything," he said.

"Pétur's a vaulter," my client explained. "You should see his videos."

I asked him about his horse's diet, age, health, all the while fixing my listening-gaze just below his eyes, barely comprehending his heavily-accented answers.

It would be a chaste courtship. I convinced myself he wasn't queer.

**M**y siblings and I binge on the phone like white girls. I have four younger brothers—high school and college age—so while I stood at my forge, we'd always be on the Bluetooth, bullshitting. They didn't know I was into guys. My dad didn't know. Moms might've known.

One night, when I was just out of college, I was on the phone with her. My roommates were downstairs having margaritas and I had nabbed the tequila—taking it up to my room and sipping it like medicine.

"Mijo," Moms said. "Are you going to bring another new girl to Thanksgiving?"

"I don't know, Amá."

"You have so many different girlfriends."

"I know...I know..."

"Tienes un big heart."

"Right."

"Don't you want to be in love with one?"

"Yeah..."

"Have you even been in love?"

That pint of Patrón made my brain spin with honesty.

"Yeah," I said. "Yeah, I've been in love."

"Qué bien, mijo."

"His name is Roger. I'm in love with this guy named Roger."

My jaw tightened as soon as I said his name. She was such an awkward lady and I could almost see her then, a smile still plastered on her outlined lips, her eyes going inward while she tightened her grip on the phone.

"Look," I said, "I gotta go." I hung up and finished the rest of the bottle.

When Thanksgiving finally happened, I brought a new girl like I always did. I broke up with Roger a month later, convincing myself he didn't really love me. Moms and I never talked about what I said on the phone that night.

**P**étur Dahlberg turned out to be a world champion equestrian vaulter and trick rider. He did commercials for Pepsi, Epson, and Microsoft which involved him hanging from one leg off the side of a galloping steed or holding a girl up with one arm while he stood on his Belgian's croup—all this to sell soda, printer cartridges, and computers.

Occasionally, Pétur did performances with a pair of Japanese twins named Yuka and Kokona Fujiwara. The three of them invented stunts that had never been attempted before, stunts that involved fire, acrobatics, and horses without bridles.

I watched all of this on YouTube the day I shod his gelding.

After the third or seventeenth video, I texted my client and asked her if she had Mr. Dahlberg's number.

"Awe..." she texted back.

"????" I replied.

Finally, she gave it to me.

"Good luck," she added.

We dated the way twelve year olds date—never saying what we were doing—me keeping my hands in my pockets and my eyes just beneath eye contact, all the while telling myself over and over again "he's not queer, he's not queer, he's not queer."

I followed Pétur as he walked the Dark Lord through Marsland, ready to jump in with the necessary smiling and social graces should we encounter a neighbor. Animals knew Pétur to be trustworthy, but fellow humans— so conditioned to the ritual of public relations—grew suspicious when their instincts to like him clashed with their expectations that he should grin and talk.

There were neighbors around when we moved in just a few weeks previous, I knew we saw them. But now as we passed the little blue house on the corner of Belmont and Nottingham we saw no cars in the front, no horses in the back pen. Turning onto Niobrara, each house stood empty, their driveways vacant.

Before sunset, we took our horses down the gravel hill. Reaching the main highway, we turned around and headed home. The little homes remained dark. Not a single truck on the road.

"Only nine people live here," I said. "They probably all went out to the Fiddle Contest in Crawford."

"An took their horses and sheeps and cows with them?"

During the Dark Lord's second night with us he slept under Pétur's arm, the length of the dog's body contoured against his side. Both of us sleep on our backs by nature, but ever since taking Pétur to my bed, I grew accustomed to curling up on my side, my hand on his chest, and my leg over his.

I heard the howling in my dream. When I tried to run from it, my limbs felt weak. My feet, barefoot and heavy, stuck to the pavement. When I tried to lift them, they melted like plastic as the howling continued.

I woke to find Pétur hugging the howling dog, stroking his brindled fur. The Dark Lord panted. So did I. I felt like I was having a heart attack.

Pétur laughed. It was the first time I'd ever seen him laugh—nearly two years together and not so much as a chuckle! And what a shock it was, like the first time you see someone without his glasses. His pale eyebrows curved upwards, his mouth became strangely wide.

"Is just so scareful," Pétur said between chuckles. "Very scareful the way he makes his howlings."

**We**'d been seeing each other for three weeks and never even held hands. He sat in my garage with a beer watching me weld and forge. I hung around his barn as he spun the Japanese girls and balanced on the back of his cantering mare. We visited the animal shelter and took home redlisted pit bulls, fostering them until they found forever homes. Each time we parted, it became increasingly impossible that we would ever touch. Our chastity had settled into a comfortable habit.

Alone in my bed I thought about the past and how it all just happened with waiting, eventually a guy would lock eyes with me—say something clumsy. Such a thing appeared impossible with Pétur—Pétur who had that strange forcefield that kept growing and growing all around him.

One night he was doing a show and I sat in the audience next to his mother. She had a long upper lip and straight gray hair down to her knees. Smiling, she stammered a few things in her language and I smiled back with a "Yeah, yeah, yeah." I said a few things to her and she replied with: "Ja, ja, ja." Once the lights went down, Pétur's mom held my wrist as we watched him and the girls spring onto the back of his thundering mare, flip, contort and throw each other around the arena.

We found him after the show. A thick-legged woman had positioned herself by Pétur's side. She spoke to Pétur's mom—a fast, rusty stream of vowels and constants.

"Sergio," Pétur said, "this is my trainer, Nienke."

I can't remember what Nienke looked like or if I even shook her hand because of what Pétur said next. He was wearing a black hoodie and zipping it up as he spoke—speaking with such ease it made me go deaf for a few seconds.

"Nienke," he said, "this is my boyfriend, Sergio."

Indeed, the Dark Lord did make the Marsland house complicated. A procedure needed to be followed in order to allow the house animals time outside for potty without riot and bloodshed breaking out. After Pétur's boys relieved themselves, he locked them up in his studio and went back into the house for the Dark Lord.

"Sergio," Pétur called to me, "come look at this."

I latched the kitchen door and went to him.

"I don't know," he said, "I don't know what happen."

His knuckles tightened around the doorknob.

"What?"

Pétur finally let me see the bedroom where the Dark Lord stood in a pool of blood. It dripped in dotted streams from his fur. He shook, bounded over. His pink tongue was drooling. His smiling mouth, panting.

"Your boys didn't get to him," I asked, "did they?"

"They are in my studio. I only left him for three minutes. They never even saw him."

"Maybe he cut himself on something."

Pétur washed the Dark Lord in the bathtub again, searching every inch of him for wounds. There were no wounds. There were no dead creatures under the bed. There were no open windows for this blood to somehow rain onto the floor. There was, however, enough of it soaked into the carpet to require that the whole thing be torn out.

In the early days we never did speak a whole lot and that kind of silence was new for me—me who spent evenings holding Bluetooth marathons with my brothers, dissecting their girlfriends' every accusation.

After his show I found myself at the barn with him, platonically in person. My fists—once more—in my pockets, my eyes cast downward. He hauled the barn door shut for the night, brushed the alfalfa dust off his track pants. I reached for his hand.

It was painful: the shock of the breach, the way it startled him, the clumsiness of it. I forced myself to see him then and it was pain once more—to finally notice the freckles on his cheekbones and the nakedness in his eyes.

"Come over tonight," I said, clenching his fingers tighter.

His expression resembled that of a scolded child.

"I have to feed the dogs first."

In the morning, I woke to the cords of his hoodie cutting into my cheek, my belt buckle making a red dent in my abdomen. What happened was this: he came over, I kissed him, took him to my room, and we went to sleep fully clothed, folded up against each other.

Other things happened that night—dialog and nuance. After I gave my dogs their dinner, a chill came over me. It built steadily until I heard his truck pull into my apartment complex.

The tallness of him would be a problem. There was a great expanse of time and space I had to overcome in order to bring my hand up to his neck, pull him down against my lips. To ponder the physics of it might lead to hesitation. I set my jaw, that was when the coldness really set in—the determination.

Heading outside, I barely gave him time to get out of his truck before I yanked on his neck, making him kiss me. A terrible shaking overtook his body. He shivered even though it was warm out. When I released him he continued to tremble all over.

"I would very like to have a drink if there are one."

We went inside and sat on the edge of my mattress with our beers—Pugilista resting at our feet. The air around us grew so heavy and hollow it felt like speaking would tear my lungs open.

"Guys become unhappy with me," he said.

"Why's that?"

"I am not very affectioness."

His long arm hung off his knee, his fingertips drifting back and forth along my dog's neck.

I awoke to a dim morning—just the faintest glint off the zipper that was pulled up to his chin, a subtle shine on the yellow stubble that roughened his jaw. He didn't stir when I slid away.

There was a railroad spike somewhere in the garage. I worried I might have used them all up, but after a few minutes of searching, I found one left under the shelves.

With the hot forge taking the chill out of the garage, I hammered the glowing spike into a knife, put a twist in the handle, and ground the edge into a brutal sharpness.

I went back to him, sat on the mattress, and nearly hesitated when he opened his eyes. Taking his wrist, I opened his palm and put the knife into it.

"Tonight I'll come to your house," I said. "I'll bring Chinese or something."

His fingers folded around my gift and I got up to make breakfast. Some men say, "I love you." I make knives out of railroad spikes.

It was the Dark Lord's third night with us. Usually, we rotated the dogs and their sleeping arrangements, but Pétur brought him to bed without any explanation.

"Five bucks says 2:45 AM," I said.

"Maybe closer do three o'clock."

Three in the morning arrived and the Dark Lord's howling struck me from my sleep and into a furor of pounding adrenaline. Pétur flung himself at the light switch while I pulled the covers up to my neck. This time the dog's wailing woke the others: barking and growling from the spare bedroom, howling and whimpering from the living room. Pétur hugged and stroked the dog, but the rest of the household continued in a frenzy.

That was when I realized our home was shaking.

"It's an earthquake," I said, gazing at each of my iron creations as they wobbled on the walls and crashed to the floor. "There are earthquakes in Nebraska?"

With his arms around the dog, Pétur started laughing again. He looked like a little boy when he did it, trying so hard to stop but continuing to spit and bellow despite his best efforts.

"What if this is the end of the world?" I said. "What if this dog is some kind of harbinger?"

The earthquake subsided with an orgasmic groan and I went to check on the rest of the pack. They had avoided being struck by any falling pieces and I took the remaining metalwork off the walls just in case there were aftershocks. It was a good thing I was a blacksmith and not a glass smith.

When I returned, Pétur was all dimples and smirks.

"I wish I knew what was going on in that head of yours," I told him.

"We broke Nebraska," he said. "We broke Nebraska by being so awesome."

A few months ago, when Pétur signed the paperwork on the Marsland house, my second oldest younger brother, Armand, called. I hadn't told anyone in my family I was moving. Such a thing would involve mentioning my boyfriend.

"Hey, man," Armand said, "it's been a while."

"Yeah," I said to my Bluetooth as I fired up my forge.

"No, man. It's been a long while."

"I guess it has."

"Juan says he hasn't talked to you all year."

"Really?" I put the glowing barstock to the anvil. "All year?"

"He says you never call him back."

I struck my hammer against the iron, working it out into a long blade.

"Tell him I said 'sorry.'"

"When are we gonna see you, man?"

I turned the rod and hammered the other side.

"I've been kind of busy," I said.

"You seeing anyone?"

"Dude, aren't you in college now?"

"Yeah," he said.

"Yeah?" Time for another heat; I put the stock back in the fire. "How's college?"

"It's weird, bro."

"Yeah?"

"Yeah."

"How's it weird?"

"The girls, man."

"They're weird?"

"Yeah," he said. "There are all these Muslim girls. Like a whole bunch of them."

"Huh."

"They wear hijabs and stuff," he said. "Like those scarves that cover their hair."

"That's cool."

"Why you say that?"

I brought the rod to the vice and put a twist in it.

"I dunno, dude," I said. "Just something to say, I guess."

"I've been talking to this one Muslim girl a lot."

"Yeah?"

"I dunno. There's this other girl who's really fun and everyone really likes her and she's really into me."

"This is the Muslim girl?"

"No...no," he said. "This is the other girl. See...I think I kind of like Fatima."

"Fatima's the Muslim girl?"

"Yeah. She wears a hijab and everything."

I shoved the stock back into the flame.

"Is that weird," he said. "That I like a Muslim girl?"

"Should it be?" I asked.

"I mean, like, what would that mean if she was my girlfriend?"

"It would probably destroy the universe." I took the stock out of the fire and went to hammering again.

"You know what I mean," he said. "Maybe I should ask out this other girl. She's really into me and everyone likes her."

"It sounds like you like Fatima."

"Yeah."

I turned the stock over and hammered the other side.

"I don't know what to do," he said.

"I don't know what to tell ya."

"If I went out with Fatima," he said, "what would that be like?"

"I guess there's only one way to find out."

"This other girl is really fun."

"But you like Fatima," I said.

"I do," he said.

I was ready to take the thing to the grinder, but I couldn't talk and grind at the same time, so I dropped the knife into the bath and sat on my bench.

"You still there, bro?" he said.

"Yeah."

"Dude, what's with you? Usually you're like Dr. Phil."

I needed a beer.

"You still there?" he asked.

"I'm just going to the kitchen for a beer."

"If I dated Fatima I wouldn't even know what her hair color is."

"Pro tip," I said, flipping the bottle opener. "Same color as her eyebrows."

I drank. Went into the living room.

"When are we gonna see you again, man?" he asked.

"Dunno."

"Fuck's that supposed to mean?"

I drained the bottle and went back to the kitchen for a second.

"Armand, bro," I said. "I'm gonna tell you something, 'kay?"

"Dude, what?"

"I'm moving to Nebraska."

"No you aren't."

"Yes I am."

"Shut up."

"I'm serious."

"Dude, why you moving to Nebraska?"

"I don't want you to talk about this to anyone. I'm not sure if I wanna tell anyone else, but I trust you, Armand."

"Okay. Why are you moving to Nebraska?"

Here it goes. I took a swig off my beer.

"You can buy a farm out there for like forty thousand, so my boyfriend bought one and we're going to live off his royalty checks and rent from his house here."

"Wait. What?"

"My boyfriend. He's weird but he's cool. You might like him. Or maybe not. He's weird."

"The fuck are you talking about, Sergio?"

"Dude, I'm a fucking homo, you dumbass," I said. "That's what I'm fucking telling you."

"Shit. Okay."

I drank some more.

"Dude," he said. "You're not a homo."

"I am. I have been for a long time."

"How long?"

"Since I was born, asshole."

"Mom and Dad know?"

"Of course not."

"Well, I'm gonna come visit you one weekend before you go. I wanna meet him, 'kay? What's his name?"

"Pétur. He's foreign."

"That's cool. I'm sure he's cool. I won't tell anyone."

"He's weird," I said. "Just warning you."

"Okay."

"When are you gonna see Fatima?"

"I guess in class tomorrow morning. I think I'm gonna ask her out."

"That's good," I said.

"Yeah, I think so."

The smell of smoke filled our noses. I worried it had something to do with my forge lighting up during the earthquake, but when I went to the garage, everything looked normal. In the morning we saddled Pétur's horses and took a ride through Marsland. A fire had blackened the area south of Niobrara Street and a small crew worked to put out the remaining flames.

I hopped down, handing my reins to Pétur.

"Anything we can do to help?" I asked one of the volunteers.

"Naw," the woman said. "It's almost out. Didn't think there was anyone still in this town."

"We bought the white house on Belmont," I said. "In case there's another fire, be sure to—you know—wake us up. How'd it happen?"

She shrugged.

"This place has been empty, you know. Who called it in?"

She shrugged again.

"You sure you all don't need anything?"

"I think we're good."

"How about coffee?"

"Okay."

So we went back to the house and returned with coffee for the fire volunteers.

"It's lucky someone saw the fire and called it in," I said.

"Maybe a trucker," Pétur said.

"Yeah. Maybe a trucker or something. 'Cause if it crossed Niobrara, we'd be dead."

"The dogs would wake us."

"Yeah, they probably would."

"I will try not to do it again," Pétur said.

"Do what?"

"Break Nebraska by being so awesome."

The Dark Lord continued howling around three o'clock each morning for a number of months. I don't know what caused him to be covered in blood that one time any more than I know what caused the earthquake, the fire, or the disappearance of our neighbors.

Sometime in the fall, I rolled out of bed with a strange tingling in my stomach. I went to the window, watching the horses grazing in their pasture. I tried to figure out why I felt so strange. There was a mist over the valley and everything looked blue and lonely.

Pétur finally sat up and called the dog onto his lap.

"What a good boy," he said. "Asleep all night with no howlings."

I laughed. That was what it was!

Two more nights passed without any howling, so we decided to resume the dog rotation—giving the ladies a chance to come back into the bedroom, and then Pétur's boys the following night. Even when he stayed in the living room or the spare bedroom, the Dark Lord slept soundly.

Soon after that, the Dark Lord began to lose weight and the vet said he had cancer. During those final weeks, we stopped the rotation again, had him sleep with us until one morning he didn't wake up. Pétur handled it with stoicism, going out into the field alone to bury him. For some reason, the loss hit me really hard.

I went to the garage, lit up the forge, and spent a few days making knives and axes and tomahawks. There was a miserable knot in my throat that seemed like it would never go away. Armand called. I almost didn't answer.

"Hey," he said.

"Hey, Armand," I said.

"What's up, man?"

"My hellhound died and I'm all fucked up about it."

"Yeah, I know."

"You know?"

"Pétur told me—"

"—you talked to him?"

"Yeah."

"On the phone?"

"Yeah," he said.

"How do you understand what that fucker's saying?"

"I dunno," he said. "But he asked 'vould you dalk vith Sergio about de dog dying?' and so here I am dalking vith you about de dog dying."

I laughed and wiped the damn tears from my eyes. He told me about school and said I should call Juan back sometime.

I forgot to ask him what happened with him and Fatima, but I'm sure however it went things ended up all right.

# Fat Faggots Barter Drugs for Sex

## THOMAS KEARNES

"**W**hat took you so goddamn long, boy?" Margene demanded. "I been calling your name since the commercial." On the plasma-screen television, a perky blonde with dazzling teeth cooed about the efficacy of scented douche. Whenever Margene needed another wine cooler or wanted to empty the ashtray, she wailed for her son, Dewey, to leave his computer and assist her. He shuffled from the back of their mobile home, past all the piles of cardboard boxes lining the hall, and into the living room. Cigarette dangling from her lips and remote control clenched in her grip, she growled for Dewey to complete the tasks her sloth made untenable.

"I was chatting with someone," Dewey answered.

"Shouldn't talk to people that don't exist."

"Whaddya need, Mama?"

Margene was little more than a skeleton gloved inside pore-ridden flesh. Her ribs, her shoulder blades, and her hips realigned as she looked at her son. Why was it so hard to label her as *frail?* "The methadone ain't kickin' in like it should," she said. "We got Xanax left, right?"

"I dunno."

"Well, shit, take a look," she said.

Dewey bowed his head. He couldn't remember ever feeling brave enough to openly glare at his anorexic, needling mother. Knowing each day brought nothing but more demands, more game shows at thundering volume, more Virginia Slims—the concept of *future* was too painful to contemplate.

The tiny bathroom shared a wall with the living room. While scanning the medicine cabinet, Dewey heard a huckster bark about his batch of used Fords, little kids orgasmic over fruit punch, and finally a plea for those who'd taken a certain growth hormone to join a class-action lawsuit.

He found the Xanax behind an empty jar of Oil of Olay. Three or four pills rattled in the bottle. His reflection in the cabinet door confronted him. His mouth grew long, the corners turning neither up nor down. *Fat fuck*, he thought. *Not fat like Daddy in heaven, but give it time. It's a slippery slope, little pig.*

"Goddammit, boy!" Margene cried. "You get lost in there?"

"Jus' second, Mama."

Dewey had tricks to appear more appetizing to the men on the hookup websites. He pressed his hand beneath his jowls, momentarily mashing his double chin. Relieved that this ruse provided hope, he cupped his hands over his two drooping pecs. No, that asshole kid down the road was right: they were bitch tits. He lifted the sagging flesh of each breast up and to the side. What if his pectorals bulged with firmness as they did in his fantasies?

There were other attempts at deception, elaborate series of gestures, rehearsed like a soliloquy. In less than half an hour, Christopher would arrive—tall, lean, and smooth Christopher with his eight-inches of carnal delight. It had taken three weeks of sexting and lewd online chatting to compel him toward the mobile home park, outside Longview. Dewey had also promised an eight ball of crystal meth for the privilege of sucking that long, thick sexy stick.

The Xanax rattled in their bottle. He planned to suggest Margene take all the pills. While he lacked the audacity to entertain Christopher in his own bedroom, he wished nonetheless to neutralize his mother. Christopher's wait after he knocked would allow plenty of time for her to humiliate the host. Dewey offered the pills, but she stared as if he were a stain.

"You trying to knock me out cold, boy?" she asked, eyes narrowed to slits.

Dewey shifted his feet, stared into a far corner. He could hide nothing from her. She was his mother. That meant something. It meant too god-damn much. He said he was expecting company.

"You ain't got no friends. At least none you bring here."

"I didn't wanna bother you." He gestured toward the television. "Judge Judy is coming on."

Margene lit another Virginia Slim and took the Xanax bottle. "Is he one of those faggots?" she asked, her voice low and froggy, as if the word were difficult to pronounce.

"No!"

"The government ain't payin' me to run some queer whorehouse, boy."

"Take the pills, Mama. You're too excited."

After further instructions not to disgrace their family name, Margene dismissed him. He zipped into his bedroom and checked for texts. Nothing. *Don't panic*, he told himself. Christopher was on his way. Maybe he didn't like to text while driving. Dewey lay atop his bed, knowing his immediate future offered no rest. He'd smoked some meth an hour ago. Without it, he would've cancelled, certain humiliation loomed. He waited for a knock and went into a sort of trance, so fixated on the wheeze from the air conditioner outside his window that he failed to register the quick trio of knocks at the front door. Another three knocks followed. Christopher was nearly an hour late. Dewey didn't care, thrilled the young man hadn't flaked, like most others, even after his promise of crystal meth.

Dewey dashed to the front door, catching a glimpse of his mother motionless on the couch. Even Xanax didn't hit that fast. Maybe it was all the wine coolers since *Good Morning America*. If she hadn't taken the Xanax, maybe he could sneak one for himself. Christopher must not detect his deep-rooted conviction that the afternoon would go wrong, and soon.

The vision that revealed itself, the creaky screen door opening, filled the fat young man with hope. Suddenly, his sad and sordid world seemed alive with possibility, knowing this gorgeous man would surrender to him. Dewey had already decided he'd swallow Christopher's load if given the chance. He asked if Christopher had any problems finding the place. Dewey babbled about the hardships of living in the backwoods, how grateful he was for company.

"You got diarrhea of the mouth, big boy," Christopher said, laughing. Dewey stopped at once. The biggest disappointment he'd experienced since starting to hook up was how no man was witty and charming like in sitcoms and frothy romantic comedies. Instead, they spoke in a primitive language of veiled insults and sexual commands. Christopher, however, possessed a true wit. Better yet, he assumed Dewey must possess one, too.

"I'm sorry, cutie," Dewey said, gripping the doorframe for balance. "I always get so nervous, and my hands sweat, and it feels like I haven't eaten in a fucking week, and—"

"How are you gonna suck me off if you can't stop jabbering." Christopher slipped past Dewey into his home. While passing, his hand grazed Dewey's love handle. Dewey wasn't sure how to interpret the gesture. This was the worst time to be reminded of his weight...but beautiful Christopher had touched him! The contact hadn't left him repulsed. Christopher flashed a megawatt grin and casually gazed about. Dewey fought the urge to drag him out the front door. Of course, he'd obsessed over Christopher's array of pictures on the website, especially the one of his long, smooth body completely nude, the image abruptly ending at his neck. Dewey marveled at any man with the discipline—and optimism—to work out.

Even though Christopher claimed online to be twenty-two, he could've passed for a high school senior, in Dewey's estimation. An unkempt bush of rust-colored curls drifted atop his head like low clouds at dawn. One of his eyes was a bright hazel while the other was a pale blue. He moved with the staccato rhythms of a tap dancer, all seductive excess motion. His only flaw was that his front tooth was chipped. Dewey's own mouth was full of neglected cavities and rotting teeth stained yellow from his daily pack of Camel menthols. He'd lied when Christopher had asked if he smoked. He'd forgotten to gargle with Listerine before answering the door.

Christopher drifted toward the living room, but thrust his head forward, as if waiting for Dewey to begin a proper tour. Margene grunted. Dewey prayed her stupor was lifting.

"You don't wanna see this dump." He slid past Christopher to block his entrance. "I set up the perfect place."

"You put mucho effort into silly things, big boy."

"We have the whole afternoon," Dewey breathed.

"Actually, I only have an hour. My girlfriend needs me to pick up a dime bag. The weed in Tyler is crap." Christopher went on to explain his visit was the product of pure coincidence—and past experience. "You fat boys are expert cocksuckers," he muttered, smiling so wide that Dewey started counting his teeth. He'd would return to his girlfriend and pretend her talent while on her knees came anywhere close to Dewey's.

The host rubbed his bulging belly without realizing Christopher watched him. Why draw attention there? How Dewey could please him was all that mattered. Christopher asked if the dope was righteous after Dewey disclosed that he'd picked it up that morning.

"I haven't tried it," Dewey replied, lying with aplomb. He knew hookups were games of deception and concealment. Each man wielded an orchestrated image for the other's enjoyment. There was no shame in this charade. Dewey had joined the website three years ago, not long after his twentieth birthday. His late father had bought the computer years ago, hoping to interest Dewey in *Tetris* and other math-based video games.

He asked Dewey if he had a pipe. He asked him if he was discreet.

"This afternoon is just between you and me," Dewey promised, thrilled to speak those words aloud. He guided Christopher toward the screen door, still hanging open. He kept gentle pressure at the small of Christopher's back, breathless over how tightly his guest's simple black T-shirt clung to his physique.

"Good. I like boys who keep their traps shut." Christopher ducked to avoid the doorframe. "You let some faggot suck your dick, and next week, the whole fucking town knows."

"I hate guys like that," Dewey said quickly.

"Where the fuck are we going?"

"This trailer down the street. No one lives there now that Mrs. Zuckerman is dead."

The two young men walked with purpose across the park grounds. Some of the trailers featured scattershot attempts at decoration or comfort—a wobbly wooden deck, garden gnomes with evil faces, wind chimes that hung uninspired in the still, humid afternoon. Dewey risked a glance through a particular trailer's window as he and Christopher passed. He wasn't surprised to see Professor Pete glaring back as if he'd been waiting for him. That morning, Dewey had struggled with his gag reflex, desperate to please, Pete shedding pubic hairs inside his mouth. For dope, Professor Pete never accepted cash. Dewey didn't have enough anyway.

What would a person think, seeing him accompany gorgeous Christopher? It was silly to speculate—he knew the answer. He was guilty, himself, of reaching the same conclusion. Obviously, when one half of a couple was far more attractive than the other, everyone knew the beautiful one held all the power. Dewey was sometimes tempted to invite homely men for quick, shameful sex. Every bastard who glared with disgust conjured Margene. She'd scorned him since his father was killed, instead of him, on that icy interstate three years ago. The memory of his father's final breaths filling the overturned pickup chilled Dewey. When Margene had asked if he'd died quick and painless, Dewey lied.

After another minute, Dewey left the pebble-strewn road and lumbered up the steps to a mobile home. He was tempted to glance over his shoulder to make sure Christopher hadn't deserted. His guest, however, clomped up the stairs close behind. *I am not a freak*, he told himself. *I can attract a worthy man. Mama's wrong. She's wrong about everything.*

"I need to smoke a bowl or two to stay in this shithole," Christopher announced, following Dewey inside. The mobile home was decorated with taste and thrift. Little touches of warmth littered the trailer: a crocheted maroon blanket folded neatly atop a sofa, bright yellow kitchen curtains allowing the afternoon sunlight, a beige cloth bag holding outdated housekeeping magazines. Nothing, however, could distract the men from the foul, pungent odor permeating each room. How long did Mrs. Zuckerman lie dead before her corpse was discovered?

"Follow me," Dewey said with forced mirth. "I've got the bedroom all set up."

"This place reminds me of Grandma's house. Man, I hate that bitch."

"My grandma sometimes forgets my name."

"Actually, I forgot your name, too," Christopher admitted. "Don't take it personal. Names aren't really important."

Dewey halted at the bedroom doorway. At least Christopher was talking. That was more than some tricks managed. He convinced himself

Christopher's candor was a good thing, an indication of his comfort with his homely, heavy host. The downside of having a trick that spoke, however, was that it obligated his host to reply.

"I'm Dewey," he said. "Actually, it's Dwight, but only my dad called me that. He's dead." He hadn't planned to disclose his loss. The mood was already too delicate.

Christopher grinned and Dewey was reminded of the door greeter he knew from his job at Wal-Mart. He envied people, attractive or not, whose smiles compelled others to trust without reservation. People rarely returned Dewey's smile.

Leaning against the doorframe, Christopher's spooky eyes were alight with mischief. Men so seldom flirted with Dewey, he was ill-prepared to recognize it.

"Remember my name," Christopher said, "and I might let you do more than suck me off."

Dewey giggled. "Of course I remember your name. You've been on my buddy list since our first chat. We chatted over an hour."

"When I'm online, all I see are dicks and assholes."

"Your name is Christopher," Dewey said quietly. He risked a step toward. His guest did not withdraw in disgust. At all these tiny omens of impending success, Dewey marveled. "I don't know your last name," he added, glancing up into the taller man's face. Perhaps Dewey had learned this classic submissive pose from all those black-and-white movies Margene watched after midnight. He occasionally joined her but didn't feel safe until she'd passed out from the wine coolers or methadone.

"Unless you're my probation officer, last names are irrelevant."

"Mine is Langtree."

"Dewey Langtree." Christopher brightened. "Maybe it should be *Dwight* Langtree. That's the name you like best, right?"

Not knowing how to respond to this oddball kindness, Dewey withdrew into the bedroom, pausing beside the bed. A quilted comforter with a floral design promised a far more genteel encounter than what Dewey had planned. He slipped the glass pipe from his pocket then fished in the opposite one for the dope. Christopher scurried toward him when he produced the tiny baggie of clear crystals.

"Some nice fat shards in there," Christopher said.

"That's the cool thing about living in the sticks," Dewey said. "The dope is so much better."

"You ever sell this shit?"

"I don't know how to be a dealer."

"If you can count, you'll do just fine."

Dewey gazed at the baggie. He and Margene certainly could use the cash. Dewey, however, possessed so little imagination that he couldn't fathom a life in which dealing drugs was his second career. He couldn't imagine anything better than what God had dumped over his head. Margene would want him to walk two miles, once Christopher left, for more Virginia Slims.

Impatient, Christopher snatched both the baggie and the pipe. "I told you," he said, "I'm on a tight schedule."

"We won't need to smoke it all," Dewey said too quickly. "It's strong stuff. You can take the rest home like I promised." He paused. "Does your girlfriend smoke it, too?"

"I thought you hadn't tried this."

Dewey's heart dropped into his stomach. He felt himself sinking onto the bed, his head bowed like a puppy disciplined for pissing on the carpet. *He knows I'm a liar*, Dewey thought. *Nobody likes liars.* Dewey glanced at Christopher and was relieved his guest was ignoring him, too busy loading the pipe with a fat shard.

Dewey pretended he hadn't been caught. To his relief, Christopher pocketed the baggie after finishing the bowl and produced a disposable lighter. Dewey watched in rapture as the immense and bright clouds of white smoke escaped his lips. He'd always found it deeply erotic, men expelling crystal-meth smoke. He liked to imagine those same mouths ravenous for him, whether or not he was satisfied never occurring to his tricks.

Christopher took five hits from the pipe before offering it to Dewey, but Dewey didn't mind. After all, Christopher was under no obligation to share. One or two of the men Dewey had serviced didn't share at all. Dewey took an enormous hit, sucking on the stem. He exhaled endless white smoke, and Christopher chuckled. "Damn impressive, big boy," he said.

"I can do a lot of cool shit with my mouth."

"Let me see that pipe again."

They passed it back and forth, Christopher always taking more hits than Dewey. They finished the first bowl and began another. Once that was cashed, Dewey succumbed to a floating sensation, atop a jet stream, fluttering over continents. He forgot about Christopher. The opening zipper slapped him back to reality. There was the business of the blowjob.

"Get on your knees, big boy," Christopher said with surprising softness.

"I'm an expert at getting guys off."

"Like I said, you fat boys are the best-kept secret on the internet."

Dewey couldn't understand why the experience of sucking a man never changed, regardless of the diversity in his list of former tricks. Dewey lost himself in a torrent of silent commands and stern warnings to not fail the man in his mouth. There was no ecstasy until Dewey convinced himself, as always, that sexual subservience all alone can bring one joy.

Christopher actually warned him before climax. After a messy finale, Dewey excused himself and washed his face. He didn't want to return and find the bedroom empty, as if the encounter were imagined. Christopher lay on his back atop the bed. He wasn't relaxed, though. Dewey noticed the tension in his limbs, his jaw. He dreaded this part of each encounter.

"How much longer do we have?" Dewey asked.

"I'm too lazy to look at my watch."

"You're welcome to stay."

"Actually, would it be okay if I chilled by myself alone? I gotta get my shit together. That was strong dope."

Dewey had never been discarded so gently. Typically, the men couldn't bolt fast enough. Why did Christopher wish for solitude? Dewey lacked the courage to ask for an explanation. Instead, he shuffled toward the doorway. Christopher called his name. His *true* name, not Dewey.

Mrs. Zuckerman had probably died in that bed.

"Yeah?" Dewey felt an optimism he didn't trust for a moment.

"Suck cock like that every time, and no one will care if you're fat."

Dewey couldn't remember the last time he'd been complimented. Unsure if he was smiling, his face contorted into a shape he'd forgotten, but Christopher returned his grin. Dewey silently vowed to abandon the website, at least for a while. This memory would surely sustain him.

"Now beat it, big boy," Christopher said, chuckling. "You're killing my buzz."

Dewey trotted home, sick with possibility. All the sad, despairing homesteads didn't dampen his merriment. He felt he should hum a song, something life-affirming, but he never listened to music. Dewey's life was a silent one, excluding Margene's inescapable television.

His jolly mood curdled when he spotted Professor Pete glaring out his window. Typically, Dewey would've bowed his head and shuffled away... unless he needed dope. Today, however guile overtook him. He stood firm and shot him the bird. Professor Pete narrowed his gaze. A moment later, the window was empty. The ease of his victory stunned Dewey. The vindication mingled with the remnants of his bliss. Coming home, for once, didn't crush him like a cigarette butt beneath a steel-toed boot.

He didn't check on Margene before sauntering toward his bedroom. When he heard her voice ricochet through their home, it shocked him. The world, after all, had not stopped. As he spun with all the planet's other soul, Dewey hoped enough gravity remained to anchor him.

"You fat bastard," she brayed. "I know where you were. I know every fuckin' thing."

Dewey considered slamming his door and pretending he didn't hear, but he couldn't let that vile woman berate him for untold minutes. He wanted to respect himself. If he did, perhaps others would follow suit. He wanted to smile at the shoppers in Wal-Mart and smile wider still when they returned it.

"Where I went is none of your goddamn business," he said. He crossed to the couch, opposite Margene. She puffed a Virginia Slim, television remote in hand. A portly weatherman warned about severe weather tomorrow.

"I went back to your room, boy," she said. "I got on that damn computer you can't live without. What pervert lets the whole world see pictures like that?"

"You can't come in my room," he said. "We had a deal."

"What you do with men Jesus don't allow."

"You haven't been to church since Daddy died."

"Don't speak to me about that fine man. It should've been *your* fat ass we put in the ground."

Professor Pete was a house of cards, easily toppled, compared to Margene. Dewey knew she'd wear him down until his treasured memories of Christopher faded into oblivion. The horrible woman squatted on her cushioned throne, day after day, and demanded the world obey. Dewey was that world's only soul. Margene opened her mouth, hot pink lipstick staining her teeth.

"Shut your fucking pie hole, you dumb bitch!"

Margene froze, her gaze nervous, like a predator wrongly targeting a superior creature. "What did you say, boy?"

"I said shut up, Mama." On the television, the weatherman flirted with the pretty lead anchor. Dewey glimpsed the screen. The weatherman was nearly as big as him, and he was on fucking television. People watched and trusted him.

Margene hurled the remote at Dewey's head, smacking him upon his eyebrow. He wailed and grabbed his head. The remote clattered to the floor. He couldn't remember the last time Margene had struck him. She was so small, so puny, she had to rely on words to snuff out his hope. Dewey knew what he must do.

He grabbed the remote and smacked Margene across the face, the device making a loud *crack* as it struck her jaw. The batteries popped out, falling to the floor. She raised her hand in fury and horror. "Boy," she muttered, "I got good reason to get off this couch..."

"You're gonna die in front of that television," Dewey snapped.

"I need a doctor." Margene absently smeared blood across her forehead.

"You need a life," her son replied. He didn't need the excuse that answering the door provided. It was a trio of knocks, actually. What greeted Dewey was yet another surprise in an afternoon abundant with them.

"You busy?" Christopher leaned upon the doorframe, posed like a classic James Dean publicity shot. A man of typical sexual experience would've surmised Christopher's intent, but Dewey was not such a man.

"I thought you had to leave," he said.

"My girlfriend called. Typical bullshit. Don't worry about her."

"What do you want?" Dewey asked weakly. He was terrified whatever happened next would sour their wonderful moments before leaving Mrs. Zuckerman's. He desired Christopher, but he knew desire led to disappointment. Always.

"I'm horny again, dude. I was wondering if…"

Both young men heard, from the living room, Margene moan in pain. Christopher's gaze sharpened but he didn't step closer. Dewey knew this home was now under his command.

"You haven't got another stud waiting, do ya?" For the first time, vulnerability unspooled from his guest. Dewey liked it. He liked it a lot.

He gazed directly into Christopher's odd, shimmering eyes. One hazel and one blue, like birthstones. "If you want me to suck you off again, spit it out. Hints are a waste of time." He paused, grinned like a guilty schoolboy.

Christopher swallowed, his face twitching. Dewey lacked the experience to know most men lose their bearings when suddenly forced from the position of hunter to that of the hunted. "You suck cock like a champ," Christopher finally said.

Margene moaned again. Christopher said nothing. Dewey calmly followed him down the steps. He left both doors wide open. A neighbor might help his mother, he supposed. Or maybe not. Christopher required Dewey's mouth. As they returned to Mrs. Zuckerman's trailer, Dwight Langtree had faith Christopher would call him whatever name the portly man desired.

# Logging in Old Algonquin

## M. ARBON

D uncan loved Algonquin Park at this time of year. The summer campers and the mosquitos had cleared out, and it was quiet during the
week; the nights were cool and the days were golden. He'd scored a campsite at the secluded end of the radio-free zone looking out over Pog Lake,
with no one in the lots to either side. He'd made a stop in Barry's Bay for
food and stove fuel, and filled his two collapsible water jugs as well; he
drove in and parked by mid-afternoon with no intention of moving either
himself or his van for at least a few days.

Duncan clambered out of the driver's seat and stretched his arms above
his head, breathing from the bottom of his lungs for the first time in what
felt like months. Dried evergreen needles cushioned the ground, and everything smelled of wood smoke and white pine. He left the door open
and went around the back of the van to open the double doors there, letting the breeze off the lake carry away the acrid whiff of gasoline and the
greasy memory of the french fries he'd ordered in a moment of weakness
on his way up through Bancroft. He stretched again, and yawned; the long
drive had taken it out of him. He crawled onto the padded floor of the van
and rolled over onto his back, just for a moment, and then, he told himself,
he would get up and make a cup of tea or take a stroll. He woke up almost
three hours later, his stomach rumbling.

That was about all he did for the next two and a half days: nap, eat, wan-
der down to the beach and back, try to read a book but more likely than
not nod off again. There was nowhere else he needed to be, and from how

thinly stretched he'd been feeling, he could tell he needed the rest. His last job had demanded a string of all-nighters, which was unusual; the dead tended to keep daylight hours, just like the living. And the thing he thought of as a door—the door he had the ability to guide spirits to and through, the door that led to wherever living things went when their lives on earth were over—had been wildly erratic lately. He couldn't open it; half the time he could barely find it, until it opened on him like a tsunami and knocked him flat. Work that had been as instinctual as breathing was now like spinning plates while balancing on an ice floe. It had something to do with a last-ditch effort that had saved a job in May, when a spirit had taken a scrap of Duncan's own life energy with her through the door when she went. That had been a new one on him—none of the other spirits he'd tried the same thing with had done that—and maybe, he'd come to admit to himself, he hadn't thought that strategy quite through. Now there was some kind of unpredictable counterweight to his power, constantly heaving him off balance. It was exhausting, it was extremely damn annoying, and Duncan had no idea what to do to fix it.

So he was relieved to leave it be for now, and doze in the tree-filtered afternoon sunlight, the shimmering white not-really-noise of creatures being conceived and dying a low hum at the back of his awareness. The other campers were far enough away that their thoughts weren't intrusive, and aside from rote greetings at the communal water tap, he had a few restorative days of not talking to a single soul.

He did find himself checking his phone. The first bar flickered in and out of existence according to no schedule he could fathom, but even two bars brought him no emoji strings or enthusiastically unpunctuated texts. Radio silence wasn't exactly Peter's MO, but he did have an actual paying job as well as the work; maybe he was just busy.

On the fourth day, Duncan hiked over to the comfort station to have a shower and shave and do a badly needed load of laundry. Back at the campsite, he strung up a line to dry his clothes on, and fussed enough over the knots that he recognized he was ready for something new to do. The summer programs had wound down for the season, but there was always the visitor centre, and it had been a while since he'd visited the logging museum. Duncan had been a pretty lousy student even before his power had shown up and knocked him for a loop right before high school, but he enjoyed historical plaques, nature trails, museums, and guided tours of any kind, just as long as he wasn't expected to parrot it all back on paper.

He got into the van and headed down 60 to the museum, which was just this side of the eastern gate. He easily found space in the sparsely populated parking lot, and followed the path to the orientation building. He vaguely remembered the video introduction from last time, and he skirted the building to enter the outdoor part of the museum, where a forested trail looped through time as well as space, starting with replicas of early logging-camp buildings, water chutes and horse-powered cranes through to the amphibious alligator boat and steam locomotive. In the old photographs on the text panels, men stood in the snow with cold-darkened cheeks and beards clotted with ice, or balanced on cut tree trunks the width of sidewalks, with a flotilla of logs spreading out over the water behind them. The woods must have seemed endless in those days. Certainly, plenty of men had never come out of them.

In the low, square log camboose, Duncan sat down on one of the bottom bunks. Everything smelled of cut wood and earth. Light leaked in between the logs and under the eaves, down from the broad chimney hole and through the open door. In the centre of the room, an iron pot hung over the huge square hearth, cold now; then, it would have been the heart of everything. The upper bunk above his head made the space feel even more enclosed, almost cozy.

Footsteps scraped the gravelled path outside. "Daddy, watch me, watch me! Take my picture!" a young voice shrilled. Duncan shook his head at his fleeting rose-coloured glasses. The room would have been less appealing filled with smoke and wet wool socks and fifty other men who hadn't showered all winter. There were stories of loggers who had walked out into the snow one day and were never seen again; Duncan couldn't swear he wouldn't have been one of them.

On his way back to the parking lot, he stopped to check his phone again—one bar; no messages—and read the bulletin board at the front of the museum he'd skipped on his way in.

"Have you seen the dig?"

When he turned, the park ranger smiled at him and pointed at a notice on the board. "This summer we've been excavating the site of an old logging camp. It will take a while for us to put together an exhibit of the artifacts, but the dig site itself is open to the public. I don't know if anyone's working on it today, but they have daily logs and some photographs on display, if you're interested." Duncan nodded. "Are you staying in the park? Oh, Pog Lake? It's before your turn-off, then, past Eucalia Lake, on the north side. You can't miss the sign."

"Thanks," he said, and she smiled again and continued into the museum.

The sign was indeed very visible, a growing spot of fluorescent pink against the green and dun that lined the two-lane highway. Up close it revealed itself to be a wilted piece of bristol board with *DIG* and an arrow written on it in black marker. Duncan pulled into the cleared spot beside the road. There were no other vehicles there. A wide path of dried mud and wood chips led into a tunnel of forest, the green-black of pines punctuated with autumn's first scarlet maple and cadmium-yellow aspen leaves.

This wasn't one of the old growth areas of Algonquin, but the trees were still forty feet high or more, thick enough to create twilight on this overcast day. Opportunistic saplings made a lower ceiling layer, and boulders and fallen limbs and logs emerald with moss cluttered the uneven forest floor, so that the landscape seemed to crowd close around him. *A whole lot of nothing,* his dad would have called it, except that to Duncan it wasn't nothing; it was crammed from here to the edges of his awareness with life.

The dig was in a cleared space, smaller than Duncan had expected. A grid of stakes bristled up from an indentation in the ground; the excavation itself was concealed by tarps held down by rocks and logs. Where the path ended, at the edge of the dig, was another of those peaked-roofed bulletin boards that were everywhere in the park. There were print-outs of photographs pinned up: tanned people in shorts and hiking boots with bandannas tied around their heads; a strip of blackened earth against brown; a half-buried, half-rusted iron pot; ivory dice, a belt buckle, a pipe. There was a hand-drawn map, with one square for the dig and another kitty-corner at a distance from it.

The page of typing that described the project had probably been there all summer, and was rain-spotted and wrinkled with damp. The current excavation was of a camboose from the late nineteenth century (*1860s??* someone had annotated in pen) that had probably burned down (a pencil checkmark). Northwest of it was another, later structure, of which some logs still remained. The corroded chains and tackle of a broken jammer had been found nearer the highway, which had led to the rediscovery of the site in the first place; original documentation was thin, human memory was short, and the forest tended to eat what got left behind.

Duncan walked to the edge of the low pit. Leaves whispered above him. An edge of plastic tarp shuffled in the breeze. A hot shiver vibrated straight up Duncan's spine and along his arms like the ringing of a bell.

He backed up from the excavation until he felt underbrush against the backs of his thighs. He rubbed his arms over his jacket. *Burned,* had the notice said?

He looked again at the edge of the excavation, focusing the sense of sight that used more than just his eyes...

Someone was watching him.

Duncan stared back at the man who stood twenty feet from him in a fringe of ferns. In the eye-blink after wondering why the man was knee-deep in forest, he realized that it was because that spot had been the middle of a path when the man had been alive.

Duncan blew out a steadying breath. "Hello."

"You, sir," the man said, and looked at Duncan levelly. "You see me."

"Yes. Do you need my help with something?"

"Happens that I do. Something's taking my boys."

Unlike the first camboose, of which there was little left but layers of char, this one had simply been abandoned to rot and dissolve into the forest floor. Now that he knew it was here, Duncan could see where the walls had been, fallen logs sketching an improbable square in the undergrowth. From his seat on a younger, sturdier log within the square, he could also see, in disorienting double vision, the camboose as it had been and still was for the man who stood in front of him: the blanket-covered bunk

Duncan sat on, the amber glow of the central fire, the shadows in the corners that laid a darker filter over the already-dim woods.

"Now we're settled in, first things first," the man said. "Name's Briggs. This is my place."

"I'm Duncan Coburn. Are you a guardian?" He'd met them once or twice before, spirits who had planted themselves to guard a place. He wasn't sure if that was the right term. Peter would know what to call them.

"I'm a foreman. I look after my boys."

Duncan could see them, too, a handful of men in a semicircle behind Briggs, none as solid as he was, a few just wavers of light. "Why have you all stayed here?"

"A lot of my boys think they won't be going to a good place when they go." He glanced back at them with grim affection. "I reckon at least some of them are right."

That was easy to set straight. "The door takes everyone," Duncan said. "We all go to the same place."

"So you say. Not my concern. Thing is, some of them are gone."

"How do you mean gone?"

"I mean they *ain't here*. And I don't mean they've gone on. Now and then one'll go, but this ain't in the natural run of things. It's too many, too fast."

"How many?"

Briggs slipped his thumbs behind his suspenders as he thought. "Paulson. The Ogre. Sam-Sam. Tall Johnny…"

"Hawkins," said one of the men behind him, as if speaking from a long way off.

*Smithy*, whispered someone else, a low gust like the wind through dry leaves.

"When did it start?"

Briggs' forehead wrinkled; day-to-day time tended to be slippery for even the most aware spirits. "In the summer? You understand, some of them tend to go quiet for a while and then wake back up again. Might've been earlier and we didn't notice."

Duncan eyed the spirits behind Briggs. "Before they went, were they upset? Angry?"

Briggs gave him a look. "Lot of my boys are, yeah."

"More than usual?"

Briggs shrugged. Duncan folded his arms and looked around the forest. Briggs' thoughts made boulders and clumps of trees light up as landmarks: there was the clearing where they squared the logs, that was where they stored the water barrels for icing the roads. Duncan stood up. "Show me everywhere you and your men go."

It was awkward travelling, Briggs striding ahead of him straight through saplings and brush, Duncan picking his way across uneven ground and crossing his fingers that he didn't break his ankle in some burrowing animal's front door. A few times he stopped abruptly, hands up to protect his face from impact, before realizing that the tree the width of an eighteen-wheeler cab was something he was seeing only in Briggs' memory. He'd read about the old-growth forests; actually seeing them made his skin prickle in awe.

"The Ogre liked to spend time here," Briggs said, pausing where there had been a clearing in the cathedral of trees, once. "He was never much for other people."

Duncan closed his eyes and felt. Chipmunks, a fox nearby, the perpetual hum of small lives. Nothing human.

"This is as far as we cleared, on this side." Briggs swept his hand to indicate a border Duncan couldn't differentiate now, where loggers before Briggs' crew had left a landscape of stumps, peeled bark and new scrub taking advantage of the sunshine. "We went deeper on t'other."

They worked their way in an arc around the camboose site, crossing the shadows of roads and clearings. "That's where Smithy did for himself," Briggs pointed out. "Axe in the foot. Wound went bad."

"Did he like to stay around here?"

"No, he kept with us, in the camboose. And that there's the very tree where Scotty hanged himself from, but he ain't one of the ones gone."

Duncan caught a sense of presence, like a whiff of smoke on the wind, a little ways north of them. It was focused and hazy at the same time, the way things could get when a spirit was obsessed with something. He headed towards it.

"Aw, now," Briggs said, with a tinge of embarrassment, "you don't need to go disturbing those two."

"Why, what are they—"

It was two, yes, though they were intimately close together, an undulating blur against a tree. Duncan could sense them individually, but barely, like two layers of tissue paper melting into one in the rain.

"You get that, in camp," Briggs said gruffly. "Those two, it ain't like they got much other pleasure out of life. Leave them be. They ain't hurting anyone."

"It's all right, I agree with you." This was just a reconnoitre, anyway. He'd come back again to talk to them, alone, without Briggs being growlingly protective in all directions. "Are they always in this spot?"

"Naw, they drift around."

They kept walking. Duncan was forced to stop to disentangle his shaggy hair from a clutching twig, and realized that he was hunching his shoulders. It was an effort to straighten; pain undulated out from his chest like a raindrop making ripples in water, sending throbs up through his skull, down to his wrists and shins.

He took a deep breath and grounded himself in his own body, flexing his toes in his boots, noticing the cool damp of the air against his cheeks, reminding himself of the integrity of his physical borders. The pain dulled. Then he cast his awareness out to find what had caused it, and flinched when he found it.

"Jonah Bailey," Briggs said, as they came up on something that Duncan didn't want to look too closely at, a broken huddle at the base of a tree. "That was a nasty death. I reckon he never got over it."

This, now, this was a thing Duncan could do something about. He steeled himself and crouched down, trying not to focus too closely on the red bubbles that breath made seeping out of the crushed ruin of a chest, or the clotted remains of Bailey's face.

"Jonah Bailey, you don't have to be in pain," he said. "You can go on at any time."

There was no sign that Bailey even noticed him, mired in his own agony, struggling to take in a last breath that had been denied him for over a century.

"Everyone goes through the door," Duncan said. "Whatever you've done, whatever you think you deserve punishment for, it doesn't matter now. The door will take you in."

He reached out with whatever sense it was that he used to touch the door, trying to find that bud of possibility, the promise of ease and warmth. *Help me*, he thought at it. *Help him.*

A grey jay chattered somewhere in the treetops, earning grating echoes from farther away. A car hissed past on the highway, a distant sound like rushing water.

Duncan tamped down frustration, shook his head to clear it, and reached out again. *He's in pain. Please come take him.* He felt his hand, instinctively mirroring his efforts, grasp empty air. Bailey's breath wheezed wetly. Duncan gritted his teeth and pushed further, knowing that he was on the verge of fucking this up by trying too hard and unable, in this moment, to stop. There was so much suffering he could do nothing about, he read it in people's minds every day, felt their loneliness and uncertainty and misery and flat-out despair; this one thing he could do, this one thing the door could do, so why wasn't it *happening*—

Something in him gave way. Anguish tore through Duncan as his back bowed, and he collapsed onto the twigs and moss beside Bailey's labouring ghost.

He might have lost consciousness for a moment. When he became aware again, there was a slick of cold sweat under his arms and a drumbeat of pain rolling against one temple.

*Well, that was stupid.*

He rolled onto his hands and knees. As he pushed himself to standing, his back started to clench. He froze and breathed through the spasm, then straightened and put one hand up to his temple to keep his pulse from bursting right through it.

"Looks like that didn't do the trick," Briggs observed dryly.

"Yeah." Duncan staggered. He felt almost high, not in a good way but in a strained, butter-scraped-over-too-much-bread way. "How much else did you need to show me?"

"Couple more places over thisaway you might want to take a look at."

They tromped through the woods for another fifteen minutes. By the time they got back to the camboose, Duncan was drenched with sweat and breathing as shallowly as he could; deep breaths hurt.

"I'll come back soon and take a closer look," he promised.

"Yep. Best to get someone to rub some liniment on that back."

The first thing Duncan did when he crawled into the back of his van was to swallow a couple of ibuprofen, chased with lukewarm water. He wished he'd thought to make himself a thermos of tea before he left the campsite. He wished Peter were here to smooth down his agitation and shore up his energy with warm, bare skin. But he'd made do alone for a lot of years. His emergency food supply contained a couple of a Jokerz bars, and he fished one out and took a bite of chocolate and nougat and peanuts. He wasn't a huge fan of sweets, but sugar and caffeine were the best alternative to touch that he'd found.

As he was driving back to the campsite, his phone let out a musical typewriter burst. Duncan pulled over onto the shoulder of the highway and took it out of his pocket.

Peter's number. *Hey so*

Duncan waited for the followup for a counted minute before he typed back, *What's up?* When he tried to send it, all he got was a circled red exclamation point and a stern *Not Delivered*.

He spent the evening and the next morning moving slowing and figuring out which postures did not send warning cramps rippling up his back. At least the stretched-thin feeling had abated.

After breakfast he drove out to the dig again. There was another car parked on the cleared patch. Duncan hesitated but then pulled in anyway, and as he walked down the path, nodded at the older couple on their way out. What day was it? Thursday, he saw, checking his phone. He wondered whether it was going to get busy on the weekend.

The dig was still tarped. Duncan stood on the bare ground and directed a tentative thread of awareness like a root into the soil.

The hairs rose on the back of his neck, and he backed away a step before he could stop himself. Something was near; he could sense it as though he were on a frozen surface looking down to a dark body blundering in the deep.

He had no illusions that whoever or whatever it was wasn't connected with Briggs' men going missing. But it clearly wasn't going to welcome him. And with things with the door the way they were, well, it couldn't hurt to know a bit more before he made a move.

He avoided Briggs' camboose for now, and, guiltily, the spot where Jonah Bailey lay. He would get Bailey through the door. He would find a way. Just not right this second.

He found the lovers lying in the sheltered cave formed by the lowest boughs of a pine. Now that he knew what they were doing, their misty outline against the red-brown carpet of fallen needles was suggestive: someone bent on his hands and knees, someone kneeling behind him, an easy rhythm rolling through them both. Duncan chose a seat on a lichen-spotted boulder a polite distance away and settled in to wait for them to finish.

When you could hear other people's thoughts, sex was weird in a way that, Duncan gathered, was different from all the ways it was weird for everybody else. For one thing, although his own experience was well on the vanilla end of things, he'd been through a whole travelogue of positions and kinks and illicit adventures in his head. It was amazing what people thought about while killing time at the laundromat or lining up to pay for gas.

The lovers had drifted, not so much apart as into a different shape, now with one of them leaning against the tree trunk and the other kneeling at his feet.

It was like having watched thousands of hours of incredibly varied but also very specific niche porn, if porn were something that got unexpectedly beamed into your head while you were just trying to buy groceries. At least he didn't have to deal with inconvenient boners. The static of everyone else's thoughts tended to white out physical arousal for Duncan under most circumstances. Though that was a mixed blessing, since it also cancelled out *convenient* boners.

The fog against the tree trunk had thickened, as if two people now leaned and thrust together, still rippling at that same easy, steady pace.

It was difficult to explain to some people how sex could be pleasurable without involving an orgasm or even a hard-on. The kindest, most generous men he'd met in truck stops and parks and the bathrooms of small-town bars—the men he'd known it was safe to approach—had also been the ones to feel the most conflicted about not going down on their knees for him in turn, or at least jerking him off. It could be hard to convince them that just getting his hands on their naked skin was all he needed.

The lovers were back on the ground again, face to face or one sitting behind the other—Duncan couldn't tell—still rocking together. Duncan wondered if they'd had this much stamina when they'd been alive.

And then there was Peter, who not only was kind and generous but also had sunk a lot of his self-worth into being able to meet other people's needs. Peter, who, on the first job they'd worked together, faced with a Duncan who was exhausted and dizzy and shocky from losing a part of his soul to whatever was behind the door, had stripped them both down and plastered his body against Duncan's. Peter, who had selflessly tried to deny his own need out of a fear of exploiting Duncan, even as Duncan had happily stroked him off. Duncan had not made it clear enough to Peter, it occurred to him now, that that had been the most satisfying physical experience he'd had in years.

Were they ever going to finish? he wondered, watching the surging mist flow into another supine form. He focused his attention a little more directly on them, shrugging off self-consciousness. They felt the same as they had when he'd arrived, the same as they had the day before, in fact. They weren't going to finish, he realized. Ever. Without physical bodies, there was no climax to interrupt them; they could just keep going, spirits wrapped around one another, inside one another, forever at the sweet spot between desire and urgency...

At the thought of that eternal touch, he felt himself blush. He turned away from the pair and looked into the cooling, distant green until the disconcerting thrill of arousal had faded and he felt able to pay attention to the work in front of him.

He approached the pair making both physical and psychic noise. They noticed him as he stopped at the edge of the pine's protected circle, although their undulation continued.

"I'm sorry for disturbing you. I'm trying to find out what happened to some people who have disappeared. May I ask you a few questions?"

They answered with wordless assent.

"Briggs said you move around the forest. Have you seen any spirits in trouble, maybe trying to run away from something or struggling with something, being taken somewhere they don't want to be?"

*Forest,* they agreed, more idea than word. Duncan caught a sense of longing and satisfaction both. But they didn't give the impression of having seen anyone in distress.

"Have you seen the door opening recently?" Maybe Briggs was mistaken, and the spirits had simply moved on after all. But all he got at the mention of the door was indifference. They ignored it when it came; they weren't ready for that kind of change.

"Have you noticed anything new or different?"

They paused thoughtfully, taking the opportunity to drift into another against-the-tree pose. There were still two of them, he could tell, but they felt identical to him. They had been two who were different, and now they were two who were the same, each made up two halves of what they'd been. Someday, if the door didn't take them before that, they'd be one, like red and blue Plasticine being slowly kneaded together into purple.

*Fire, smoke. Smoke, fire.*

He'd guessed as much. "I understand. Anything else?"

They considered. *Save them.*

He didn't like the sound of that. Duncan sighed. "I'll try."

He thanked them and left them swaying against one another. He made his way back to the camboose and sat on the log. "Briggs?"

The foreman appeared, two of his more solid men flanking him. Duncan could feel their regard: distrust of him, old resentments and fears, anxiety hot in one like a smouldering firecracker.

"What can you tell me about the older camboose, the one that burned?"

Briggs scratched his beard. "Well, now, it was before my time, but I remember one of the old-timers saying it was a bad business. Happened at night. Not everybody got out."

"Is there anyone from then still around?"

"Never seen any."

Duncan stuck his hands in his pockets. "I think someone's been woken up by the dig there. I'm going to go talk to them."

"Might need more than talking," said one of the other men, and his form darkened into shadow, looming up towards the treetops.

"That's not how I do things," Duncan said.

Briggs turned his head towards the man. "It's under control," he said, and Duncan ducked his head against an unexpected swell of pride.

When he got back to the dig, he listened for voices or the sound of a car out in the parking lot, but heard nothing. He contemplated the tarped hollow.

"I'd like to talk to you," he said.

Silence.

"I'm looking for some people who've disappeared. Their friends are wondering what happened to them. Have you seen them?"

Nothing.

The tarp shivered in the breeze. Duncan looked down at it unhappily, knowing what he was going to have to do.

Under the tarp, the excavation was at least broad enough to not immediately remind him of a grave. Nearest him was the deepest trench, with two more in ranks like steps up to the level of the cleared forest floor. Fortunately, it hadn't rained heavily in the last week, so there was no standing water at the bottom. Duncan cast a last look at the path, mentally apologized to archaeologists everywhere, and lowered himself into the dig.

He lay down on his back, spreading the hood of his hoodie so his hair wouldn't be in the dirt. He couldn't quite bring himself to pull the tarp back over himself. Far above, dark branches and leaves traced a lattice on grey sky. The still air around him smelled of soil, damp, and rotting leaves.

Duncan closed his eyes. He pressed his palms against the ground, let his fingertips push divots into the dirt. Tiny lives glittered around him.

"I want to help," he said into the silence.

A shiver ran along his skin. He shied away from the thought of many-legged things crawling in the dirt. "How can I help?"

*Help. Save them*

His own heart boomed so loudly that Duncan started. *Get them.* Panic raced up his body. *Save them save them get them save them*

"Yes," he sent into the dark. "I'll help you save them. What's wrong?"

*Save them get them* SAVE THEM SAVE THEM

"Where are they?" It was hard to see, everything was murk and confusion. "I'll help. Where are you?"

*No way out lost lost* SAVE THEM

Duncan inhaled smoke, choking hot. He could feel other spirits, disoriented and isolated in featureless roaring light. He coughed and reached out for them. His touch fell short.

*LOST*

Despair crashed down on Duncan, followed in an instant by searing agony on the side of his head. He rocketed to his feet and flailed at the flames.

"Drop!" demanded a different voice. "Drop and roll, yeh fuckin' idiot!"

Duncan heaved himself out of the dig, onto flatter ground, and rolled over and over in the dirt. The pain retreated. He could see again, breathe again. He sat up. His back felt as though someone were grinding knuckles into the side of his spine.

"Trying to run away from fire like a damn fool," groused Briggs.

Duncan put a cautious hand to the side of his head. A handful of charred hair crumbled, blackening his fingers. His skin was stubbled and tender.

"They're there," he said.

"What's got them?" Briggs asked grimly.

Someone else's memory of flames that blotted out all other sight and sound jolted through him. Duncan strained a breath through his teeth before realizing that the air around him was clear and cool. "He's another logger. He got trapped, and he thinks he's helping them, trying to save them from the fire. He's holding onto them and trying to get out."

"But my boys? How do I get them out?"

The answer was the same as it always was: "I have to find a way to get him through the door."

Duncan had come prepared this time. Back in the van, he drank a thermosful of strong, sweet tea, and swallowed a peanut butter sandwich without tasting it. Then, because he felt about to crumble into ash himself, he wrapped himself in his sleeping bag and fell asleep for two solid hours. He needed it, but it messed up his sleep schedule; he spent that night dozing through tangled dreams of smoke and doorless hallways, startling awake every hour with a gasp to find himself surrounded by the clean, chill air of an Algonquin October. Once, deep in the night, he woke to the sound of wolves howling out to one another across the dark distances. The back of his neck prickled, and he remembered an Ojibway guy he'd met once from way up in Temagami First Nation, who'd said, "Man, there is shit out in those woods that just needs to be left the hell *alone.*"

On Friday, he cooked himself a stick-to-your-ribs breakfast of oatmeal and dried apricots. He used his Coleman stove rather than the campfire, and checked three times to make sure the flame was out. Then he headed out to the dig for the fourth time. He'd come across a lot of thorny cases this year, he reflected as he drove. But then, spirits usually stuck around for strongly felt reasons. Only occasionally did he find one who had simply lost their way and needed to be ushered in the direction of the door like a lost tourist. *Hello, goodbye, and home in time for second breakfast,* as Peter liked to say.

There were two cars already in the dig parking lot. Duncan hesitated, then carried on by and out of the park into town, where he grabbed some groceries. He also stopped at a drugstore and got a good look at himself in a mirror. A patch the size of his fist on the left side of his scalp was almost bare; the skin looked pink and tight. His next stop was the town barber, who buzzed his shoulder-length hair down to velvet on the rest of his head to match. Duncan hadn't had his hair that short since grade school, and he felt so exposed that he had to dig his grey toque out of his box of winter clothing.

When he passed the dig on the way back, there were three cars in the parking lot.

Duncan drove back to the campground and spent the rest of the day reading and napping—which would confuse his sleep rhythm even further, but later on, he suspected, he'd be glad of the rest. More cars pulled into the lots around him as the afternoon wore on, and the rust-and-green landscape sprouted lemon-lime tents and fuchsia Gore-Tex jackets and acid-blue canoes.

At twilight, as campfires sprouted among the trees, Duncan drove back to the dig for what he hoped would be the last time. He parked in the empty lot as close to the trees as he could get, and propped up on the dash the sign he'd scrawled on scrap paper for this kind of job: *Engine trouble, back soon.* Then he made his way into the woods.

There was a quarter moon, and he left his flashlight in his pocket to let his night vision develop. Getting to the dig was easy, the wood chips crunching softly under his tread. Once there, Duncan looked in the direction of the second camboose, not too eager to traipse through the undergrowth in the dark unless he had to. "Briggs?"

He sensed the foreman appear next to him. "Yeah?"

"Do you know where the entrance to this camboose was?"

Briggs surveyed the site. "Well, now, we always cleared a space in front, so...likely right about there." Duncan moved to where Briggs pointed, about the middle of the eastern edge of the dig. "What are you about?"

Duncan sat on the ground. The chill immediately began to seep into his legs. "I'm going to try to show him the door."

"And if he sets you on fire again?"

"I'm hoping if I can lead him out, that won't happen." It was a risk, no question, and if it was just the man in the burned camboose, maybe he wouldn't have tried it. But it wasn't just him; it was all the others, Briggs' friends and maybe others he didn't know about, who knew how many, trapped down there, lost and choking. He couldn't leave them to an eternity of that.

He centred himself and reached out. "Are you there? I'm here, at the door. Come towards me."

What seemed a long time passed. Then, from below: *Out*

"Yes. Bring them out."

*Bring them save them save them*

Duncan tried to keep his breathing steady against a surge of adrenalin. "You can save them. You can get them out. Bring them towards me."

*Out save them lost lost*

"Towards me." He could sense them all, spirits he had seen briefly in Briggs' memories, now milling around each other in a close space, snared in panic and disorientation. "Bring them out. You can save them."

*Save them*

Now would be a good time for the door to show up, Duncan thought, and cast out a thought for it. He felt the spirit's attention leave the churning confusion around him, fountain out to focus on what Duncan was doing. *Save save save* The naked side of Duncan's head tingled.

"You can save them," he repeated with half his concentration, trying to pull the budding possibility that was the door out of the ether. His face prickled, as though tiny flying cinders had landed on his skin. He hoped that if fire manifested again, Briggs would be able to call him out of it in time.

*Save* The spirit swooped in close. Electricity ran along Duncan's arms, and a growing heat like the beginnings of a sunburn. Then a pull, as though the spirit were looking outward. *Save save save them ALL*

Duncan's eyes began to water in intangible smoke. "Yes, save th—"

A force like a pickup truck in high gear slammed into his chest and knocked him into the dirt. Agony ground his breastbone into fragments. He heard his own gasp, too shocked to even draw breath to scream.

Bailey. The spirit had found him, gathered him in.

Duncan fought to distance himself from Bailey's pain. He was not that broken body; he was whole, living, separate.

Another force hit him, lower than his chest this time. The lovers. Heat surged into Duncan's groin. He honestly couldn't tell whether he was physically responding or not; the thought or memory of intimate touch was more visceral right now than his own body.

*Out* demanded the spirit. Duncan felt his skin tighten and itch as the fire licked closer. Sensation racked him, anguish and lust and flames, all of it heat, blending together and winding tighter and higher.

He thought fleetingly of the door. All his concentration had scattered like cold ashes kicked into the dirt. He sent a tendril of appeal out to it, the faintest plea, the weakest touch, knowing it was futile.

And the door answered.

*Out* The spirit's vast, exhausted, disbelieving relief washed over him. The door began to open, just a thread of light and harmony, and the spirit moved towards it.

Taking them with him. Bailey, the lovers, the Ogre and Smithy and all of Briggs' men, Briggs now too, all of them dragged along by the spirit's conviction. All of them, including Duncan.

*Stop,* he thought at the spirit, unable to speak, and struggled against a rip tide of solace that soothed the agony away.

*Saved* the spirit promised.

*Yes. You saved them. Now let them go.*

*Go* the spirit agreed. The door was about to open, pulsing with comfort and light. Tears of longing pricked Duncan's eyes.

*Stop. It's not right. Not like this.* That was a fundamental of the work, practicality and his own ethics in parallel; the door itself might be able to compel people, but Duncan could only bring them to it and try to persuade them. He got a sense of incomprehension back from the spirit. Of course; who wouldn't choose to be saved from a fire?

Duncan tried to drop away from the spirit's hold, but it had him fast. He could feel the door's consolation, like hearing a favourite song indistinctly through apartment walls. Some poor park ranger would find his body in the morning. Would Peter ever know why Duncan had stopped replying to his messages? Would he think Duncan was just ignoring him until Peter left him alone?

"That's far enough." Briggs' voice was hoarse, as though he had breathed smoke, but firm.

The spirit wavered. *Saved*

"Yeah. You did well. I'll take it from here." His authority was bedrock. Duncan felt the grip on him loosen.

*Go* Now the spirit was uncertain.

"Yeah, you go. You've earned it. You let me worry about them now. It's my job."

The door bloomed open.

There was a sense of giving in, both reluctant and longed-for. The spirit didn't let them go so much as set them all down gently. Duncan felt himself settle back fully into his own cold, aching body. The spirit slid away into glory. Others, freed now, followed him regardless: Bailey, leaving his agony behind at last; the one Briggs had called the Ogre; a few more. The light of the door eclipsed them, and then they and the door were gone.

The lovers drifted away into the trees. Spirits around him dissolved back to the camboose or their favourite spots. Duncan groaned and relaxed into the dirt. Constellations invisible in the city glittered above him.

He felt Briggs beside him, squatting down. "You all right?"

Duncan rolled onto his side and managed to push himself up to sitting. Everything, physical and psychic, felt battered. "Yeah…" He was shivering. "Good thing he listened to you."

"A good logger knows when to heed his foreman." And then, as if in response to the thought that Duncan was trying to keep to himself: "Without your part, I couldn't have done mine. Well done."

"Yeah. You too." Duncan tried to stand. He couldn't get his trembling legs under him. Unable to help himself, he reached out; his hands went right through Briggs' arm. He flushed. "Sorry."

"I can't touch the world the way some can." Briggs pursed his lips. "Hold on, I got an idea."

He disappeared. Duncan wrapped his arms around himself. Why had he decided to leave his thermos a million miles away in his damn van?

Briggs appeared again, not alone.

*Touch?* the lovers offered.

He barely stopped himself from grabbing at them. "Do you mind?"

*Touch.* They closed around him. Warmth, connection, familiarity, pleasure. The rhythm of heartbeats, of sex, of bodies of water. Duncan swayed with them, enveloped and embracing, feeling their enjoyment at his difference and sameness, and his need gradually hushed into a smooth, gentle contentment.

The moon had moved by the time he separated himself from them. "Thank you," he said, and felt their gratification in return before they wandered away. His body was relaxed and just a little aroused, enough to feel good without him needing to do anything about it.

Duncan stood up and brushed himself off. "Briggs?" The foreman appeared again from wherever he'd vanished to to give Duncan some privacy. "That helped a lot, thank you. But I have to get going."

"Sure. It was real good working with you," Briggs said. "Now you go get some food in you, catch some sleep."

"I will. I hope you don't have any more trouble."

"It's gonna be quiet around here," Briggs said, surveying the dark forest that held fewer of his men than it had. "I *like* quiet." Duncan saw the forest through his eyes again for a moment, towering old-growth trees that three men linked could not encircle with their arms. Then Briggs faded, and Duncan made his way back to the parking lot and his van.

By the time he woke up at his campsite the next morning, most of the other campers had doused their breakfast fires and moved on to the kayaking or hiking or whatever vigorous outdoor activity had brought them out to the park. Duncan cooked himself a massive breakfast of home fries and scrambled tofu, accompanied by a litre of tea. He knew he'd probably have to pull over and have a nap later in the afternoon, but for now he felt wide awake and ready to be on his way. He left by the west gates and headed south on 60.

Ten minutes out of the park, a long string of musical typewriter arpeggios erupted from his phone, one after another after another, each punctuated with a chime. Duncan was laughing by the time they ended.

He'd need to stop in Dorset for gas, and he'd read all of Peter's messages then. In the meantime, he cradled the warm knowledge of them as he drove down the highway in the brilliant October day, the sunlight turning all the autumn trees around him to flaming crimson and gold.

# Jager

## BRETT STEVENS

Hearing the runners scrape across the kitchen's tile floor woke me from my nap. It was Adam dragging the stupid rocking horse from the garage towards the family room. My dear partner of forty-odd years was beginning to lose it. He was acting so strange some days; talking to people who weren't there, forgetting things, and even seeing things. I was worried about him.

I got out of my chair, pressing downwards on my cane. As my hips groaned and my back creaked with pain, I felt each and every one of my many years of life. Shuffling until my joints warmed up, I headed for the kitchen. I could hear Adam talking to someone now. I hoped he was on the phone.

As I rounded the corner, I was glad to see him chatting on the house phone and twisting the cord like he always did. He looked up at me and gave me his boyish, charming smirk. It was this devilish look that captured me all those years ago. I could still hear the Doobie Brothers singing about *China Grove* as we necked in the back of Adam's Oldsmobile Delta 88. That was the same night we'd met at the dance at the Unitarian Church. There weren't many good places for men like us to meet.

Adam was so brave that night. He'd always been the one of us with courage. Our eyes had met across the room in the church basement. After I pretended I wasn't looking at him, he got up and walked over to me. I remember looking up and seeing his long blond—

"How was your nap?" Adam asked as he hung up the phone. "We've got a big night planned."

"What big night?" I asked, wondering what hijinks my dear man's mind was playing on him.

"It's Valentine's Day." Adam kissed me on the lips and I felt my heart flutter. Even after all these years, he got a rise out of me. I may be taking heart medication, but he could still make it race.

"I know," I answered. I lied. I forgot it was today. It didn't matter though because I'd gotten Adam a box of his favorite candies; milk chocolate with raspberry cream inside. We'd been to the mall and I bought them when he was in the bathroom. He was under the impression we were only mall-walking for our health. I knew I had to get him his present when I had the chance. Once he disappeared around the corner, I dashed into the See's Candy and bought them.

"Why did you drag the old rocking horse in from the garage?" I finally had to ask the question. He's avoiding it, I can tell.

"We're having company later," he answered cryptically. Adam's been doing that a lot lately. It bugs the hell out of me.

"Who's coming by?"

"The usual Valentine's Day group," he says, smiling and wiping his eyes.

My other concern is Adam has been very weepy lately. He was never a sentimental fool until recently. His furtive eye-wiping makes me think there is something wrong with him. Every time I bring it up, he only gets more emotional. It hurts to see the pain etched across his heavily lined but still handsome face. His eyes are red a lot lately.

"I can help, you know. What do you need me to do?"

"Nothing, my dear. You need to rest up. There will be a houseful this evening."

There won't be a houseful. There never is. We're just two lonely old men, still loving on each other, but alone.

"Are you sure?" I ask. I'm concerned about him. I worry it's his mind that's going and then what are we going to do? I can hardly get around. My heart can't take much activity. My arms and legs have weakened. Luckily we have people come in to help us. Thank heavens.

"I'm sure. Go finish your nap. You've only been asleep for a few minutes."
Adam has a hand on each of my shoulders. His lovely blue eyes are peering into mine. I smile back, reassuring him. It's what we do for each other.
We have the other's back. Adam and Glen, the dynamic duo, in love and in charge for forty-some years.

"Are you sure?" I ask. I suddenly feel really tired. I should keep an eye on him. His mind is going I think.

**A** noise awakens me and when I open my eyes I see a little face staring at me. I start, and pull the afghan closer. Who is this little imp peering at me so happily? I pull the wrap over my head. There are voices in the other room. The slight weight which was beside me disappears. I hear the sound of little feet padding quickly across the room.

I hear Adam's laugh. It's musical, but like a trombone, not a trumpet.
The sound of it makes me grin and I pull down the cover. It's darker now with the sun having set. I struggled to pull myself up with my arms. They aren't working right. I stop and sigh.

I realize the only voice I can really hear talking is my Adam's. There are no other voices. He's doing it again, talking with people who aren't there. It has happened a lot recently. I'm worried about him. I'm worried about us, really.

What had I seen a moment ago?

I must have been having a dream to see the face of a little one right in front of me. It happens. We once planned on having a family. Adam and I were going to have a little boy or a little girl to raise and take care of. It was all planned. I sighed and it sounded so sad and weary. It felt so recent as I remembered.

*Our friend Amy found herself in the "family way" and she didn't have a boyfriend or husband. It was the late seventies and while there were plenty of women who raised kids alone, it was still looked down on.*

*Frankly, it wasn't like two men raising a baby was considered acceptable or normal. I lucked out because as Adam said, "I just don't care what they think. Fuck 'em." Like I said, he was the brave one.*

*We had a house in Brooklyn and a room for her. Amy could stay with us until the little boy or girl was born. Adam and I were putting together a little nest egg to give her. It was a gift because she was giving us something we'd never get otherwise; a family. I remember her going up to bed the night before. I met her on the stairs and kissed her on the forehead, thanking her for her sacrifice.*

*The next day, she came to us. It was evening. The air was chilly for May. I remember smelling dirt in the air from our neighbors newly planted garden. I'd started painting the baby's room, a pale foamy sea green with white trim. Amy knocked on the front door, which was odd given she was living with us.*

*As we sat at the dining room table and she told us about the abortion, I felt numb and somewhat hollow. Adam was crying, silently weeping, because we both knew the dream had died. We would never be parents. The room I'd only started to paint would become a den or a spare room no one would ever use. It would remain empty and alone.*

*Amy went upstairs to pack her things. I remember reaching out to Adam as he continued to cry and took his hand. It was cool to the touch. I pulled him closer. He scooted his chair closer to me. My lover, my partner laid his face on my chest. His tears watered my skin. I could feel the hot puffs of his breath as he sucked in air, desperately clinging to hope but feeling nothing other than despair.*

Adam's presence at the doorway brought me back to the present. I smiled at him, bleak at the memory of loss.

"Are you going to join us?" he asked, crossing his arms. Behind him, there were no other sounds. There was only the quiet.

"Oh, Adam," I sighed. Running my hand alongside my chair, I found my cane. "Who's here?"

The dread filled my chest as I waited. He was delusional. No one was here. We were two old queens on their last leg in the journey of life. We had each other.

"Come and see. You'll be surprised."

I waved him away and heard his footsteps cross the kitchen tile floor. It was the lonely sound of my man walking across a divide and away from me.

I put the cane in front of me and, heaving, I stood. My joints were stiff. My back ached. It was slow going, but eventually my torso was somewhat erect. For a moment, I thought I heard the jangling sound of a child's laughter. I couldn't have though. There were no children here. It was only Adam and I and, well, Jager.

*Jager was the rocking horse my grandparents bought for me. It had been bare wood, built by a neighbor, I'd been told. My grandpa had carefully painted it white with a red saddle and reins. There were blue accents and it was a beautiful thing. When I was presented with the gift on my birthday, my German immigrant grandmother had pointed at it and said, "Jager," nodding at me. From then on, my rocking horse was called Jager, which I later discovered meant "hunter." I loved it so much. I would get on it and ride for hours at a time, pretending I was out in the wild tracking buffalo or coyote.*

*Wearing a child's cowboy hat with a fringed vest and a holster with a toy gun, I became Roy Rogers. I was the Lone Ranger. I could become anyone I wanted to. Therefore, when we made our deal with Amy, the first thing I retrieved from my parents' house was Jager. I knew our little boy or little girl would love Jager as much as I did.*

*Jager was sitting in the middle of the baby's room when I started painting it. Every time I remembered our loss, it was the image of the rocking horse alone in the center of a half-finished room. He'd never have our son or daughter ride him. Jager's only purpose was to give a child dreams, to let him or her become whatever they wanted to be. That was a rocking horse's reason for existing.*

*Now, Jager had no reason to live.*

*That night after Amy left, I stood in the doorway and looked at the drying paint and the rocking horse and my eyes filled with tears. As the tears trickled down, it became rage. I marched into the middle of the room and grabbed it. I dragged the horse through the doorway and down the stairs. Adam was screaming at me as I pulled it around the corner. I could see his face was a contorted mask of pain. It gave me pause.*

*I wanted to take the stupid wooden toy and smash it. I wanted to turn Jager into kindling wood and burn it in the backyard. The rocking horse had no purpose anymore. It would never make a little girl or boy laugh and imagine.*

*Adam grabbed me and hugged me. He pulled me so tightly and again I felt the heat of his tears. His face found mine and his lips sucked greedily on mine.*

*He looked so sad and lost. Adam was always boyish, but that night he looked like a kid who'd lost his favorite toy. In a way, perhaps, we both had.*

*I'd calmed down and Adam made me promise not to destroy Jager. I couldn't deny him anything. Even thinking about the rocking horse and what we lost that night made my heart thud and ache. Jager was the symbol of what we'd never have.*

"Are you coming?" Adam asked, his face flushed. For the first time in some time, his eyes glowed with hope. I hadn't seen him look so happy in some time. "They're waiting for you."

I shuffled after the man, his back hunched a little. His arthritis was bothering him and it hurt me too. It could feel his pain.

When we reached the far side of the kitchen, I stepped down each stair carefully. The family room was below and I rarely went there these days. I began hearing voices, other voices, and there was something familiar about them. One sounded a little like my brother. Another sounded like someone else I knew, but I couldn't place it.

As I got to the last step, I saw a handsome young man looking at me happily and in his arms was a boy, a child of maybe five. I smiled back though I didn't know who they were. Something about them perplexed me. Hadn't we met?

"Hi, Dad," the handsome young man said confidently. "Happy Valentine's Day."

He seemed to know me, but why was he calling me Dad? I knew better than to question it though. I got by playacting and recognizing people who seemed to know me. At least, it usually worked. So I went with it.

"Isn't it good to see them?" an old man beside me asked. He looked very familiar and there was something about him. I didn't know him though. Not really.

"Dad, how're you feeling?" the young man asked. There was a woman behind him. She approached and grabbed onto his arm and spoke to me expectantly.

"You're looking good, well rested and so handsome this evening."

I didn't know who these people were. There were a couple of older people and I realized one was my brother, Will. I smiled at him. I hadn't seen my brother in a long time.

"Will? Is that you?" I asked, shading my eyes for no apparent reason in this basement room.

The man smiled hesitantly and stood up. He stepped forward and held out his hand. "I'm your nephew, Scott. Dad's been dead for several years now."

I didn't know what he meant. My brother was dead. I looked over at the familiar man, and then I recognized him. It was my Adam. He was looking at me nervously, biting his lower lip like he always did.

"Grandpa!" the little boy in the handsome young man's arms squealed. He was the little guy who woke me up earlier, at least I thought so. "Grandpa, can I ride on Jager?"

The boy squirmed and writhed until his father set him down onto the floor. He raced over to the rocking horse. He crawled onto Jager and began rocking back and forth, screaming, "Woo Hoo!" at the top of his lungs.

I felt my heart rise up and fill my throat. "Someone's using Jager." It came out like a whisper.

"Yes, first our son and now our grandson adores him. They both love Jager," Adam said. He put his arm around my shoulders and hugged me. I turned and kissed his cheek. It was hot beneath my lips.

I looked over at the handsome man and turned to the man next to me. "Is he, is he our son?" I asked softly, almost shyly.

"Yes, it's Brandon. The little boy on Jager is our grandson, Liam. They came to wish you a very happy Valentine's Day. I love you."

"But Amy...?" I said, confused again.

"We used a surrogate. He's your birth son."

I felt a flash of emotion. It was both hot and cold. My head was a little dizzy.

"Pops, I think Dad needs to sit," I heard the young man say.

"Let me help," the woman beside him offered.

I looked over and saw the little imp of a boy rocking wildly and happily on Jager, my own, dear rocking horse. I wondered who he was. I looked at the man next to me who helped me to a chair. He looked familiar.

"Do I know you?" I asked. He wiped his eyes as he pulled away.

"Pops," the young man said. "You can't do this anymore."

"I can't leave him." The old man looked so sad. I wondered why.

"Let's figure this out. I'm coming by tomorrow morning." The handsome young man seemed lost. He gave me a forlorn smile. I couldn't understand why.

Why were all these strangers looking at me?

*A day in March*

I hear drawers open and close. There is a warm patch on my left cheek. As I open my eyes, I notice the bed is angled differently. The orientation of the room isn't the same. I sit up and see him.

It's a stranger dressed in blue scrub pants and a blousy top, lemon yellow with brown figures on it. They appear to be cartoon bears. The young man is stocky, short, and built like a fire hydrant, and he is busy putting clothes into a dresser across from my bed.

"Where am I?"

The guy turns, smiles and responds, "Good morning, Glen. I hope you slept well."

I smile back, hesitantly. The room looks somewhat familiar, though it seems strange to me. Then I see a couple of picture frames next to my bed. There was one of me and of— "Where's Adam?" I ask, suddenly remembering him. "Why isn't he here?"

"I'm right here, my darling man," I hear as the door opens. There is Adam, pushing a cart with a coffee pot and a plastic dome and grinning. His face looks happier and for some reason more relaxed. "I brought us some breakfast. Are you hungry?"

"I am. Where did you go?" I ask, disturbed. "I woke up alone."

"You had a bad night so I slept next door," he said, taking off the dome, which showed a couple of croissants. Next to it is a plate of fruit. "Do you want coffee or juice?" he asked.

"Where are we?" I ask again. I see the young man has finished putting clothes away and is standing over by another door. "Who is he?"

Adam looks at me and smiles. He nods at the young man who then approaches the bed. "I'm Stevie, Glen. Don't you remember? I'm your day nurse."

A fleeting memory whips through me and then departs. I don't know what's going on, but turn and see my Adam's smile is warm and calming.

"It's okay. We're at St. Anthony's now. We moved here a little while ago. We're in our new apartment. People like Stevie help us. We're in a good place."

Adam's voice is reassuring and I feel my heartbeat begin to slow. "Is everything okay?" I ask. I'm worried about him, but he looks good, actually better, though I don't know where I got that idea.

"Everything is fine. Brandon found this place. Isn't it wonderful?" he asks me. I look around and it is a nice room. The young man, Stevie, I think, is looking at me thoughtfully. I give him a smile as I reach for a glass of juice. He looks kind and Adam seems to trust him.

"As long as I have you," I say, patting Adam's hand. I look back over and see a picture on the wall. It's a large framed photo of Adam and me and behind us is a waterfall. It's beautiful. I can remember our trip to Sioux Falls like it was yesterday. Suddenly, I'm very tired.

I fall back on my pillow. There are light butterfly kisses on my forehead. I open my eyes and see a man, old, with his face heavily lined and wrinkled. He is over me and he looks familiar. I don't know exactly who he could be. He has friendly eyes. He's a stranger though.

# Cooking Lard and Candle Wax

## RICH BARNETT

---

**B**illy was sitting at the kitchen table poring over the latest edition of *Photoplay* when Linda Katie came barging through the back door wearing a faded yellow towel wrapped around her head.

"Damn it! I've really done it this time. I can't compete in the pageant looking like this." She removed the towel to reveal a head of fiery red hair.

"Wow!"

Linda Katie was a shoo-in, everyone said, to win the title of Miss Strawberry Queen 1959. But that was yesterday, when she was the prettiest girl at Rehoboth High; today, she looked like a cross between Lucille Ball and an Atomic Fire Ball.

"All I wanted was a little red. Then I found mother's cigarettes and Carol phoned and—damn it!—I left the dye in way too long."

Billy giggled and she threw the towel at him.

"You've got to help me!"

Billy wasn't good at hitting a baseball or throwing a football. Nor was he interested in cars like most teenage boys. His dad often said Billy's engine just ran with a little sugar in the tank. That, however, didn't stop him from employing his youngest son in the family barbershop after school and on weekends, because Billy had a way with hair. His scissors could transform an average Joe into an Ivy Leaguer or a Hollywood heartthrob. The young men lined up for Billy's haircuts on Saturday mornings. Then, after lunch, he skedaddled across town to his Aunt Lottie's beauty salon to do hair for the blue-rinse brigade.

Billy grabbed a can of Comet Bleach Powder from under the kitchen sink and mixed it with some shampoo to make a gooey paste that he worked all through Linda Katie's hair. "Let it sit half an hour," he instructed.

While they waited, he read to Linda Katie from *Photoplay*. It took an additional thirty minutes, but Billy was able to tone her hair down almost to the strawberry-blonde shade she'd been aiming for.

"You're the most, Billy, the most. How can I ever pay you back?"

"How 'bout we go for ice cream?" Besides movie magazines, Billy loved ice cream. Given the chance, he'd eat it every day. He liked pistachio best because he'd read it was Tab Hunter's favorite.

That night, Billy was in line for a cone—Linda Katie was outside flirting with one of the Apostolakas brothers—when he overheard someone asking for pistachio ice cream. He craned his neck to see who it was, but he didn't recognize the handsome sullen boy with the perfect DA haircut. His family must be renting a house for the summer. Billy wormed his way to the counter.

"I'll take one too!"

The teenagers looked at each other, both holding cones of pale green ice cream. "My name is Billy." He stuck out a hand.

"Cooper," the boy replied, shaking Billy's hand.

Cooper was different from Billy's friends in Rehoboth, who were loud and always showing off for girls on the beach. Not only was he from Washington, but also he stayed mostly inside and out of the sun. Cooper had a portable phonograph and a huge stack of rhythm and blues records that he played nonstop, all the while pretending to be a radio disc jockey. He knew as much about Chess Records and the Apollo Theater as Billy did about Universal Studios and the Brown Derby Restaurant.

"Where's Rosedale Beach?" Cooper asked Billy one afternoon as they sat in Cooper's bedroom, listening to the Isley Brothers' new song, "Shout." He handed Billy an advertisement cut from the *Coast Press*—one night only, James Brown and the Fabulous Flames, nine o'clock, at the Rosedale Beach dance hall.

"It's the colored beach, over on the other side of the bay."

"Boy, wouldn't it be a blast to see James Brown in person? They say he does the splits on stage."

The advertisement got Billy thinking. Summer was coming to an end and Cooper would be leaving soon. Billy might not ever see him again. "Let's go," he blurted out. "My dad has a motorboat he keeps down on the bay. I hate to fish, but he lets me drive it."

Cooper looked directly into Billy's eyes, with an expression that was both excited and questioning, yet he said nothing.

"Tell your folks you're sleeping over at my house. I'll tell mine I'm spending the night at yours. Linda Katie and me do it all the time. Works like a charm."

It was almost twilight when Billy pushed off from the pier in his dad's aluminum bass boat. He and Cooper paddled quietly out into open water, then Billy cranked the engine to life and they sped off, past Thompson's Island with its spooky Indian burial mounds and south across shallow Rehoboth Bay. It was a smooth ride, even after they hit the cross currents of the Indian River.

Though Billy had never been to Rosedale, he had heard about its hotel, boardwalk, and dance hall. Some white people from Rehoboth went to hear the colored music on Friday and Saturday nights. They wouldn't actually go in the dance hall; they anchored their boats offshore and listened.

Rosedale attracted the best black talent traveling from Philadelphia south to Norfolk, Virginia Beach, and the Carolinas. It was one of the few hotels catering exclusively to black folk on the entire Delmarva Peninsula.

Billy and Cooper, however, weren't content only to listen. They could do that with records. No, the boys came to see James Brown, whom Cooper believed was a legend in the making. Just beyond the dance hall and the other boats, they kicked off their penny loafers, jumped out, and pulled the boat through the cool, shallow water to shore, where Billy tied it up to a large pine tree.

Barefoot, and using the cover of trees and bushes, they carefully crept over to the dance hall, a single-story, wooden, white, frame building with aluminum awnings over its windows. A loud crowd had gathered on the front steps to greet James Brown, who had just arrived. From their hiding spot they heard how Brown and his band had been stopped for speeding and then detained at the county jail for a couple of hours.

The boys took advantage of the commotion and made their way to the back of the dance hall and darted inside. Cooper seemed to know what he was doing, so Billy followed. "There's got to be somewhere in the dressing room we can hide."

Sure enough, Cooper found a supply closet. There was no door, merely a thin, green cloth nailed up. They ducked in just as James Brown and his band burst into the dressing room, carrying suitcases and band equipment.

"Gimme a drink," Brown ordered, and sat down heavily in one of the few chairs in the sparsely furnished room. A well-dressed man they called Bird handed him a bottle of Canadian whiskey. Brown took a couple of very long swigs. "Goddamn crackers," he yelled. "Thought they was keeping us locked up all night." Members of the band were unpacking their instruments and changing clothes.

"Where's the girl gonna conk my hair?" Brown hollered, feeling more relaxed from the effects of the brown liquor on an empty stomach. Bird explained that she'd gone off with her boyfriend when it looked like the band might be stuck in jail all night.

"Hellfire. Who gonna do my hair? James Brown can't go on stage looking like this." He kicked a suitcase. "People pay to see a show, they expect a show." The noise from the crowd in the dance hall was getting louder.

"Wear a hat," one of the band members yelled.

"Wear a hat? When you ever see James Brown wear a goddamn hat?" He took another swig of whiskey.

At that moment, Billy stepped out of the closet. "I can style your hair, Mr. Brown."

"Whoa, Nelly!" James Brown leaned back in his chair, almost falling over backward from surprise. "Who this skinny white boy?"

Bird pulled a gun. Cooper screamed as Bird grabbed a struggling Billy by the arm and pushed him up against a wall. "What you doin' here, boy?"

"We came to hear music."

Bird seized Cooper and shoved him up beside Billy. Both boys were trembling like wet puppies. He continued to point the gun at Billy and Cooper.

Alarmed, Brown spoke up. "Now hold on, Bird. Be cool. We just got *out* of jail and I ain't going *back*. Let me have a word with the little cracker."

Bird led Billy over to James Brown, holding the boy's arms behind his back to keep him from running. Brown eyed the barefoot blond teenager in his pressed chino pants and plaid button-up shirt with the carefully rolled up sleeves.

"You got one minute before I throw yo white ass outta here." Bird released him.

Billy quickly explained how he styled hair and his dream was to go to Hollywood and find a job doing hair for the stars when he finished high school next spring. Overly excited, he began to lisp, which caused the band members to snicker.

"You know how to do *black* hair?"

"Can't be any harder than Mrs. Dantonio's hair. I barely get a comb through it."

"Don't listen to the little sissy!" Bird, who had been part of James Brown's band from day one, was protective and cautious around new people, especially white people.

"You got a better idea, Bird? *You* want to do my hair?" Bird went silent. "Humph. I didn't think so." Brown turned back to Billy. "Got any supplies?"

"No."

"Then *how* you gonna style James Brown's hair?"

Billy reached out to feel Brown's hair, running it through his fingers. "Doesn't need to be conked. I can make pomade with cooking lard and candle wax. They'll have both in the hotel kitchen." For rollers, he had to think fast. Remembering the supplies in the closet, Billy grabbed a roll of toilet paper and pulled out the brown cardboard tube. "I'll cut and use these."

"You ain't puttin' toilet paper on James Brown," Bird yelled at Billy. "Ain't right."

Brown, however, was amused and impressed by the boy's nerve. He took the cardboard tube from Billy's hand and examined it up close. After a long silence, he finally spoke: "I'm gonna give the sissy a chance. What's your name, boy?"

"Billy."

"All right, Billy." Brown held out his hand to shake. "You got yourself a gig. Bird, take Billy to the kitchen. And tell the crowd we'll go on in an hour. Ain't no damn speeding ticket gonna stop James Brown."

After successfully procuring the needed supplies, Billy set a chair in front of a small mirror hanging on a wall. He put newspaper on the floor and draped a tablecloth over Mr. Brown to prevent the homemade pomade from dripping onto the singer. Billy carefully coated the singer's hair with the lard and wax mixture, then swept it up and wrapped it around the toilet paper tubes to create Brown's signature curls. He used tin foil to create a cap, which he put over the hair to keep it all in place.

Cooper, meanwhile, was peeking out of the door leading from the dressing room to the stage and beyond. The dance hall was full. The audience was sitting and drinking at small mismatched tables and chairs or standing by a makeshift plywood bar painted all different colors. Most of the men were wearing suits and the women were in dresses. The room was loud and smoky. Red-and-white gingham curtains fluttered from the slight breeze.

Bird came up behind Cooper and looked out. He was more relaxed now that his boss was happy. "How many you think we got tonight?"

"I'd say about two hundred. When 'Slippin' and Slidin'" played on the phonograph, everybody was dancing."

Bird looked down at Cooper. "How a white boy like you knows Little Richard?"

"I listen to WOL radio in Washington. He and Mr. Brown are my favorites."

Bird nodded. "Your daddy know you here?"

"No, sir! Billy took a boat and we sneaked over."

"That so." Bird finally cracked a smile. "Well, you boys all right."

Billy's homemade pomade and cardboard tubes worked even better than he'd expected. High on whiskey and wearing a new electric-blue suit, James Brown dazzled the crowd at Rosedale nonstop for ninety minutes, putting on one of his most energetic performances. At least that's what Bird told the boys in the dressing room after the show. Brown's shiny hair never moved an inch, and it looked just as good after the show as before.

Bird handed Cooper a bottle of whiskey. "Drink?"

Without hesitation, Cooper took a sip. Then another. "Thank you, Mr. Bird." He passed the bottle to Billy, who took a big swig. It burned going down and he coughed.

"Not too much," Bird counseled. "You ever drink before?"

"No, sir."

"Well, what you wanna do is take little sips. Enough to fly, but not get sick."

Billy nodded. "That why they call you Bird?" The musician grinned as Billy took another drink, more cautiously this time, feeling the whiskey's warm embrace.

A short time later, Brown called Billy over to where he was changing clothes and handed him an engraved white business card. Billy had never seen anything so glamorous and he said so. Brown chuckled. "You got talent, boy. When you get to Hollywood, you look up this cat named Mr. Ray. Show him this here card and tell him James Brown said give you a job. Mr. Ray styles everybody who plays the coast—Ella, Duke, Fats. He'll help you out." James was looking at his hair in the mirror. "Damn fine job."

"It's getting late." Bird interrupted James's preening. "I've lined us up some barbecue like you asked. Finest chopped barbecue in all of Rosedale."

"Sure am hungry. What's her name?" At that, the band started hollering at Bird to fetch them some barbecue too.

Brown looked over at Billy and Cooper. "You boys want some chopped barbecue?" When they didn't reply, he continued on. "No? I didn't think so. I'm guessing you like the T-bone." Billy and Cooper blushed, but Brown was amused. "It's okay by me if you got a taste for the bone. Means more barbecue for me. Plenty of fellas like a T-bone.

"Listen here, I'm gonna give some advice and I want you to pay attention to what James Brown got to say. Don't be ashamed cuz you like the

T-bone. One thing I've learned in this business is you got to be yourself. Can't try to be somebody else. Ain't nobody in music today like James Brown." The band members nodded. "But you got to be real careful, you know what I mean?" Brown continued, his tone turning serious. "Not everybody is cool like James Brown and the Flames. Lots of mean folks out there won't think twice 'bout hurting boys like you."

Motoring back down the bay toward Rehoboth, Billy kept thinking about James Brown's words. Finally, he cut the engine and the boat slowed. Soon, only the currents gently pulled them eastward. Billy opened the bottle of whiskey James Brown had given them as a token of thanks and took a swig before passing the bottle to Cooper. He watched his friend drink. Heart pounding, Billy leaned over and kissed Cooper, whose lips were wet and tasted sweet. Thankfully, he didn't pull away. Billy might have been a sissy, but nobody ever accused him of being shy.

# Escort Surgery

## MATTHEW CAPRIOLI

I hated the cold walking west on 58th Street, one a.m. on January 20th. The freezing currents had a way of trapezing down from steel-cut condos, making the walls of my nostrils suddenly raw. My arms crossed themselves as I braced my way toward 10th Avenue. I had been in New York for several months, and I was still negotiating the fact that an avenue was much longer than a block. I'm from Alaska, and studies have shown that people from the north develop thicker blood over time. Maybe this is true, but personally I don't buy it.

I cursed myself for not wearing a thicker coat. I did have a puffy red one that made me look like a tomato, but I knew most clients would prefer slimming outerwear. So I wore a drab olive, form-fitting, trench-like-coat that looked great and provided no warmth.

Most of my clients stayed in hotels in Midtown East, SoHo, or Times Square—locations that required small walking. But today, I was to meet a surgeon named Tim on the 21st floor of his apartment building.

I didn't know much about Tim. I didn't know what he looked like or sounded like, just that his emails were laconic and he was willing to pay $300 at the conclusion of our session. With that kind of money, I didn't want to offend him by asking what our session might entail. "No pain and I'm game," my profile on Rentboy.com said. I hoped he had read that.

Riding up an elevator with a glass door, I experienced the usual thrill of nerves. It was always risky meeting new clients, especially the ones like Tim who, in the name of discretion, were completely silent. But at this point, I had been a gay escort for four months. So far, I hadn't run into any kind of trouble, and as an optimistic twenty-two year old, I couldn't imagine any of my encounters ever going wrong.

I sent three firm but polite knocks into his door. Some facial muscles contracted, ready to spring into a smile as the hinge gave way.

He opened the door wide open; my smile turned on full blast.

"Hi there," I said.

He was gaunt with thin black hair combed to the right of his forehead. His voice was library-low.

"Hello," he said. His finely trimmed mustache made him look like John Waters.

I entered the amber glow of his apartment. He shut the door behind me. I stood in his kitchen.

"Mind if I place my things here?" I said, pointing to an island counter.

"Please do."

Ella Fitzgerald sung from a record player near an empty vase. I set my body to dancer mode: straight spine, all movements refined and seamless. A huge part of the job was figuring out in the first ten seconds just what a client wanted. Tim, or whoever he was, wanted an elegant call boy. So that's what I became.

He led me toward a sofa. It had an austere Bauhaus design and its leather was bleached white. It could double as a sarcophagus.

"Please, have a seat," Tim said. "I have some merlot and sauvignon blanc."

Pouring myself some white wine, I asked how his day was. He inched closer to me. He regarded me, and took a dainty sip of his merlot; his black eyes were wide and unremitting. I felt a dint in my smile. I looked around his apartment. He had a lot of abstract art whose maker I couldn't place. He didn't seem to have a bookshelf.

"You have a great view," I told him, taking a sip.

He let out a "Mmmmm."

Then his right hand reached out. His wan fingertips brushed my cheek. They rested there. They pulsated along my jaw. I imagined him reciting the anatomical names: index on the mandible, thumb on the submandibular fossa, pinkie on the mental foramen.

His hand withdrew. Then moved in toward my ear. His fingers ran up and past my cartilage; I thought of a girl brushing her hair back.

"So what do you want to do," I blurted out.

He grinned.

"Drink your wine," he said.

I smiled, and took another sip.

His hand planted itself on my stomach. It crept to my hip bone and around to the back of my pelvis. Then, like he was zipping me up, his fingers shot up the side of my torso.

"You can remove your clothes now," he said. "All of your clothes. Then please meet me in the bedroom. Lie face up."

I watched him, trying to figure out what came next. He saw my hesitation, and repeated himself that I should get undressed now. I started to remove my shirt.

"Don't mind me," he said. "I'll be preparing dinner. It's a time-consuming dish."

"Of course," I said.

I undressed looking at a dark Hudson River through his window. I folded the clothes on top of his white leather sofa. He removed some green peppers from his fridge, ignoring me.

I walked down the hall. An accordion door covered what I assumed to be a closet. I passed a bathroom with a deep blue tile floor. The room Tim had sent me to was surprisingly slender. I wondered if the main bedroom was behind the closed door; this room belonged to a fresh-out-of-college type in Bushwick, not a surgeon in his fifties near Columbus Circle.

There was no comforter on the bed, just a thin white cotton sheet. I wondered if I should lie above or below it. I supposed he had a thing for walking into his room to find a young naked boy waiting for an examination. So I laid myself out above the sheet, naked.

I heard chopping noises from the kitchen. I thought of Dexter, and all the other stories of hookers getting killed in the line of duty. But what was the probability of that happening to me, I wondered.

I looked around the room for sharp objects. A nondescript red pen lay near a journal. If he did try to maim me, I imagined slamming it into his jugular. "That would buy me some time," I thought.

I waited.

I tried to think of a sexy way to just lie there face up. But sexiness didn't seem to be the point with Tim. He probably wanted me how he met most of his unconscious patients before surgery. So I just lay there, supine, focusing on my breathing, ignoring the chilled wind permeating past his window.

He walked in wearing a pair of black, wispy briefs. He grinned at me. My face made some sign of mutual recognition. His cutlery had stayed in the kitchen.

He sat on the side of the bed, his eyes scanning my body. I waited, staring at the ceiling. I gathered that I wasn't supposed to move as his eyes dissected me. He roved through the bones of my feet, the vellus hairs on each toe. He saw from my thin shins that I was into tennis and running. He scanned all the way up to my neck, and stopped.

Then his two hands reached for my stomach. I tried not to flinch. One hand coasted toward my pubes, the other to my chest. His palms brushed the interior of my arms. They smoothed past my thighs. He nudged them apart, and I spread my legs wider. He gripped one of my testicles and ran it between his thumb and middle finger. His other hand pinched my semi-erect penis and massaged it up and down with the same excitement a maid would have bringing up a pail of water. A hand examined my nipple; it pinched the tip.

"Please turn around," he said.

I quickly turned over: acting before thinking was key to success as an escort.

His inspection of my person repeated itself. The back of his fingernails traced down my spine. He squeezed my calves. He scratched the arch of my heel.

"I will return," he said. He left the room. I heard the bathroom door shut.

I flipped over. If he was going to kill me, I was going to see it coming.

Again, I waited.

A few minutes later, I heard the toilet flush. He returned to the room in a white robe, the previous reserve on his face finally released.

"Thank you, Matt," he said. "You may leave now."

I gave him, what I hoped to be, a calm and gracious smile.

I gathered my clothes from the couch. He went back to the kitchen and continued to cook. I replaced my clothes rapidly, then stepped into my shoes. His eyes caught mine. He inclined his head toward a white envelope on the table. I smiled and picked it up. The weight felt right.

"Thank you, Tim," I said. "Have a great night."

"Wait wait," he said. I paused at the doorstep. "Let me look at you one more time."

I smiled as his slim pointer fingers moved toward my eyes. I imagined him gouging them out, but they coursed below my eyes to the bay of my bags, then around and up to my eyebrows. They drew a line down my forehead, through my pinched nose, past the puddle above my lips, through my lips, terminating at my round chin.

He smiled for the first time that evening. "Stay warm," he said.

# His Own Secret Sharer

## LOU DELLAGUZZO

"You've got some bare spots here," Lenora says. "And over there too." She reclines on her parlor couch, waving her cigarette in a zigzag motion.

Paul has trouble following his mother's gesture. He steps away from the Christmas tree for a better view. "So what's left?"

With her foot she nudges an empty box lying on the floor. It collides with the others Paul stacked as he worked. She scans the boxes for remaining ornaments.

"Nothing here but cardboard."

She seems a little drunk, even though she doesn't indulge, except for the occasional daiquiri. Must be her new pills. The nighttime ones. They have the opposite effect of the pink tablets that energize her days.

Paul drapes more tinsel on the branches. The chubby Norwegian spruce rises over six feet. His father bought the fragrant evergreen a few days ago. It was a surprise. Max is full of surprises lately. Ever since his son's brush with the law.

Lenora's attention shifts from the tree to the holiday drama on TV. It's sponsored by a greeting card company. "You know what I think, Paulie? I think she's going to take him back." Her words emerge in a smoke cloud.

Paul looks at the handsome, estranged couple on screen. "You think so or know so?"

"I've never seen this program before. It's a worldwide premiere."

"But it's still a Christmas story. The guy's been nice to her since before the first commercial. And he keeps saying he's changed. That their kid needs a father."

"Talk is cheap," Lenora says, like she's enjoying a private joke.

"How about that gift he gave her she always wanted? That wasn't cheap."

"It wouldn't surprise me if he bought it secondhand. Where's the receipt?"

"It was a present."

"But she might have to take it back if she doesn't want to reconcile."

"I doubt she'd return that gift. Or any of the others."

"Why not?"

"She's not the type."

"The type?" Lenora's face stiffens. She wraps her new, kimono-style robe tighter around her chest. Some dancing white cranes disappear in the folds. "So Mr. Shakespeare, how do you think the story'll end?"

Paul shrugs.

"No, I really want to know." With some effort she sits up, looks at her son intently. "How'd you like the story to finish if you could write the ending?"

"I don't care one way or the other. It's only a movie, right?"

"Right," she says after a long pause. "Since you don't care how it ends, I'll watch the rest in my room. Unless you need more help with the tree."

Paul looks at the mess of boxes she made on the floor. "No thanks, I'll be fine."

Lenora stops midway and snaps her fingers. "I just remembered. We got more stashed in your closet."

"I'll go get them." Though tall for a thirteen year old, he still needs a footstool for the top shelf. He finds three boxes in a back corner. He turns off the TV after Lenora shuts her bedroom door. Muted voices seep through it. They come from the new portable set Max bought her. Or is it secondhand?

Alone in the darkened room he plugs in the tree lights. They're designed as small candles complete with holders. Each one has a tiny light bulb sealed within the plastic base. The reedy candle part is filled with liquid tinted different colors. Once they heat up, the candles bubble. They animate every branch with constant movement, making the sea-green spruce appear vaguely aquatic.

Paul decides he should polish off the tree tomorrow. Better to get his homework done first. He still has an essay to finish on that big wall in Berlin. The one the Russians started building last summer.

Later that night he dreams about the bubbling Christmas lights, the fluid purring they make up close. The relaxing sound amplifies. It turns into a steady tapping. Soon the lights start to explode. Each candle makes a popping noise a shade louder than its predecessor. The last awakens him.

Eyes closed, he listens hard. He begins to realize the noise doesn't come from the parlor or any other room in the dingy flat. It comes from outside. At his back window. Made *by* his window. The tapping has a jazzy beat. A syncopated rhythm no wind can create. His heart races. His muscles tense. Visions of movie monsters flash in his mind. Some hideous man wants to lure him to certain death.

And what about Lenora?

Like a cat he springs off his bed. He reaches into his closet for a baseball bat never used for sport. Shut tight, the venetian blind gives no hint of what's outside. What lies in wait on the back roof of the tavern he and his mother live above. He grabs the drawstring and tugs. Nothing happens. He pulls harder. Harder still. The blind at last obeys. He sees a form in the darkness and jumps back. He hears a voice, subdued but unmistakable. Half wondering if he's still asleep he raises the blind.

It's true. Hal's really out there, bent low on the tarpaper.

"Open up. It's fucking cold out here."

Paul works fast. Hal seems unsteady, a dangerous thing since he's near the roof's side edge. Free to enter, he tumbles over the night table. He lands on his back with a thump. Paul kneels beside the laughing boy, gestures for silence. He opens his door, listens for any sound of his mother stirring, ready to say he tripped on his way back from the john. Once certain it's safe he shuts the door.

"You okay?"

"Couldn't be better."

"Couldn't be...what're you doing here?"

Hal frowns. His eyes narrow. "I can split if you like. Don't want to spoil your frigging beauty sleep."

"You're not going anywhere. I'm worried is all. About you. The crazy way you came in." Paul shuts the window. He turns around to find his buddy standing close behind.

"Boo!" Hal laughs. "Still a scaredy-cat, I see."

"You have to calm down or we'll get caught. I can't lock the door anymore. My mom took the key." Paul examines his buddy's face. He searches for any wound from the security guard's assault on the boy.

Hal slips off his coat and throws it on the bed. "That look familiar?"

"It's the coat you wanted to swipe from the store."

"*Did* swipe. Walked out that place like any other shopper."

Hal smacks his fist against his open hand. "That fucking guard. I creamed him good soon as he let his eyes off me. Used his own paperweight like a sledge hammer. Went straight for his temple."

"I was real worried you were hurt," Paul says, "but afraid to get help."

"I got help all right." Hal doesn't sound happy about it.

"Then you *were* hurt."

"Just got my face smacked raw. It ain't like that prick busted my bones."

"Sure sounded that way from the room I got put in."

"And look who walked out." Hal spreads his arms in victory. In only a few weeks he seems taller, his voice, a little deeper. But he's wobbly from his tumble.

"You better sit down. That was a rough somersault."

Hal plops onto the double bed as if it were a trampoline. His feet dangle from the mattress. He slips off one shoe, then the other. Paul catches both as they fall to keep them from making noise. One of the soles has a small hole. If he didn't know better, he'd think his buddy wanted more trouble, might even want to get caught. "What's wrong?"

"You got to ask?"

"I mean right now. The way you're acting."

"How'm I acting?"

"Like you don't care."

"About what?"

"What happens to you."

"I know what'll happen to me. Got it all figured out."

"For real?"

"No, for fake. You're the dreamer."

"Maybe, but I'm not on the lam either." Paul kneels on the bed next to his secret visitor. He has so many questions to ask, doesn't know where to start without ticking off his buddy, whose mood he finds impossible to gauge. He makes a cautious start. "You thirsty or hungry? I'll try and get anything you want."

"I'm good. Stuffed myself at the party."

"The party?" In his worst imaginings, on which he often dwelled, Paul saw his buddy hiding from the law in an alleyway, living off scraps.

"It was way up in Belleville," Hal says, "But I got out at the railroad tracks."

"Out of what?"

"The car."

"There was a party in a car?"

"Of course not. I told you it was in Belleville. A *house* in Belleville. Real classy. I was riding back and felt like seeing you."

"How'd you get on the roof?"

"Climbed the telephone pole near it and jumped on." Hal snaps his fingers. "Piece a cake."

"Was someone driving you home?" Paul's buddy doesn't answer, only stares at the sloped ceiling. "So where've you been the past two weeks? When you didn't show up at school, and anywhere else I could think of, I called your home to see if you were there. Or in jail maybe. Your mom got all hysterical. She yelled that she didn't know where you were. Told me never to call again. Then she slammed the phone down."

Hal's long sigh smells of alcohol. "She wasn't angry at you, only worried about the cops. They might've tapped the phone. Might have the neighborhood patrol car doing special watch on the place. That's how my brother Richie got snatched last year. And what're you griping about? Here you are sacked out in your own bed. It ain't like you're in trouble. You didn't steal nothing, much less whack a store guard flat with a paperweight. The cops can't touch you. Unless you were dumb enough to spill about our plan."

"Not a word," Paul says. "Honest." His buddy doesn't look convinced, so he crosses his heart twice, hopes to die. "I swore up and down I never saw you take any coat."

"Nice to hear you didn't rat at least. Not that it makes any difference."

"How'd you know I didn't take anything?"

"You kidding me? When I wasn't getting slapped in that pig's office, I heard you next door whining to the guard who held you. Telling him what a good little boy you were." Hal makes a crybaby face, mimics how Paul pleaded with the man to let him go. "Always figured you might chicken out the last minute."

"You should've made the same move."

"Too late now," Hal says like it's no big deal.

Paul fights a strong urge to shake him. "So where've you been? Two weeks is a long time for a kid to disappear." He lies down facing his buddy, less worried the boy might bolt for some mysterious reason.

Hal turns on his side. He tucks an arm under his pillow. It's the same pillow he used during his sleepover a few months ago when they first became friends. "Been staying with a guy," he says. "Some old guy. Like in his fifties or more. I met him after I split the store. He lives on a little side street off Broad. It's right across from the 280 ramp. I hung out under that damn ramp a long time after I escaped. Thinking what to do next. Freezing my ass off. I sure as hell couldn't go home. So this guy. He kept watching me from his window. Had a big smile on his droopy puss. He called me over. We talked a while. Then he asked if I wanted to come inside."

"That was nice of him," Paul says. "Was it?"

"Real nice." Hal doesn't sound like he means it.

"Where'd you go after that?"

"Ain't no after that. It's where I'm staying for now."

"This guy live all by himself?"

"Except for me. The place is a big boarding house. He's got a room on the first floor. Even got his own john and kitchenette. I keep out of sight when the landlord collects the rent or checks on things. And he checks a lot. The building's real old and full of characters."

"Your friend a character too?" Paul says.

"He likes to make me feel good."

"Make you feel good?"

"I lie on my back like I am now and he blows me. It's what he wants in return for a safe place to stay."

Safe. Paul thought he understood the word before tonight. He gazes at his buddy as if examining a stranger. Though more beautiful than ever, Hal seems pale. Thinner too. His large brown eyes have lost their glow, the sense that someone's behind them. And what does he do all day without going to school, having to stay in hiding? From what Paul's learned so far, he'd rather not ask. He gets off his bed, starts to pace.

"Got ants in your pants?" Hal says.

"Just nervous."

"I know how to calm you down."

"That's not a good idea."

"Since when? Since I told you about—"

"The guard at the store," Paul says. "The one who hit you. It was all self-defense what you did. You were protecting yourself from a grown man. My mom said so."

"Your mom?"

"After you ran off, the cops came to the store and took me down the station. They called my dad. I was there a long time getting grilled by a detective. And yelled at by my old man."

"What'd you say about me?"

"Same thing I told the store guard who held me. The detective kept wanting me to fink on you. But I swore I never saw you steal anything. That we never planned to. I kept going back to how the guard beat you up. That was something the cop didn't want to hear.

"My dad drove me home after I got released. Him and Mom and me talked about everything that happened. I got another big lecture but that was all. Somewhere around the end my mom said that the guard never should've hit you like that. She thought he was in bigger trouble than you. My dad thought otherwise. Said you got what you deserved. But he's nosing around to move back in with us and let it drop."

"So what're you telling me?" Hal says. "I should give myself up because your old lady thinks I might get off?"

"Don't mean that exactly."

"Then what do you mean?" Hal springs up and hauls Paul onto the mattress, straddling him. "What if I told you I'd do whatever you want? Put my frigging life in your hands? But before you start shelling out dumb advice, remember I got priors. I could get a long rap in some reform school like my brother."

The question overwhelms Paul. The responsibility it carries. More than anything he wants his buddy's mess smoothed over, made right. Wants Hal back home and away from that man. But what if Lenora's wrong? What does she know about anything except soap operas, much less how the law works?

"Never mind," he says. "I was only wishing. But what'll you do otherwise? You can't keep living where you're at now. And you can't quit school."

"Ain't going to. I'll be leaving Newark soon. I can go to school in Syracuse."

"Where's that?"

"Upstate New York. I got family there. A stepbrother. He's older than me and Richie. Like ten years older. He kicked around the country when he was a kid. Got in lots of trouble too. He knows the score. Gonna take me in and get me resettled. I called him collect from a pay phone a few nights after it happened. Told him everything."

"I didn't even know you had another brother. You never said."

"Never had to." Hal rubs his head like he's washing it, running long fingers through wavy brown hair that looks black in the weak light. He gets off Paul, lands softly on the floor. "Man, I'm thirsty. And I got to use the john." He reaches for the doorknob.

"Let me check first." Paul sticks his head out the door. The kitchen nightlight casts the room in dramatic shadows. A faint glow reaches the parlor. He can see a few branches of the spruce tree.

"Make me wait any longer and I'll pee out the window."

"Okay, okay. Just stay quiet." Paul follows his buddy into the kitchen, hands him a plastic cup from the dish rack. "Drink in there."

With Hal in the john, Paul steals into the parlor. He makes his way to his mother's bedroom at the other end. He presses his ear to the sliding doors. He can hear a buzz, more like purring static. Lenora must've fallen asleep with the TV on. No wonder she didn't hear his buddy's clumsy entrance. Meanwhile the flushing sound from the toilet seems endless. The bathroom door creaks open.

Hal walks into the parlor despite being signaled not to.

"Go back to my room," Paul says.

Hal ignores him. He stares at the Christmas tree as if mesmerized. He gets down on all fours, paws his way around the red-and-glitter felt wrapped along the base.

Paul kneels beside him. "What're you doing?"

"Where's the plug? I want to see the lights on."

"You what?"

"Found it."

Paul stays his hand.

"Said I want to see the damn lights."

Paul envisions the two of them in a reckless struggle to control the cord. The tree topples down in a tangled mess. A mess Lenora didn't create.

"Let me check my mom first." He gets a terse okay and hops into action. Inch by inch, he slides open one of the heavy doors. Lenora's fast asleep. Across from her the TV's gone dark. White noise that pours from the speaker has a steady, soothing tone. He shuts the door and rejoins his buddy.

Hal rubs his hands together. "Here we go." He connects the extension cord. The tree lights blaze in a flash that dazzles up close.

"They'll bubble once they get warm," Paul tells him.

Hal notices the three boxes Paul found in the closet. He reaches for an ornament.

"Careful," Paul says. "They're glass. Real thin and old."

Hal removes an angel from its tissue paper. He runs a finger along the translucent wings. "I could use a pair of these right now. Let's do some."

"Are you kidding?" Paul thumbs at Lenora's bedroom.

"I didn't get to do my tree this year. That's the best part of Christmas." Hal sounds plaintive as a five year old, his stubbornness suddenly gone. His eyes are bright and shiny, the irises like melted chocolate. He seems really back again.

Paul can't resist. "Maybe you can do one box until the lights bubble."

He knows they'll start up soon. He watches his buddy hang the ornaments in the same thoughtful manner the boy makes a drawing—or picks a lock. Hal seems calm, content. In the multicolored glow he's so beautiful, seems so fragile, Paul feels emptied out with affection. He hates to break the silence, but there are things he needs to know. Hal may have to steal away at any moment, down the back stairs and out of his life. Perhaps forever. The thought unsteadies him. Their friendship's been so brief. This should be only the beginning.

He takes a deep breath. "When you plan on leaving?"

"Day after Christmas. Traffic should be light then, Ralph thinks. He's giving me a ride far as Kingston. I'll meet up with my brother there."

"Who's Ralph?"

"Who I'm staying with."

"Does your mom know?"

"About Ralph?"

"No." And if she does, Paul doesn't want to hear. "About your brother and Syracuse."

"Johnny called a good buddy of his down here. He got word to her."

"What's your dad think?" Paul has to wait for an answer.

"He didn't come back from his last truck run. Just stayed in Cleveland. He's shacking up with someone again. But he sent me ten bucks. Stuck it in a card that said he was sorry."

"You never told me."

"Who says you got to know everything? Hey, the lights. They're starting to bubble!"

"And it's time to quit," Paul says. "Like we agreed."

"There ain't that many left to hang. Let's do the rest."

"You're making me nuts."

"Oh no I ain't. You were nuts when I met you. Talking to yourself. Living in a dream world. I made you a whole lot better."

"And now you're leaving."

"Yeah, well." Hal proffers another box of ornaments, and together they finish. He looks at their work from every angle, as if he were trying to absorb the glittering tree with his eyes. He yawns and stretches. "I need to lie down before I head out. Got a long walk back."

Paul hesitates answering. He wants more time with Hal, wants to forestall the agony of goodbye. But he better not press their luck. It's after three in the morning. The sooner his buddy leaves, the better.

"It's okay, ain't it?" Hal says.

"Sure. But only a little while, you know, because."

"I know." Hal stuffs his hands in his pockets, gazes at his feet. He seems even sadder next to the festive tree.

Paul takes his buddy by the shoulders and rubs them. The gesture becomes an embrace. He could stay this way until his legs give out. But he has to think for two. "We need to cut the lights." He watches Hal take a final look at the tree before pulling the plug. He turns back to Lenora's room. Maybe he should switch off her TV as well. Then again, the abrupt silence might awaken her. "You know when they start broadcasting again?"

"Who?"

"The morning shows on TV." Paul nods at his mother's door.

"I'll be long gone before that."

The heavy sleet that hits the tar roof sounds like corn popping in a hot pan. Half awake, his arm draped around his buddy, the first thing Paul sees in the dark room is the back of Hal's head. He presses his nose against the boy's nape, enjoys its warm, toasty smell. His left arm's numb from resting his head on it. He can't get himself to move. Not yet. Why should he? Only been a few minutes. At most a half hour since they lay down together. But then he notices the clock atop his bureau. An icy feeling coats his gut. He climbs out of bed and listens at his door. He shakes his buddy hard, has to dodge a slow, reflexive swing.

"What the fuck?" Hal's eyes are half shut and puffy.

"Keep your voice down. It's late. I mean it's morning. You got to leave before—" Paul hears music. Military music, coming from the front of the apartment. "That's her set."

"Her what?"

"My mom's TV. It's going to wake her."

Hal fumbles out of bed. Good thing he's dressed. It seems to take forever to get his shoes and coat on.

Paul peeks out his room in time to see Lenora's door sliding open. He shuts his own.

"You got to hide in the closet quick!"

Like an animal prowling jungle growth, Hal makes his way past shoes and boxes and hanging clothes. His commotion tips over the baseball bat Paul grabbed for defense last night when he feared a monster invasion. The bat lands hard on linoleum. It bounces a few times.

"Paulie?" Lenora says from the kitchen. "What was that?"

"What?"

"What do you mean 'what'?"

"My baseball bat."

"In December?"

"It got in my way last night when I was looking for the Christmas ornaments. Forgot to put it back."

He rearranges the hanging clothes to give Hal cover and shuts him in just as Lenora barges in. She frowns at the bat leaning against the bureau.

"Damn TV woke me up."

"I heard," he says.

"From here? Christ, you're like a dog."

"Was coming out the bathroom."

"That's where I'm heading," she says, "then back to bed. The tree, by the way, it turned out nice. You did a good job."

"Yeah, *we* did."

She offers a tired smile and pads away. Once she's in the john he keeps his door ajar so he can hear. He opens the closet where his buddy sits on an old trunk jammed against the wall.

"That was close," Hal says and gets up.

"Stay put."

"Why?"

"You heard her. She's going back to bed. Be safer then. A sure thing."

"I'm getting stir-crazy in here." Hal shrugs off his coat and folds it in his lap. "Don't like tight places."

"Won't be long."

"Better not be or I'll split in front of her. What can she do?"

"Help my father kill me."

"Okay, okay," Hal says.

Paul gives him a quizzical look.

"What's the matter now?"

"Sometimes I think part of you wants to get caught."

"You really do got a screw loose." But Hal's blush is obvious even in the closet.

The bathroom pipes start working. Paul shuts his scowling buddy in again.

Lenora stops for a glass of water. Ankles crossed, she leans against the sink while she sips. "Your father's coming for dinner tonight."

"I know."

"I'm fixing him something special."

"Sounds good."

"Don't you want to know what it is?"

"Tripe," Paul says. "You told me yesterday."

"It's a lot of work. Not sure I feel up to it. There's so much to do with Christmas coming, and your father moving in next week."

"Dad's moving back in? When'd you decide that?"

"Last night before I fell asleep. Maybe it was that TV show. When I woke up I felt the same way. But don't let on. I want to tell him myself."

"I won't say a word."

"We'll have Christmas together the way we used to."

Paul's tight smile freezes in place. He should say more, show enthusiasm, but he can't take the risk. What if Hal makes a noise? What if he carries out his dumb threat and saunters out the bedroom in front of bleary-eyed Lenora?

"You look real tired," he tells her. "We should talk about Dad's moving in after you've slept more. I can help with the tripe. I watched Grandma make it."

"Her tripe's thicker and spicier."

"But it's all still tripe."

"It sure is," Lenora says like she means something else. She refills her glass and heads out the gloomy kitchen. "Wake me up at nine. And no loud TV before."

Soon as Paul opens the closet door Hal shoves the hanging clothes aside. He jumps over the floor clutter and lands on the bed. "She took her sweet time," he says. "You two going through Santa's list?"

"You're out now." Paul sits beside his buddy and rubs his back.

"My shirttail's coming loose."

"Want me to stop?"

"Didn't say that."

With a deft hand, Paul tucks in the boy's shirt, noting again the thin waist. "That guy been feeding you enough?"

"I should get moving." Hal brushes away the hand.

Paul grabs the black umbrella hanging in his closet. "It's snowing kind of heavy now." He remembers the hole in his buddy's shoe. "You'll need my galoshes too."

"My dogs won't fit in those."

"They're loose on me. And they can stretch a lot."

"My head hurts when I bend over."

"Sit back, I'll do it." With some effort, and a long-handled shoehorn, Paul manages to slip the galoshes on. He opens his bedroom door and checks out the flat. He nods an okay and they walk through the kitchen to the back door.

Hallway stairs creak as they wend their way down in the dark. They linger within the small, unheated vestibule.

"So this is it," Hal says.

Paul shuffles his feet on the worn tiles. "Any idea if you might be coming back sometime?"

Hal shrugs, his grim expression barely visible.

"That's okay." Paul starts to shiver from the cold.

"Should've grabbed yourself a coat."

"Yeah, I should've."

"This'll help." Hal gives him a rough, long hug. Paul melts into it, his mouth pressing against the other boy's neck, his chin resting on the stolen coat that ruined everything. He holds tight, won't let go. His buddy has to make that move.

"Your address for up in Syracuse. I never got it from you."

"Don't have anything to write with."

"I'll get something. Be right back."

Paul climbs the stairs and sprints to the kitchen wall phone. He grabs a pad and pen Lenora keeps on the nearby cabinet. His descent is hasty. He rounds the curve and almost trips. There's daylight at the bottom. The vestibule's empty and bitterly cold. The door's unlocked and wide open.

He careens his way through the alley. Out on the street, well into the distance, a lone figure under an umbrella walks fast in the snow.

# The National Gallery

## STEFEN STYRSKY

I t was because of the bike crash that I volunteered for an HIV-vaccine trial. I blame Brian. For the crash, not the trial. Well, I volunteered for various reasons, the accident was one, but mostly because I needed the money.

This was sometime around the summer of '01, before Memorial Day, before the winter and the cold that blurred us into '02. I ran a bike for www.vroom.com (corporate logo: VrooM!), a customized delivery service. The idea that you could order things online and have them delivered to your home was in those days a crazy novelty. But people seemed to like it. No time to hustle out for cat food? We'd get it for you. Have a craving for Ben and Jerry's Triple Fudge Chunk but don't want to miss your favorite television show? A VrooM! courier would have the pint on your doorstep in half an hour.

Our founder and president was a small man we called Mr. Fiji because he was forever sucking at those rectangular bottles of Fiji water. He was younger than me, and I was only two years out of school. He had broad hands outsized for his narrow body, knuckles like marbles and fingers both thick and long. Between runs, he gave the couriers pep talks. He'd say how "good organizational citizenship" would earn us IPO options, and wave his hands around, flipping them front to back like semaphores, or with a fingertip describe invisible trend lines and market fluctuations.

Toilet paper, floppy disks, a frying pan, DVDs from Blockbuster—I had couriered it. But mostly it was pizza, sandwiches and burritos, and related items: six packs of Coke, cigarettes, beer. I worked part time. The tips were good. On big nights, Oscars, Super Bowl, *Sopranos*, I made decent money. VrooM!'s delivery radius was Logan Circle and parts nearby. I wasn't pedaling across town to Capitol Hill because some legislative type was too embarrassed to rent porn videos in person.

"Whoa," you say. "Back then Logan Circle was a scary place." Sure, guys who've come through it, they'll brag: "Everybody I knew was mugged at least once," or "Every Saturday night we'd chase the prostitutes off our porch." One time I did get a flat from a needle and occasionally I heard gunshots, though mostly distant pops. A steady traffic of Virginia- and Maryland-license-plated cars clogged the streets, near-idling engines coughing pucka, pucka, pucka as the drivers prowled for hookers. The pimps would bite their lips as I rode past, appraising my danger to their livelihood. But really, the worst threat was my allergies flaring up after pedaling through car exhaust.

The brave new world of VrooM! delivery ended the night I hit a Mercedes head-on. My phone had rung, the double beep that meant Brian called, and I'd looked down to fish it from my pocket. I never saw the car. I landed feet over scalp onto the silver hood, my tennis-shoe treads flat against the windshield, arms splayed as if I was making a snow angel. The crash bent the bike's frame and turned the front tire into a Dalí clock. A large pepperoni with extra cheese was the other casualty.

I remember staggering to a bus stop as the Mercedes squealed off. I plopped onto the aluminum bench and used my reflection in the poster ad's plexiglass to check my scalp for wounds. Someone had scrawled "faggots" over the covering in permanent marker. That was when I noticed the ad. It showed a crowd of smiling men, a multicultural array—white, black, Asian, my ghostly half-image now as well. The text promised money to volunteers for a vaccine study at the NIH. Threading marinara out of my hair, I thought, Perfect.

Let me explain. In those days, jobs came and went fast. None of us remained employed for long. I say us, meaning a couple friends and a few other guys I was friendly with.

I can't tell you what we wanted. Maybe a psychologist could parse it now, diagnose us in denial of everything fate had spooled out for us. But it meant that we had certain requirements of a job, certain expectations as part of our identity: hours we could set, pay in cash, and no responsibility past the front door.

My friend Brian stripped at Wet three nights a week. After shunting gyros or shampoo around the city all night, I usually caught the end of his show. Up there on the stage, he looked so lean you imagined you could wrap one hand around his waist. Closer—and yes, I once jokingly stuck a dollar bill in his g-string—you realized the fan of his back only made him seem that thin. Every Sunday morning he'd wave a sweaty, beer-smelling bouquet of ones and fives in our greedy faces.

Brian and I were walking home from the P Street pool when I told him about the study. Blue sky that day. The late summer wind gently pushing from the north carried with it only the mildest of chills. We'd gone to the pool because Brian said it was a good place to find lost wallets. I think he just liked showing off that body of his, god-given, sharp and segmented as a scorpion's tail. I only found a quarter in the deep end.

"You're crazy," he said. "You should dance."

"I wouldn't make any money."

Brian took a hard look at my face. His eyes flicked to my feet spread over flip-flops, then the damp bathing suit that clung to the spud of my dick.

"You're young," he said as if noticing my age for the first time. "Come out mid-show when the old farts are drunk."

Here's how I met Brian. I shared a basement apartment on 2nd Street with a guy who called himself DJ St. Jon. He was way too cool for me—our low ceilings forever thumped with Martha W's belting gospel or Tiesto-inspired mixes that St. Jon claimed were "the thing" at Ibiza. I simply nodded at his testimony. St. Jon and I got along. The guy before me was a deadbeat; I was still working as a newspaper reporter and could always pay my share of the rent.

Like a tolerant older brother, St. Jon would invite me to his shows. Nightclubs and groups, people in general, weren't my thing. I was a solitary person and didn't know how to belong. Whenever he left for a gig, fedora slung low over his eyes, his stash of vinyl in a briefcase handcuffed to a wrist, his G-man look, I'd give him the old show business sendoff—"Break a leg!"—and settle on the couch behind a library book.

But there were nights I'd panic. I imagined I was missing something, an experience or sight I'd remember until I died, and I'd find myself in a froth to go out. Of course, once I paid the cover, got my hand stamped, and finally passed through the pat-down line, the crowd of shirtless guys twisting in the strobe lights would send me scurrying for the DJ booth. I'd bang on the door until St. Jon let me in.

I ventured out only when I needed a drink.

One night, I was tapping at the booth door, trying not to spill my vodka-tonic, when someone behind me asked, "How come you get to do that?" It was Brian, though right then I didn't know his name or anything else.

"Friend of the DJ."

"Let me show you something." Brian yanked me into a corner, ice and vodka sloshing into the dark at our feet. His shoulders eclipsed the strobe lights, and I froze beneath his winged shadow. I hoped he was going to kiss me. A glassine baggy and a key appeared. Balanced on the key's edge was a powdery, white pile. It went up my left nostril as if I'd practiced for the moment my entire life.

"Party starts now," Brian said.

In the booth I introduced Brian. He passed the bag and key to St. Jon. Later, I'd learn that Brian was forever with a stash. And every time I thought of him—and I thought of Brian a lot—I'd imagine him with his hand in his pocket, thumb and forefinger rubbing the slick plastic the way someone might worry a rosary.

The NIH's lobby was a cathedral of steel beams and slanting shafts of sunlight. A nurse gave me a clipboard piled with forms to complete. Height: 5′ 10″. Weight: 145. Allergies: none. There was a page for family background. My official story was that I arrived without origin. Mentioning the past, I feared, like the superstition about uttering the name Mephistopheles, might conjure what I'd been so desperately avoiding. "How important is this?" I asked.

"We need to know everything." She stood over me, her lab coat draped and pendulously circling her legs, the pockets heavy with thermometer, stethoscope, reflex hammer, otoscope; devices that peered inside people.

Pen poised, the bleach fumes wafting up from the sanitized floor threatening to make me sneeze, it occurred to me that we lived in the age of self-invention. So I invented stuff: my father shouldered his tour in Vietnam like a dirty rucksack; my mother spoke of her time as a Peace Corps volunteer in Kenya the way someone brags about a favored child. History was irrelevant. The emptiness of those blank lines, where any event was possible, seemed to endorse that notion.

I peed in a cup. The nurse drew blood.

She looked over the forms. "That's really not the kind of family history we mean."

I shrugged. "I wasn't sure."

"And you didn't list an emergency contact."

I'd hoped she wouldn't notice. It's not like anyone would come running. I put in Brian's name.

"Who's Brian?"

"My brother."

"Brother?" Her pen scratched something on the clipboard.

"Same mother, different father." I regretted not writing that my dad had hit me with a belt. That would've made good copy.

The nurse said, "You understand this is a safety trial." Meaning they just wanted assurance the stuff wouldn't kill anyone outright. I patted her white-sleeved wrist and said, "I'm not worried." Future glory was all that mattered. In a hundred years, after they declassified the research files, historians would read my name and know I was part of it. Movies would have bit parts inspired by my life. When I was a doddering centenarian, handsome young men would interview me, and I would tell them the whole story while my heart pumped alongside us in a glass case.

The first guy I picked up at a bar, ever, had a spot at the back of his skull where hair didn't grow. I know because he cut his hair short, military fade, exposing the patch. This was the third time I'd done crystal, and it must've been the good stuff, as much as that's possible. Right after the first bump, I had an enormous erection. I beat off twice, the first time working my hand in rhythm to a mix of *Domino Dancing* whomping from St. Jon's bedroom; the second, my fist in time with a dance version of the *American Beauty* title track. I got about five minutes of relief. My dick pressed painfully against the elastic band in my underwear and I loved how good it felt. I needed to fuck someone or someone to fuck me and it had to be soon or I'd take an axe to the furniture. I worried what I'd gotten myself into. I put in my contacts and left the apartment.

Cobalt was the nearest place. It was two floors of bars and a large dance area, and on Saturday nights the main customers were guys my age. My jaw grinding from the speed, I put on a big smile that probably more resembled death's grin than a seductive lure, and waded into the boys hopping underneath the strobe lights. Dry-ice smoke hissed from a tube overhead. It burned my eyes and I was soon wiping at tears.

"It's not that bad," a guy yelled, leaning into my ear. He was the one I mentioned with the short hair. A star tattoo decorated his forearm just below the elbow.

"My contacts are killing me."

"I'm a sucker for a weeping boy."

"Then I guess we're ready," I said.

We went to his place. He had a condo in a new building on P Street, the advance scout for a gentrifying wave that would soon follow and change the neighborhood forever. A nice enough place if you like the generic of beige carpets, marble counters, and doorway trim so new and clean it looked capable of razoring open your skin if you brushed against it. The marble counters were handy for cutting lines and hoovering up every last, little grain.

He led me into a back room and that was when I saw the empty patch on his scalp, a slice as long and thin as a cigarette, crossing diagonally from the nape. I wondered if he was born without follicles there, a serial killer, or a brain tumor survivor.

Hanging on the wall was a flat-screen television as large as a mattress. He triggered it with a remote. I shielded my face as porn flared to life, two boys almost life-sized pounding away at each other. The guy stepped into another room and brought back blankets and pillows and spread them on the carpet. "I don't do this in my bedroom," he said.

I shrugged. Whatever. He took off his shirt. A star to the right of his navel mimicked the one on his forearm, the tattoo ink diluted by a pad of fat that must've come in after he was marked. The light here was better than in Cobalt. He was older than I'd realized, on his last party days. I was just starting out. The crystal made me think I deserved hot guys like the pair pumping away on the TV. The crystal made me horny as fuck. I could've serviced a crew of scurvy Vikings.

He lay face down and said, "Touch me."

Not a serial killer I guessed. I peeled off my shirt and tossed it across the back of his head. He laughed into the blanket, a sound like a muffled cough. I unzipped my jeans and my dick sprang free. I kicked off my pants. I massaged his shoulders, firm and willing muscles, and sighed as I settled my balls against his warm back.

"Wow, I am rolling," he said.

"A real one-man party."

I'm thinking this might be easy: a naked massage and a jerk-off session for a couple of hefty bumps. After that I planned to hit Cobalt again and find a really cute boy. But then he rolled over and wormed out of his pants. I heard the rustle of a foil wrapper and the burp of a gel bottle and then his cold finger coated my asshole. I exhaled as he pushed into me. I focused on the dark-haired boy on the TV, his face clenched as he endured the same punishment. A ball of electricity deep inside my navel conducted straight up my dick. I glanced down; afraid I'd see his dick, like the creature from *Alien*, pushing outward from inside my stomach. My cock head was swollen, purple, and gossamer skinned. Everything hurt. I wanted to keep hurting.

My phone rang with the double-beep that meant Brian called, its LCD light flashing from the cave that was my jeans pocket. I scrambled away, the guys dick thumping wetly against his hip, me flooded with relief and agony. I flipped open the phone.

"Have you heard from Victor?" Brian asked. Victor was our dealer.

The guy looked betrayed. I held out a hand: one second. "No."

"We were supposed to meet before I went on."

The lube around my ass chilled in the air. I watched the screen as Brian rambled about how he'd been searching for Victor all night. The dark-haired boy had traded places and mounted the blond. Their smooth, seal-like bodies writhed on a wrestling mat in a high school gym. They rolled outside the competition circle and the action paused, a clenched ass, hip-bones and hamstrings pressed tight. The camera held their faces smiling at each other, the blond boy's thick salmon lips mouthed "Still in" and they went back to it.

"I have to go," I said to Brian. To the guy I said, "Sorry. My friend's cracking out."

"Problem?" He was a seesaw of light and dark in the television's shifting glow.

"He dances at Wet. Likes to be high when he does. He can't find our dealer."

My eyes kept jumping to the screen. I couldn't look away. And the boys made me want to leave, to go back to Cobalt and see who else I could score.

"Sounds like Brian," he said.

The screen went dark, a pause before the next scene, and the guy disappeared. When it came back on, I grabbed the crack bag and snorted a bump off my pinky. I titled my head back. Everything slid into place.

I squatted down over the guy. "No, that's not my friend's name."

I still had a bank account so there was no problem cashing the first check from the NIH. Bumps were my treat that Saturday night. With a dead credit card, while Brian and St. Jon looked on, I powered lines on the glass plant stand St. Jon and I called a coffee table. We shared two other pieces of furniture: a rickety IKEA television stand that wobbled more from my incompetent assembly than deficient materials; and a bus seat for a couch. I'd found it outside an auto mechanic's garage that was being demolished to make way for an apartment building. Someone had taped a handwritten sign to the seat-back cushion: FREE.

"Your tax dollars at work," I said, offering St. Jon the first line by holding up a drinking straw cut down to a quarter-length.

Brian wore tank tops for easy removal. Tonight it was red, a griffin rampant on the chest as if squaring its paws to bridge the cleft between his pec muscles. He saluted, exposing an armpit shaved smooth. "It makes me want to enlist."

"They'd bounce you out of the army so fast," St. Jon said. His eyes were wide, pupils swollen, from drugs, from desire, as he took in Brian's body.

"Don't Ask, Don't Tell," Brian said. "And I bet they'd take me now."

We parted at the club. St. Jon to his booth; Brian into the crowd chasing a slim, shirtless Adonis rippling in the strobe lights. I took up with a guy who recognized me from my VrooM! job. Furniture polish. Late Monday morning I found myself laid out in a wicker deck chair on someone's balcony, sipping the tweaker's post-party cocktail of orange juice and swirl, and watching the sun, like my aching head, slug through low clouds.

My phone rang. It was the nurse. "Your bilirubin is elevated."

"You got me." I stood, hoping that would make me sound sober.

"Usually it goes up when someone fasts."

I tended not to eat much when high. "I watch my weight," I said. "Sometimes I overdo it."

"If it's this high again we'll have to drop you from the study."

It was time to go home. The balcony came off a bedroom. Inside, the bed's rumpled sheets and a familiar ache in my body conjured images from last night. (Or was it the night before? Or both?) My shoes were lined up by the door.

In the living room I approached a tall, blond man. He made me think of televised college basketball. "Thanks for everything," I said. "But I have to go."

"Do I know you?"

"Isn't this your place?" I looked around. The window shades were drawn against the daylight. At the center of the dining table stood a bong, its smoke tube languidly hanging over the edge. The television's flicker blued the knees of two men on the couch.

I turned back towards the tall man. He gazed down at me with a stare intimate to the heavily self-medicated.

"Where's the flat's owner?" I asked.

"He just called your place a flat," he said, talking across my shoulder.

This time when I turned around a moment of vertigo almost knocked me over. Even if I wanted to stay things were winding down.

The condo owner worked a piece of gum between his front teeth; the neon-green wad flickered in and out of sight like a second tongue. An image flashed—the edges of those teeth scissoring my nipples. "Bump of K?" he held out a bag.

"I'm in a study," I announced. "I need a break."

My host raised an eyebrow. A head on the couch lolled my direction. "A vaccine trial," I continued, launching into a synopsis of the study. Then I realized there were details I couldn't drop, and so described the NIH, the stethoscope's cold disk against my chest, and the forms I'd filled out. The tall guy shook his head and walked away. When the owner started scratching his stubbled chin, his eyes on something in the corner near the ceiling, I eased towards the door, wrapping up with a blithe dismissal of the experiment's lurking danger, and then I'm pretty sure, as I stood halfway in the corridor, one foot still planted inside the threshold, a reference to myself as a biological commando.

The door slammed shut. From behind the steel someone called out, "Good luck."

Before all this started, when I still wrote for a newspaper, and before I met Brian, I spent a lot of time at the National Gallery. A reporter's typical week was seventy-two hours of straight work in the rush to deadline, pounding out copy as the sun rose. I lived on breakfasts of leftover turkey sandwiches oozing mayo, sidewalk cigarette breaks, and so much adrenaline I could barely fit my apartment key into the door handle when I finally got home.

Even then the work kept going. I remember once standing in the tub, water dripping from my elbows into the pool around my shins, and arguing quotes with an editor. That I had the phone with me in the bathroom never seemed strange.

After press time was two days frittering the hours in bed recuperating, thinking about next week's headlines, pitching stories, and planning a Saturday night that would begin with cocktails right after lunch.

Monday it began again.

Me: I'm here to see the Senator. [flashes press pass, offers business card.]

Secretary: [picking up phone] Do you have an appointment?

Me: I thought she'd like to discuss the general's comment about the unfitness of gay soldiers.

Secretary: [phone back in cradle] I'm sorry, she's not available.

Me: I can certainly write she had no comment. [notepad and pen out]

Secretary: [phone back in hand] Her campaign manager can speak with you.

Me: [smiling] Wonderful.

You can see why I enjoyed it. As I said, this was before I discovered drugs.

The museum had no admission fee. There were people. I could mingle, lurking unnoticed alongside the other lonely and dislocated, while the city pulsed around us.

One time I came upon a young man, part of a mother-father-daughter-son quartet. The four pressed to their ears those translators the museum rented to foreign tourists. The boy wore a souvenir Washington Nationals baseball cap. His jeans cuffs fell over his shoes and the frayed edges seemed to polish the marble floor like soft mops. I trailed them through the rooms, past arch studies of myth and swollen hells, and the angel announcing. By the time we reached Rembrandt's darkly static self-portraits, Dad had finally caught on and came right up to me brandishing a face of clenched teeth.

I'll admit that while I was following them my gaze might've danced mostly across his son, but not in the way you think. I was imagining what it'd be like seeing things from his angle. As I glided away, the plastic carriage of dad's device creaked in his fist, and I knew that even if we spoke the same language, he wouldn't have understood.

Within a week of the nurse's phone call, a semblance of my normal sleep patterns returned. No more three days awake, and then four in front of the television spooning up bowls of rocky road ice cream and napping in between reruns of the *Golden Girls*. But only a semblance. I'd drift off around ten, ten-thirty, and stay unconscious for a couple hours. Then without fail I'd shoot upright, panting, the clock on the floor beside the mattress flashing 12:00, trying to remember where I was, and unsure if I'd even slept.

The first time this happened I assumed the beckoning streetlight just outside my bedroom window was to blame. The next evening I tacked up an American flag as a curtain. But still I shuddered awake in a panic. I'd toss and turn and, only after what seemed like hours, finally go back down. Around the fourth or fifth night of this, I instead paced the apartment's narrow common area, slapping my arms and legs, hoping the sting would keep me focused. The parquet floors clacked like a giant sliding puzzle. St. Jon shouted that I was keeping him up.

"I'm bored," I moaned. "Everything is the same all the time." The NIH only required I visit every Friday so they could record my vitals. Other than that, I was free.

St. Jon came out of his bedroom. He said he knew about going cold turkey. "Let's try television." He pulled me to the bus seat.

The waxy dots where long-ago passengers had stubbed out cigarettes scratched the back of my thighs. I flipped channels, never satisfied.

"You're making me crazy." St. Jon wore a silver ankh on a necklace; he was in his pharaoh period. The oozy television light gave him a beet face, round and shiny. Midweek television offered cartoons, which made me laugh, but St. Jon said he preferred cooking shows.

I tried other distractions. Sweeping. Dusting. I soaped the walls and wiped off fingerprints. One night I even cleaned the oven. The fumes woke St. Jon. He flung open his bedroom door. A t-shirt clamped over his nose and mouth, he yelled, "Are you embalming somebody?"

So I went to the National Gallery again. I made sure to ignore everyone around me: the tourists, the families, the school groups on field trips.

For a while, wandering wall to wall, I was happily secure in the air-conditioned hush. The museum is a labyrinth of small rooms and connected galleries. On a weekday afternoon, you can easily find yourself alone in a forgotten chamber lined with obscure paintings not even familiar from college textbooks.

But somewhere deep among Dutch masters, footsteps drew me around a corner. The guy I saw across the way was as familiar as my own reflection. Not that I knew him. What I mean is—watching him absently fiddle with the buttons on his blue Oxford while shifting his weight from one tasseled shoe to another—I knew that he was AWOL from a job or a college class and had no interest in the still life hanging before him. He was, like me, burning time.

I eased close behind him. "The cracked mirror symbolizes vanity," I said. Startled, he jumped, and had to resettle his glasses. My tread must've been quieter than I realized. As an opener, the line seemed better than "The fly means death."

"So they tell us." Bowing his pale head, he tried skulking away. There followed a merry little chase from room to room, me wandering out of sight for a moment, making him think I'd given up, only then to step back into view. He paused every so often to regard a canvas, an attempt to disguise his flight. But his gaze was forever split between the art and warily hunting for my presence.

Brian would've led the guy home, his words echoing on the glossy stone, "Party starts now." I lacked Brian's tools. And considering it now, I think I was after more substantial prey.

The guy broke for the open hall. I zipped ahead and cut him off beneath the rotunda dome. From the center fountain, naked bronze Mercury pointed his caduceus heavenward. We at his feet were nothing but poppies in a field of mud.

He cleared his throat. "What do you do?"

Washington had trained him well. I could've clutched my stomach and let out a great, bellowing yawp.

"Let's get a drink," I said.

At the bar he was nervous. His ID said twenty-one, but he trembled like a kid. He gripped his highball glass as if it might zoom to the ceiling.

I sipped my drink. Cool liquid washed my throat. I'd forgotten the simple pleasure of a vodka-tonic on the rocks. Brian dropped onto the stool next to me. "Haven't seen you in a while."

"I'm in that study." I leaned forward, putting myself between him and the kid.

STEFEN STYRSKY

Brian snapped his fingers. "Right." He raised a hand and ordered me another round. "Mark, take care of my friend."

The bartender poured a fresh glass. "Just say when." He let vodka flow until I said stop. He topped the drink with a click of the seltzer gun.

Already my fame spread.

"Not drinking?" I asked Brian.

He wrinkled his nose. "Messes with my tweak." He planted his forehead against my temple and whispered into my ear, "Cute boy you have there." He then sidled down the bar; cast me a wink and a thumbs-up before slapping the back of another friend slumped forward on a stool.

Suddenly I was starving. I ordered a hamburger, rare. It arrived with a mound of fries. Instead of ketchup, I swabbed them through the meat's pooling, bloody juices.

"Want something?"

The kid shook his head. His bony knee bounced, and I steadied it with a hand. His eyes widened behind his glasses.

"Don't be nervous," I said. "My sacrifice is your salvation."

# Through the Still Hours

## JONATHAN CORCORAN

---

It's Saturday. I wake up early, and after having a cup of coffee alone in the kitchen, I cook and bring him breakfast in bed. French toast and eggs. This, in my head, seems the simplest way to make romance. It's our fourth anniversary—four years since we met each other in that parking lot. I think I might catch him off guard this morning, before he has time to think of all the ways to keep me at arm's length. Food, I reason, is something that still motivates us to make nice with each other. The promise of taste and smell and drink still stirs something inside of us in the most primal ways. Sad, I know, for someone not yet thirty years of age to act fifty, but this is where I'm at—where we're at.

At first, in the bedroom, it seems I might trick him into submission. He awakens with a smile—his ash-blond hair a mess from the static of the pillow. I think, this is how it should be, two lovers naked, all proverbial walls down. I kiss him on the neck and use the stubble on my chin to trace patterns on his back. His pale white skin turns red in abstract hearts and figure eights. His initial complacency, his unmoving body, surprises me, given the defensive posturing that usually greets my attempts at sex. His lack of a defense is enough to arouse me, and I try not to overthink things. I let the smell of his night sweat pull me into his body. "I want to make love to you all day long," I say. "And then I want to make love to you some more, until the sun sets and rises again."

I wonder if I really mean these words. I try not to think about how making love, in the few times that it ever happens with us anymore, has become an almost selfish act, driven more by basic needs and less by a desire to revel in the other's pleasure. It's a letting of blood for us. A release of tension. But I don't dwell on the usual way of things. I convince myself that anniversaries can act as a reset button. In bed, as I'm blowing hot air onto his neck, he's the Gerry of day one, with a lust-inducing shyness, his falsely innocent eyes beckoning.

But this doesn't last. As he awakens and recognizes my intent, his smile melts away. His eyes harden. It's as if I've stirred him from the most sexual dream, only for him to realize that the man who's been fucking him in the clouds is not the man in his bed—is not me. "I'm tired, love. Maybe later?" He finishes with a peck of a kiss, quick and dry. He sits up and sticks his fork into the eggs. He eats with zeal.

How we found each other goes something like this: Four years ago, we message each other on one of those Web sites whose sexually punny names I prefer not to pronounce aloud. We settle on a spot in the next town over for the sake of discretion. We decide to meet just off the highway in a McDonald's parking lot. I remember seeing his face for the first time. I think of that electric sensation when I'm alone in the shower.

On that first day, we are two anonymous Internet profiles taking a chance on explicit pictures from the chest down. His car is just as he said it would be: a 1991 silver Toyota hatchback with a belt of rust along the bottom. He rolls down the window, wanting to speak, but scared. Before he can say a word, I utter, "Yes. It's me."

He leans over the gearshift and throws open the passenger door. It groans. I make him take his car, because I don't want to run the risk of anyone recognizing me, even here, twenty miles from home. I'm no fool—I know that people talk. Some people drive twenty miles to do their shopping, looking for a change of scenery. Others drive that far because they're tired of being seen. Like the preacher said at church when I was growing up, "Someone's always watching you." God, or that old woman who lives next door.

In his car, the smells wafting from the vents of the fast-food restaurant mix with the scent of his cologne. This combination—salty, florid, cheap—makes him seem younger than the age that was on his online profile. We take one long, deep look at each other, and then we both lock our vision straight ahead through the windshield. His face burns into my mind in that look, exists still in my memory: frightened blue eyes, nervous lips. I prefer that face. Even his blond hair, back then, seemed to suggest *soiled.* In my dreams, I see that face, and he says, "I'm holding back, but only for a moment."

In the car that evening, he says, "Where are we going?"

"I don't care." My heart beats too quickly. My hands clench down on the sides of the vinyl seats. "Just drive."

So we do. We drive down back roads, past rolling farms at the edge of mountains. We drive past abandoned gas stations, the victims of four-lane highways. He knows the roads by heart, as we all do, because that's where our fathers took us on joyrides to tell the dirty stories of their youth. My instinct is to recount these stories, to tell him where my father brawled with drunken men. To tell him where my father took an easy girl under a tree and asserted himself. I bite my lip, though, and say nothing. Somehow these stories feel too shocking, as if I'm not actually driving down a back road with a stranger intent on doing things that seem too embarrassing to speak of.

Gerry steals sideways glances when he takes sharp turns. I notice, then look away. We fumble. We shimmy in our seats. We become braver, in fits and starts, make eye contact, breathe heavily to fill the silence. He moves his lips, but no words come out. He puts his hand onto mine, after switching gears. He waits for me to meet him halfway, to curl my fingers into his own. It's such a teenage gesture, but for us, there's a newness to it.

"Are you a murderer?" I say, only half-joking, when his skin touches mine. "Why haven't I seen you around town? I've seen everyone."

"I'm from the next county over," he says, naming the town. It's a place I know well, not much more than a pit stop on the way down from the mountain. He looks the part, with his Sunday best on: the checkered shirt, the khaki pants, and the schoolboy cut. He sang in the church choir no doubt, bringing old women to tears with his honey baritone and startled eyes. I judge him for these things, as if being from my town of eight thousand is any better than being from his town of five hundred.

"I just moved here for work," he says.

"You look, well, normal," I say. "What do you do?"

"High school teacher."

"Are you out?"

"Define out."

"Do people know that you're into men?"

"They suspect. I don't talk about it. Why does anybody need to know?"

We drive for miles, lay down the basics, or at least as much as we feel safe revealing to a stranger who suddenly knows too many of our secrets. It's fall and everything is red—the dropping leaves, the setting sun, the fire of our cigarettes, blazing brighter as they catch the wind from the cracked windows. I see the blood in the back of my eyes with each throat-clenching heartbeat.

We pull over onto a secluded lookout: a meandering river and hay bales in the fields below. We are far from any named town: existence incognito out here. We watch the day disappear. The sky fades like a rotting peach. We sit in silence and pass a flask of whiskey to cut the tension.

At a farmhouse in the distance, a porch light shines like a nightlight or a warning. I understand this darkness. I revel in the feeling of it. One can't avoid it growing up underneath the mountains. The darkness never fails to frighten and to thrill me, to conjure ghosts and campfire stories. We get out of the car and lie back on the warm hood. Thousands of stars circle slowly above, clustered and thick, hanging over the non-forms of trees along the hillsides, the black on blacker horizon.

"Do you do this often?" I ask.

"More than I'd like," he says, his voice quiet but sultry. His admission, which I can also claim as my own, both shames and turns me on. We're pushed by the world to dark spaces, filthy bathrooms, and secret lookouts. We feel dirty always, but then at a certain point, when we become familiar with these dark terrains, we begin to like the feeling. We claim the dark spaces and the secret corridors as our own. These acts become at first an outlet, and then an addiction: an instant erection upon pulling into a highway rest stop.

Because of all this, we know what's coming without prompting. We knew what was coming before we sent the first message online. We get back into the car. We touch lips. We feel the contours of the other's body and delight in the mystery of what exists under our clothing. We recline our seats.

But just as we're beginning, the headlights of a vehicle break the darkness. It's a half mile down the road, lumbering toward us.

"What if someone catches us?" he says.

I don't stop, though. I can't stop. The fear of getting caught is also part of the game, part of the turn-on.

"And what if?" I say, challenging him with my hand as I squeeze his inner thigh.

"Don't you…aren't you…? Oh, fuck it."

The headlights grow brighter and closer. I kiss him deeply. My hands stop touching and start pushing, forcing their way, fueled by some exhibitionist tendency. I dare the night to interfere, to trespass on this scene.

And then the lights arrive. The truck slows to a halt just outside our car. Bright white pierces the glass, blinding us. Gerry pushes me off of him, looks to the steam on the windows. His shoulders shrink inward. We are guilty and scared. I roll down the window—decipher the face of an old man in a dented pickup. The brim of his ball cap hangs down to the edge of his eyes. He nods his head at us, firm and quick. His face is clean-shaven. He looks nervously over his shoulder. Clears his throat. "You boys be careful out here," he says and drives off.

We don't finish what we started. Gerry drives me back to my car, through the night, in silence.

I watch Gerry finish his breakfast. He smiles as he eats. He tells me the food is good, raises his fork, nods his head with approval. When he finishes, he hands me his plate. I get up to walk to the kitchen.

"Happy anniversary," he calls after me.

I take his dish to the sink. I drink a glass of water. I look out the kitchen window. I see the solitary willow tree that takes up a full half of our fenced-in backyard. The willow's thin branches flutter with the breeze, caress the grass like fingers. I imagine my body as the grass. I want to be touched.

I come back to the bedroom to get dressed. Gerry plays on his laptop, as I put on jeans. When I look at him, my neck tenses. I breathe in. The air feels thick.

"Ariana just texted," he says, not looking up from his computer. "She said she really wants margaritas before we go out tonight. We have tequila, but would you mind going to pick up the mixers?"

"You know I didn't want to do this tonight," I say. I want to hit him. I want to grab him by the wrists and squeeze so hard that I leave a bruise. "I still don't understand why we can't celebrate by ourselves. It's our anniversary—not theirs."

"Because what we have is so special," he says, in his high, whiny voice. "I want them to know what we have."

I don't respond. I walk into the living room and put my shoes on. I grab my car keys. He yells goodbye as I walk out the front door.

I drive to Walmart, and as I pull into the parking lot, I think maybe I should find a secluded place in the back lot to finish alone what I had attempted to start with Gerry. But the back of the lot is too busy. Saturdays are always madness here, with every last troll and ogre lining up to do their weekend shopping. I decide to save my solo joy for a later time. I clench my teeth and walk inside.

I'm treated to a vision of every person I don't care to see. We all know each other—by face or name. If not, we could surmise enough, by the type of clothes we wear, by the way we carry ourselves. I left the house in a hurry, throwing on whatever I could find, but here, I'm a snobbish prince. I hold my head low, so as not to attract any unneeded attention.

I stop into the bathroom before I begin shopping. In the bathroom, as I'm in the middle of pissing, a wrinkly old man with a high school letterman jacket begins to jerk his dick at me two urinals down. He swings it around like he's offering me gold or a diamond or both. His all-knowing glance sizes me up, perhaps by my clothes or the way I return his eye contact. He thinks: queer, horny queer, likes-to-suck queer, takes-whatever-he-can-get queer. That's the standard around here, be it in a bathroom or on the Internet. When I refuse his ilk, I'm never sure if they're going to burst into tears or pummel me.

I've stopped trying to make sense of it. It happens once a week at least. The same old men you hear trash-talking outside the redneck bars—faggot this, faggot that. Gerry doesn't believe me when I tell him this—doesn't trust my face when I emerge red and angry from a piss at the movie the-ater. It's because he doesn't look at people—at least not directly. He's head-forward everywhere, bulldozing through air—all *excuse me* and *pardon me.* Knows his place.

Before Gerry and I started dating, I'd never kissed the same man more than once. Half of the men I met—on the Internet, in the stalls of bath-rooms like this—didn't even kiss me on the mouth. I thought that was the way life worked: a series of shady encounters with men I'd never see again. Gerry gave me something I'd never felt before. It was love, I thought, or something like it.

In the restroom, with the Walmart radio blaring upbeat country music designed to push this week's camouflage coat, my eyes settle not on the old man's dick but on the golden band on his left ring finger. Though I'm not attracted to this man, I feel myself getting hard. I smile. I laugh. I proffer him a look at my penis. "Relationships are tough, huh? I'm sorry I can't help you out."

And what does he say, in response to my gesture at civility? "Fuck you, faggot."

I leave the bathroom and continue on with my shopping, unfazed.

I return home with the mixers, and Gerry avoids me for the duration of the day. He lesson-plans for school and then putzes around on the Inter-net while I read a book. He pulls me aside before our friends arrive. "This means a lot to them," he says. "We're the only gay couple they know."

"And we're the new paradigm," I say. "We're the hope for the future."

"You can be a real dick," he says. "Don't be that way tonight. Be happy. For me."

That's the end of our conversation until evening comes and our friends arrive, couple by couple, taking seats in our living room. There's Ariana and Chris, and Karen and Michael—two pretty and talkative women who Gerry met through teaching, and their blissfully silent husbands, who are really just quiet because they're unsure of what to say to us: the nice little homos that mix such delectable drinks. There's no harm in their silence. I take no offense. It's as awkward for me as it is for them.

It's just another Saturday, slightly altered subjects: the politics du jour and the strange old man who showed up this week outside the grocery store and greets customers with cat noises. He meows if he likes you, hisses if he doesn't. Gerry receives purrs, while I receive claws. I think there must be something in that, some larger comment about the quality of my soul, but I can't quite put my finger on it.

Gerry and I sit on opposite sides of the living room in two hardback chairs. The two couples sit on the love seat and the big sofa, hands on knees, and close enough to advertise that they still feel something for each other.

We sit and the chatter rolls on. Karen regales us with the politically incorrect things that her high school students say. Ariana talks about taking a trip to Pittsburgh to go shopping for some "real" clothes. As they blather on, the room grows darkly golden with the sunset. The light always disappears sooner than expected here: the end-of-summer shrinking sun falling behind the mountains, gnawing at my psyche. A breeze blows against the trees and rocks the neighbors' wind chimes as if to say *take cover!* So I close the windows and the curtains. I switch on lamps and light tapers in brass holders on the coffee table. Our shadow figures gesture on the walls, and I wonder, how is it that the shadows seem more animated than we do?

"I always feel so comfortable here, guys," Ariana says. "You have the coziest apartment in town."

Once, I would have been flattered. Once, I would have proudly agreed with her. I remember back when Gerry and I first moved in together. We tried to create beauty and warmth in the way that we draped a curtain just so, in how we painted the walls of the living room an inviting burnt orange. We thought we were so smart in that choice, building our refuge. We wrapped ourselves in blankets on Sunday mornings and held each other until the dusk. I look back on the conversations we had, back when we thought that the burnt-orange walls were a symbol of our life to come, not a marker of stasis. "Imagine," I said then, "a world—this very world, same place, same town—where two men could go walking down the street arm and arm and the neighbors would just smile and wave." And then we'd hold each other some more, and think that maybe that future was a real possibility. We watched the television, the promise of a president. Obama, we thought, a man who would change everything. Childish optimism, I know, to think that the outside world would somehow find its way here, to our small world. But in those moments, there was a forward movement with us: a connection through hope and a sharing of secrets.

And at some point after those moments had played out, something quiet happened. After all our secrets were revealed, our fantasies confessed aloud, we began to pretend that we were just like everyone else. We played at husband and wife, though we knew it was forbidden for people like us. Or maybe we just didn't understand the game, or the rules. Or maybe, most importantly, we tried to be something that we weren't. We became like apes wearing human costumes. We could play the part, and though we were different at the core, we were close enough in kind to fool the onlookers.

Ariana moves her gaze from Gerry to me. She extends her arm and her margarita glass for emphasis. "I'll fucking kill the both of you if you ever break up."

**We** drink until we're all sure of our insobriety. Then we prepare to head off to the bar to go dancing, the second leg of our Saturday night group anniversary celebration. Gerry collects everyone's margarita glasses, and as he takes mine, he kisses me on the cheek. I feel like shivering, but I catch a warning in his eye. I reach out and touch his arm. I feel disgusted with myself for playing at this game.

"You guys are just adorable," Karen says, as if on cue, another hint of what will be an evening of excessive drunken flattery. And I know that he loves this idea: that we're the porcelain figurines missing from their otherwise perfect shadowboxes. He throws an extra shimmy into his hip as he walks. He spouts sassy one-liners stolen from bad reality television. Of course, he won't touch me once we leave the safety of our apartment.

As we walk out the door, I imagine what it would be like to fuck him, right in front of their faces. To show them what a dick looks like going into an ass. To show them that we're capable of lust and aggression and messiness. I picture tying my sweater right around his mouth, jerking his head back as I push into him. Would they remain seated? Would they drop their cocktails?

And what would Gerry do if I grabbed him by the balls and squeezed? Would he moan in pleasure? Would he call my name?

No. I think he would slap my face.

We approach the steps of our destination, which is just a short walk from our apartment. The bar is called "The Commander's Pub," and it sits on a residential street, off the main drag of the quiet downtown. It's an old Victorian house with a big wraparound porch where we escape the crowds and smoke cigarettes. The neighbors complain about the hippies and write to the newspaper about the strange music that blasts until two in the morning. It's our sanctuary, and sometimes I wish I could climb up the old wooden stairs and claim one of the Commander's extra bedrooms as my own.

We hear a trumpet and drums as we walk up to the screen door. It's salsa night. Ariana turns to us. "Chris and I've been practicing at home. We've been watching videos online. I think he's finally ready to spin me."

Gerry and I used to dance alone with the blinds pulled. We taught ourselves salsa and swing. I led him with strong arms, and he followed, turning once, twice, dipping low. I would pick him up and toss him around my body and under my legs, as I'd seen on television. We're different, the two of us. His body is light, featherlike. Skin and bones, but not fragile. Easy to push around. Easy to hold.

"I can't wait to see, honey," Gerry says to Ariana.

There's something about the way he speaks to her that makes me want to run away. I'm embarrassed to be a part of this. Sometimes I feel he's like a talking doll with a cord in his back. A jester. Their toy.

The owner of the bar, the namesake, the Commander himself, greets us as we walk inside. He's the town's favorite eccentric, with his bald head and white beard down to his hips. He hugs the girls and shakes the boys' hands. Karen stands on her tiptoes and whispers something into his ear.

"Esmé," the Commander says to his pretty young wife standing behind the bar. "Drinks on the house for Cliff and Gerry."

She pours us two whiskeys on the rocks—our regular drink. "What's the occasion?"

"Our anniversary," Gerry whispers and winks. The words roll from his mouth so easily that I feel guilty. "Four years."

"Congratulations," she says. "Drink up, lovebirds."

Gerry forces a toast, clanks his glass against mine and bottoms out the whiskey. I can't even bring myself to sip—I just swish it in a circle.

"I'll have another," he says.

I know this is the beginning of many more drinks for him, which means when we go home he'll crawl into the bed and fall asleep in minutes. I used to try to kiss him after nights like these. I would kiss his neck and touch his back, and he'd say he was too tired. He'd roll over, mumbling about how there'd be time in the morning. When the morning came, he'd say he was too hungover.

A half-dozen couples have started dancing in front of the band. We watch the band for a moment: a trumpeter, drummer, and a piano player. Gerry is tapping his feet and his fingers to the rhythm. I lean over to his ear and whisper: "If you love me, then dance with me."

He looks shocked, then angry, then hurt. "You know we can't do that here," he says.

I recognize all the faces: the same ones who have been coming to this bar for years. Every one of them knows about us, though I can't think of a single person who has ever brought it up without prompting. They never ask questions—as if that would be some sort of transgression. They don't need qualifications. Or really, they don't want to know the details. We're just us: Gerry and Cliff, those boys, two names that go together.

A few drinks in, and our friends are all out on the dance floor. We sit alone, Gerry looks away, and I look at him.

"We haven't fucked in a month," I say. "Happy anniversary."

"Why are you acting like this?" he asks, and then turns away.

We sip the whiskeys and watch the dancing couples: carefree, ridiculous, completely wrong but right. I swallow the last of my drink, and feel an anger-fueled intoxication streaming through me.

"Just fucking dance with me," I say. I reach for his hand, but he pulls away. He reaches for his cigarettes, takes his glass, and heads to the porch.

I follow him out the door. From the porch, the music bends into something different, creates a tunnel-like dream world. There's the life inside and the quiet reality of the streets just down the steps.

Gerry sits in a rusty metal chair around the corner, out of the light, almost invisible. I go to him. I get down on my knees so that we're face to face.

"I'm sorry," I say. "But what do you expect me to do?"

He seems to consider my words, as he looks into my eyes. His face fades in and out of the shadows, picks up a bit of fire from the cherry of his cigarette. "Why don't we dance together, Cliff? Why don't we hold hands? Do you need me to explain it to you? Do you need me to tell you, step by step, about what happens to men like us in towns like this? Are we really going to go over this right now?" His eyes look like glaciers: reflective and uninviting. "If you don't want to be with me," he says, "then go."

"I can only try so much," I say. "This isn't my fault."

"It's no one's fault," he says. "No. It's everyone's fault."

He's crying now. I want to comfort him, but I can't. We've done this one too many times. I walk off the porch and leave.

I weave through the side streets to avoid the main drag. The night is mostly quiet, but with sudden bursts of sound. Yips and yells, and tire squeals that smash the stillness unexpectedly and send chills through my body. The sounds fade just long enough to surprise again when they return.

I walk by the rows of old houses. Brick and clapboard. The lights are mostly off, but television screens flicker blue and white and beckon. The windows sit framed by low-hanging sycamore and maple trees. I want to be home. I want to go into my bedroom and curl under the blankets, pull them over my head, and seal off the world. But I continue to walk along because the home I'm thinking of is not the home in which I live. I'm not sure where that home is.

As I'm walking, I sometimes stop and close my eyes—the sidewalk curves, familiar as a recurring dream. I imagine Gerry taking my arm, and I jump a little, surprised by the vividness of this thought. In my mind, he holds me tightly and leans his head on my shoulder as we walk. People smile when they see us. And then their smiles make us want to take off our clothes. Then we're making love on the streets, and the audience is cheering.

I walk past the homes of the people I've known all of my life. I can assign names to most doors. I meander down sidewalks and look at the moon, and try to imagine what life would be like there, on the bright side, when a shadow is always a shadow, never shifting with the position of the sun.

I take a turn and pick up the pace. Now I'm rushing through the main street of the downtown, past the rough-and-tumble pool halls that I'm afraid to enter. The handful of gruff men who smoke outside these places utter prophecies in my direction: *broken neck, fuck your pussy.* Some of them blow kisses and lick their lips. They call me with two fingers: *here, queer.* But this only fuels me. I smile back at them, with teeth. I watch them retreat, then, their heads going down, like dogs backing off from a fight.

I walk past all there is to see in the downtown, which isn't much more than the same old buildings that have been here for a hundred years. Half of them are boarded up and empty. I walk across a swinging footbridge over the town's shallow, dirty river. The river seems so much more enchanting here and now, as it reflects the moonlight and the lamplight from the windows of an adjacent apartment building. I cross the river and leave the downtown, heading back toward my apartment. I look at my watch and realize I've been walking for over an hour. I wonder if Gerry is home now. I wonder if we will apologize to each other and then cuddle, sexlessly, until we fall asleep. Or more likely, we'll say nothing at all, and then in the morning, we'll say even less.

I'm only two blocks from home. I don't see the truck at first. I hear it, sense its presence—air moving different than the wind. I turn around, watch as it drives toward me, a dark form with no headlights turned on. It appears as a living, moving thing under the street lamps: an animate beast of sorts, with instincts, on the hunt. I don't see the driver. Instead, I see the fluorescent reflection of the streetlights in the windshield.

The truck slows down as it nears me, and I look straight ahead, to show that I have a destination. The confidence that I showed to the men earlier is gone, though, and I fear that the driver can sense it. The truck rolls along beside me. I pick up the pace, expecting the worst—though I'm ready for it, prepared to be beaten, can already feel my face against the ground, head stomped by a steel-toed boot, teeth loosened. The thought doesn't bother me—almost delights me, in fact. I can already feel the sidewalk, cold and comforting, like when you have the flu and you collapse onto the bathroom floor. I wonder if I will call out to my lover, as the attacker calls out to me, "Dirty faggot."

The truck drives away, though, and in that moment, lucidity returns. I finger my cell phone in my pocket. Should I call the police? Should I call Gerry to come meet me? I'm only a block from home now. I can see our porch light just down the street. I could run, and that seems smart, but I don't. I have the urge to test fate, or maybe just experience a thrill—anything but home, anything but Gerry.

The truck returns, as I expect. The same pattern—slowing down as if to escort me. The passenger window is rolled down. I see the man's shadow of a face—sad, hard-leather skin. This villain has a backstory, I think, full of broken hearts. His own heart included.

"What do you want with me?" I ask.

I think the man smiles, though in the obscured light I cannot tell. There is some movement in the truck. I can hear the shifting of the man's weight, and his breathing.

"Do you wanna go for a ride?" he asks.

We have stopped moving: two parallel souls in the dark night. There are stars out, and televisions flickering. There are people dancing in bars, and the thought enters my mind that there are children writing wishes in diaries by the light of the moon shining through their bedroom windows.

I wonder if Gerry can see us—if he has hitched a ride home, feeling lonely and raw, and now sits at the kitchen window, watching for moving shadows, my body hulking through the dark streetscape.

I take one step toward the man and pause, waiting for his reaction. He leans across the seat and opens the door. "You don't have to be afraid," he says.

And in this man's voice, in his face, in the darkness of the night, and the still intact body I inhabit, I know I can trust him, this man who wanders alone through the still hours of the earliest morning, looking for people like me, offering comfort in a familiar phrase: "You have nothing to fear."

"Where are we going?" I ask.

"Wherever you want," he says, as if he were sucking in the words, not speaking them.

He is me four years ago. He is Gerry four years ago. His aged face is unimportant. What matters is the tone of his voice.

"I know a few places," I say, and get into his truck, settling into the seat as if I've always belonged there.

As he drives off, without asking any directions, a surge of feeling emanates from my gut and into my throat. And it's in that feeling that I know this is both exactly where I should and shouldn't be.

# Unresolved Sexual Tension Between Friends

## JERRY PORTWOOD

It wasn't meant to feel like a date, but when Guillem arrived outside our apartment, helmet in hand, he looked like my silver suitor ready to whisk me away for a night of romance on his bike. I'd cleared it with Patricio, asking him several times if he was okay with my heading out with Guillem, and he'd told me he wasn't jealous.

"Sure—I want you to go," Patricio assured me. He knew I missed having a social life these past three months after we'd moved to Barcelona together.

While I lived in Atlanta, I'd been a dedicated culture vulture, usually going to a gallery opening, a concert, the theater, or dance event five nights a week. Our long-distance relationship—he lived two hours away from me, where he taught architecture at a South Carolina university—turned out to be perfect for that first year of dating. I'd spend weeknights absorbing whatever the city threw at me; weekends were our time together. Exhausted from his week of teaching, Patricio wasn't much for spending two hours in a dark theater. I didn't try to force it. Maybe we'd go out dancing, or I'd coax him to the latest Malaysian restaurant I was reviewing, but mostly we spent our time together in bed—which worked. We didn't have to share every interest; I didn't have to parade him around with my friends. But now living in Spain together meant new negotiations. So when Guillem mentioned he had free tickets to a production of a Catalan version of *Glengarry Glen Ross*, something that sounded bizarre and intrigued me, I wanted to go. But I needed reassurance.

"You're sure you don't mind?" I asked again.

"Stop asking. Just go," Patricio said. I realized he might be just as glad to have an evening free of me. It was the first time either of us had lived with a lover, and we'd spent every waking and sleeping moment together for the past three months in Barcelona. I'd introduced Guillem to Patricio and they had hit it off. Guillem had dark hair, a sexy goatee, and piercing eyes. He was attractive and, unlike most of the Spanish guys I'd met, worked out regularly at a gym; he liked to show off his sculpted chest and biceps in tight shirts. Patricio had explained that it was next to impossible to make a Catalan friend, and he was impressed that I'd managed it in such a short period of time.

Guillem was a writer for the most popular Catalan soap opera, *El Cor de la Ciutat*. Although the show meant nothing to me, Patricio had explained it was the most popular TV program in Barcelona. Since Catalan had been forbidden during the Franco dictatorship and could have been lost for future generations, the regional government now supported any artistic endeavor that developed the language and supported the national identity, so this soap reigned as the most beloved family entertainment for millions. It was like *Dynasty*, without any other competition. I was excited to join him for a night of theater.

"Have you ever been on the back of a moto before?" Guillem asked.

"A what?" I wasn't sure if he was attempting some sort of a flirtatious tease, and I was just missing the subtlety. "I like your Vespa."

"My moto is a Suzuki," he clarified and told me to snuggle up behind him. He helped me with my helmet as I fumbled with the straps, buckling it below my chin. "Put your arms around me. Nos vamos, here we go!"

We slowly inched backward until we faced north and he gunned it. I tried to hold on to the plastic of the seat, but when we lurched forward, I instinctively gripped Guillem's waist. He glanced over his right shoulder and said something, but it was lost in the road's rumble.

I was wary of the cars in Barcelona, but the mopeds, motos, scooters, and motorcycles that dominated the streets were entirely different beasts. They didn't seem to obey any rules as they hopped curbs, hurtling toward you down the middle of the sidewalk. Women wearing skimpy skirts and high heels weaved through cars to mark their spot at the front of the pack.

Then, seconds before the light turned green, they'd zoom by you, ignoring crosswalks, crouched for sudden impact. Now I was one of them.

I tried to remember if I was supposed to lean in for the turn, or worried that, if I slouched the wrong way, we'd suddenly lose control and plow through the people in front of us. My hands on Guillem's waist, I felt that erotic thrill of being nuzzled against a man on a machine. At the red light, I would make space between Guillem and myself, and he leaned back. "Move with me," he explained. "Or you might make me fall over." He gunned the engine, and I gripped his hips harder.

When we made it to the theater, intact, he told me I could bring my helmet inside with me. It felt like a badge of honor, proof that I lived here, I wasn't a tourist. Of course, how many tourists would show up opening weekend to see Mamet's *Glengarry Glen Ross* entirely translated into Catalan?

The theater was beautiful, inserted into the agricultural building from the 1929 Expo and, for the purposes of this play, the stage was converted into a "black-box" viewing space. I felt I had already cheated on Guillem: Before he showed up, I read a complete scene-by-scene synopsis of the play, since it had been years since I'd seen the movie. I wanted to at least imagine I knew what was going on as people spat epithets in a foreign tongue.

So as these slimy real estate salesmen tried to swindle people with bogus property in Arizona and Florida, I attempted to fill in blanks. Somehow Mamet's Chicago setting wasn't American enough, so the designers had created an abstract Texas-like terrain with a big cactus next to a glass cube that represented Chop Suey, the Chinese restaurant where the first act's action takes place. As the cube turned slowly on a circular dais, I glanced at Guillem who was concentrating on the subtleties of the actors' deliveries. He caught my eye and leaned over and whispered, "Do you hate me?" thinking that I was despairing over the difficulty of the opaque verbal barrage.

True, I had no clue what they were saying—except for a few *joders* (fucks), *putas* (bitch/whores), and some nicely punctuated *merdas* (shits)—until a strange interlude in which all the characters suddenly broke out into an English language rock & roll song for a major set change. "This director always has people singing in his plays," Guillem had warned. After the bows, Guillem admitted he was nervous that I was going to come out dazed and confused and once again he asked, "Do you hate me?" apologetically.

"No, I don't hate you," I said. "I'm so happy. This is one of the best nights I've had since moving to Barcelona. Plus, I learned all sorts of new Catalan cuss words."

"Well, actually Catalan doesn't have enough coarse language, so they have to use Spanish words when they want to curse," he explained. "Catalan is too refined. It's why I like having sex in Spanish. It's sexier. But fucking in English is the best."

Seeing my confusion, he went on to explain. "There's nothing sexy to say, nothing *fuerte*, very strong, in Catalan. It's all a little weak. But telling a guy, 'I want to fuck,' that's the best. Fuck is the best English word, sometimes it's the only one that works."

I laughed and agreed, filing away that bit of intel. I remembered how awkward Spanish still felt on my tongue, making me feel like an impostor when I tried to deploy it during an intimate moment.

"There was one word I didn't understand," I said, slightly changing the subject. "And they said it like a thousand times. Oh-stee-ya?"

"Ah, you did learn the queen of all curse words," he said and smiled. "*Ostia*. It's the Spanish word for the communion wafer? We use it like damn. It's like taking the Lord's name in vain."

Part of me felt guilty for having such a great evening without Patricio, so we called him and told him to meet us at a bar in the Raval area. Guillem and I hopped on his moto and headed off to the Merry Ant, a sort of speakeasy where we had to know the correct, unmarked door and then a secret knock. I was worried that Patricio might decide he didn't want to join, but I was glad when he showed up, and I threw my arms around him, relieved that he didn't seem mad after my date night without him. We ordered Estrellas, the weak Spanish beer I'd resigned myself to, and the three of us talked about books, theater, movies, boyfriends. It was the type of casual hanging out I'd been craving the entire time in Spain, and I'd finally found it. Although I felt the intense attraction to him, I vowed to make Guillem my friend and not screw it up by screwing him. I didn't want to lose my one Catalan friend.

I showed up around nine-thirty for dinner and a movie. Guillem was still on his healthy kick and had prepared a simple, yet tasty meal: a spinach salad with sunflower seeds and golden pasas (the word sounded so much better than raisins), followed by arroz con setas (rice with mushrooms), and a big salmon steak in a soy-sauce glaze. I had picked up a nice bottle of Spanish red—"Any Crianza will do," Guillem had instructed since I confessed I was nervous I'd make a poor wine selection—to get us lubricated for our night in.

He'd invited me over after I'd gushed about *Hedwig and the Angry Inch*, the indie film about a transgender rock & roll troubadour searching for love. He'd never seen it, and I'd brought the DVD to Spain with me but couldn't watch it on our player due to regional restrictions. Guillem, who was obsessed with American pop culture, had a machine that could read the American format. So we made a date.

We'd invited Patricio to join us, but he'd already tired of my preoccupation with the film, which he'd bought me as a birthday gift, and begged off, preferring to stay home alone. It felt sophisticated to be dining together at Guillem's table, since Patricio and I had transformed our dining table into a desk and ended up eating our meals in front of the TV most nights. After eating, we sat together on Guillem's small sofa and watched the film with English subtitles for extra language reinforcement. I resisted singing along to the songs I knew by heart and glanced over to notice if Guillem was enjoying himself. The awkwardness of the situation hit me: This definitely felt like a date.

Although Patricio and I had easily agreed upon our own version of an open relationship, it meant we had sex with other men, not romantic flings. Our rules were fairly basic: 1. no sleepovers; 2. no repeats; 3. be honest and tell one another everything. The idea was to curb the possibility of emotional attachments. Having an affair wasn't what we desired, so dating was definitely off the table. Although the movie watching was intended as a friendly get together, I now wondered if it was an excuse so we could easily fall into one another's arms. Plus, Guillem was clearly boyfriend material. But I already had a boyfriend. I wasn't looking for another.

The truth is, I'm a romantic. Although many people would claim the opposite because I can be blunt and critical—and I believed their assertions for years, convincing me that I didn't have a romantic bone in my body—I'm a sucker for a great love story. The trouble was I didn't believe in the cheeseball stuff found in most pop songs or what Hollywood tried to sell us.

The *Hedwig* plot, loosely adapted from Plato, was that we had another half and were searching for that part to make us whole again, a concept I'd romanticized from an early age. I remember in adolescence saying I didn't care if it was a man or a woman—I wanted to find the person that "understood" me. That was my thirteen-year-old way to articulate the idea of a soulmate. And through the years I'd tried, unsuccessfully, to jam myself together with someone even when that fit wasn't there. It's an ongoing, solitary crusade for billions: How do we join with our other half, and how do we know when we found that person?

With Patricio, I felt like I'd finally found that person. I was too self-conscious to use the term soulmate, but when I learned the Spanish word for it, *media naranja*, I understood it. A half of an orange: The phrase sounded strange, but I identified with the image of two juicy halves that come together but also function as separate parts—that should be squeezed and enjoyed.

I felt guilty. I was already thinking how I'd explain to Patricio that it was something less than a date when I got home. I didn't want him to think Guillem was trying to seduce me since that could mean I'd lose the only friend I'd made since moving here.

Guillem must have felt something too because, when we paused the film for a bathroom break and a refill of Rioja, he returned, saying, "You know, when we write soap opera scripts, we have this term we use. We call it URST."

"URST?" I thought I'd misunderstood him. He spoke English fluidly, with a sexy accent and enough Britishisms to make it sound incorruptible. "What's that?"

"When we have a scene between characters that have some chemistry, we use the English acronym: URST. It stands for Un-Resolved Sexual Tension."

"Hmm," I replied, unsure what I was supposed say. "That's fun. An interesting concept."

"So?" he said. "I think there's some URST between us, don't you?"

"I don't know," I said and laughed, trying to defuse the situation. Part of me was thrilled that he found me attractive, especially since he was a total catch, but I tried to play naïve, not sure if this sort of seduction fit into my relationship rules or was somehow outside the boundaries. If I pretended it wasn't true, maybe that could get me off the hook. "I guess so. Sure. I think you're great."

I wasn't sure what I should do. If he made a move, would I stop him? But I knew I shouldn't be the aggressive one. Playing stupid, a passive player to someone else's wishes, seemed like my best defense.

"Well, I thought I'd get it out," Guillem said, picking up the remote.

"Want to finish the movie?" I asked, not sure if I'd ruined the mood.

He pushed play and it resumed. I'd already watched the film a dozen times, but I couldn't focus on the familiar story. I imagined a director reading our night's script, taking a red pen and marking it everywhere. It would be bloody with URST.

I'd confessed the night's sexual tension to Patricio, and he wasn't surprised. "Well, why didn't you get it over with then?" he asked.

"I don't know," I said. "I guess I thought maybe you'd be mad? That maybe it was against the rules?" I knew he wouldn't kick me to the curb over such an indiscretion, but what if he forbade me from seeing Guillem again? I wasn't willing to lose my first friend in a foreign place.

"Nah," he said. "He's hot, but I'm not worried."

I was anxious though: That once this particular URST was satisfied, perhaps Guillem might not find me as interesting. What if it was that unresolvedness that was keeping us on friendly terms?

I'd been telling Guillem that I wanted to repay the dinner by inviting him to a meal at our place, so I returned the favor by offering to create a big curry stir fry, something outside his comfort zone. "Catalans don't like spicy, don't make it spicy," he urged. I promised I wouldn't scorch his sensitive palate—but I did want to push his boundaries.

I chose a night that I thought would work for the three of us, but then Patricio reminded me he had a dinner with a colleague visiting from the States. "Do you want me to join?" I asked. "I could cancel."

"No, you'd probably be bored. You and Guillem have dinner," he said. "I won't be late."

Guillem brought the wine, and I tried to memorize the labels, so I knew the best bottles to purchase next time. He complained the food was still spicy, and I teased him that he was a wimp. We got toasted soon enough, and when we curled up on the love seat, I told him, "Bésame." I said it in Spanish, partly as a provocation, partly because it didn't seems as real in a foreign tongue. The words still worked, and he did. He kissed me.

I felt the shock of the lip contact, that powerful surge of passion that comes with finally getting the thing that you've imagined and withheld far longer than normal. Luckily, I liked kissing Guillem. We fit together and our arms were around one another. We stood up and I started pulling his shirt over his head. We giggled as we unbuckled and pulled at one another's clothes. This felt right. We were soon naked on the bed, squeezing each other and shivering in anticipation.

Then I heard the door lock click.

"Shit!" I said.

"¿Qué?"

"Shhh. It's Patricio."

"Hey, are you there?" Patricio called from the front of the apartment. It was a small space so I knew in a few more steps he'd see us sprawled naked together on the bed.

"Oh, well, I guess you guys got that over with," he said as he reached the wide-open room. "Get up and get dressed. Let's go out—I want a drink." He laughed and left us there as we scrambled to get our clothes. We laughed too, realizing how stupid we must look, naked on the bed, like two children caught stealing a cookie. Still feeling awkward and silly, I tried to smooth things over.

"Sorry we got interrupted so soon," I apologized to Guillem. "I didn't know. But…"

"Is everything okay?" he asked.

"Yes, I think so."

Although I thought I had made up my mind not to act on the URST, part of me wanted to get it over with. It seemed our roles were already written, and, luckily, we were in a romantic comedy, not a Lifetime television drama. Now that it was over, we could finally be friends.

The fact is, over the years I've had an intimate naked moment with most of my good friends—and many gay men I know share a similar bond. After I met Patricio, I've spent the next fifteen years figuring out how our puzzle pieces fit together, but it doesn't mean that one doesn't remain curious about the curves and hidden places of others. Those encounters with other men aren't just a notch in the belt—rather it's proof: No, we don't fit together in that way; that was fun, let's move on. We may understand it, but it can make for awkward moments at a dinner party.

When a straight woman asks gay guys how they met, we hem and haw, trying to figure out a palatable explanation if we hadn't already come up with some sort of euphemistic backstory. Unlike many heterosexual groupings, where I've seen men awkwardly try to talk to female friends, the URST thick in the room, many of us have managed to neutralize that strain on familiarity to get closer. "We hooked up," was the easiest rejoinder. "And now we're the best of friends."

# Whatever Makes You Happy

## TROY ERNEST HILL

**A**t least I know I'm not sweating from low blood sugar because it's hot as hell by eleven in the AM. Now I'm not a church guy, but at least they've got air-conditioning in those places, but my granddaughter insisted on having the damn wedding outside in the backyard of some old restaurant in July. I don't really mean the wedding is damned. I'm happy for her—I really am, even if the guy is black, but I don't mind that either. I don't. They all think I do. They all assume this and that about how I think, but I like Leroy just fine. In fact, I respect the black men for not being intimidated by a woman with curves, like Barb, the way all these neutered white boys seem to be. They can't be happy unless the girl is nothing but a stick, like some kid—can't say what all that's about, but what I am saying is I sure am happy for Barb and Leroy. I just don't like the way my sweat is soaking through my undershirt and pooling in my rented shiny black shoes. I hope Barb doesn't sweat through her dress—that would make for a sour picture for the mantle. We Jacksons do that way—sweat like nobody's business. But all in all, the weather's not what really matters, I keep telling myself. What matters is giving Barb away. My girl.

My own daughter, Lisa, she passed before I had the chance to do it for her. Didn't even get to see my son Henry married since he damned eloped. And he's not here to see Barb off because twelve years into his marriage he disappeared like Houdini, except there was no magic in it. Just pain. A great big old empty place and questions we'll never answer. That little shit.

Raised our grandkids Barb and Jimbo like our own—me and Sheila did. Probably did a better job of it, too, than we did—or I did anyway—with Henry and Lisa. Less stress later in life. Not so much pressure, trying to make ends meet, paying off the loan on the truck and equipment, paying the mortgage, you name it. Plus I guess you mellow with age—not that I'm inclined in the ways of the hippies, but mellow like a fine wine or a barrel-aged scotch, I'd like to think.

I walk the grounds here to get the lay of the land, big old house from the 1920s turned restaurant turned what they call an event space—somebody's making a few bucks is what I call it. A couple big old oaks out front, parking on the side, and a trim lawn in the back with a variety of flowers along the edges. They got roses—red, white, and pink, yellow iris, something Sheila used to grow called gooseneck, all shapes, sizes, and colors of bloom. Guess you'd better if you want people paying to have their wedding at the place.

A few folks are already sitting in the rows of white chairs they've got set up back here facing the podium that stands in front of a white lattice kind of wall stand. Mostly family at this point, but a few other guests are starting to arrive. Car doors slamming, hushed talk, couples quietly wrapping up the bickering that got started on the way, kids pouting about being dressed up, people picking up the programs off the seats to use as fans. I'm gonna bet Barb and Leroy are inside the house, lucky bastards, each with their own rooms upstairs to get dressed in. Don't figure this old house has central air, but you can see the window units sticking their butts out up there, almost shaking they're cranked so high.

I spy Jimbo, sitting over there with somebody I'm going to guess is his date, the two of them sitting there reading on their screens, silent and still with their noses pointed down like scholars in a library. He's something else, let me tell you. Last time I seen him he had this Edwardian kind of twirly mustache, coming off his face it was so long and twisted into points at the end. He tells me the thing is some kind of a joke. I'm saying, hold on a minute, how can something on your body—on your face, that you put there on purpose, be a joke? I just don't get it. But then he shows up at the rehearsal dinner last night, hadn't seen him in a good year or two, and he's got this long, untrimmed beard like some character from Appalachia.

So I'm thinking, the joke had to go further and further to stay funny, I guess. So I says to him, I say, "Hey, Jimbo, good one. Bet your keeping 'em laughing with that thing." I stroke my chin to show I'm talking about the beard. And wouldn't you know, he rolls his eyes like I'm the one with a few screws hanging loose and tells me, "No, Pupa. The mustache was ironic. My beard is sincere."

These kids, I'm telling you. I can't make heads or tails out of 'em. I would've thought these guys, the ones who go in for each other, I'd a thought they'd go for a real clean look, more on the girly side, you know? But I guess it makes sense that at least one in a couple would be more like a man. His friend there sure looks like a girl. I'm not trying to be smart, I'm just describing what looks like what. I wonder, does that mean Jimbo's the one who—I don't want to think about that. I really don't.

All these friends of Barb's and Leroy's seem to think it's perfectly all right—I mean Jimbo and all. Nobody seems to care these days, and so I'm glad he's got it like that in the world instead of what it used to be. I saw a program about it on television. Used to be torture for these guys. Stay underground. Run away from your family. Live in some rundown part of a city to hide. Or do it on the sly. I know it's not easy for 'em still, in a lot of ways, but it sure has gotten easier and in a way—and I *mean* in a way— ain't it better than having to prove every damn day that you're not? That you're a real man—that you never thought for a second about grabbing your buddy's butt in the locker room shower? And think about not having to deal with the women. I was lucky with Sheila, lucky as hell—I'm not saying I wasn't, but being in one of these couples where the other one's got the same stuff as you—wouldn't that be just like hanging out with your best friend? Maybe it's not, but think, too, about all the money'd you'd save. I know they're all getting married now and adopting or jumping through whatever other kind of hoops so they can have kids of their own, but hell, so many of us got married and had the first one because the thing just happened—you hadn't planned on it—and then sure—what the hell—of course you said that's what you wanted all along and that's what the plan was anyway, but if you never had it happen by mistake and had to go to a whole bunch of trouble to get the kids, well, the reality is that in plenty of cases it just wouldn't've happened. I'm not saying I didn't love my son and daughter, God rest her soul, but I run some quick numbers through my head and see how I could've retired at fifty-five, easy, if it hadn't been for the kids. Instead I worked like a dog till sixty-seven. Made good money, too, plumbing up a storm. That's right, I wasn't one of these college kids with a fancy degree, but I made my way. Always good at taking things apart and putting 'em back together. Worked construction till this fellow took me on and let me learn the plumbing trade. Studied the books. Got certified. Not always pretty, but plenty of work and more and more these young people can't even screw in a light bulb on their own without calling somebody to come out and do it for 'em. Fine with me—I'll fix you right up and send you the bill.

Jimbo. I saunter on down the aisle to say hello. I get to where he's sitting and I'm standing there while he and that friend of his are so lost in their little computer phones they don't even look up till I finally shout, "Jimbo, earth to Jimbo!" He looks up like I've just yelled something nasty in the middle of a funeral. I hold out my hand for a shake, and Jimbo gives me that look of his like I'm such an old fogey, uptight, formal, you know, because I'm trying to shake a man's hand. Well, that's just how I was raised and how I raised his father before him and how I tried to raise him, too, but now days you gotta hug with this generation. I thought at first it was just Jimbo being that way, but they all do it. Leroy, Barb's friends, male and female, hugs all around. The regular guys hug Jimbo, each other, everybody gets a hug, a half-hearted hug, sure, but a hug. I'm telling you if I decide I'm going to extend my hand, you'll find there's more in my handshake, in the look I'll give your eye, than in any of these weakling pat-on-the-back hugs. Sometimes I think they do it so they don't have to look you in the eye. They act like everybody's their friend, and I guess they are, but you just wonder how far it goes if you ever stop and watch how they act. It's like they don't care to know who and what you are. It's just hugs and jokes and rolling eyes all day long.

I think I always kind of knew about Jimbo—well, since he was about ten or so. We were out on the boat fishing. It was when Sheila and I tried living in Florida for a few years after I retired and had a boat and trailer and the whole nine yards. Used to put that sucker in the water at the landing down passed the public beach and stay out all day. We'd catch 'em all right, the fish—flounder, sheephead, black drum, you name it—even caught a young turtle once, but Sheila slipped him back in when I was looking the other way. She didn't want to hurt the damn thing, but I'd been in Korea and always remembered this turtle soup I had one night out on the town, but Sheila wouldn't hear of it. Was a cute little turtle, after all. Anyway, I'd fish just about every day back then—saved a fortune on groceries, too—dinner right out of the sea, you see. Jimbo and Barb liked going out, too, for a while—for a few years, before they got to be teenagers and wanted to be running around with their friends day and night.

One time we were out there and Jimbo was about just up to my chest in height, and he had this way of being short that caught your eye. I mean he was just a kid, but there was something about the way he stood with the fishing pole, too big for him, the end nudged into himself right around his waist there, the way he balanced himself, legs spread wider than his shoulders, riding the boat like a surfboard, afternoon sun streaking through his dirty blond hair—made more blond by his days in the ocean and pool—loved the water, that kid—that was just so damned cute. Now I know all kids are cute enough—well, maybe not all, but at least the ones who're your relations. But there was a way about Jimbo—I don't know—made people want to tousle his hair—coaches, teachers, friends' moms and dads—everybody. Whatever it was struck me that day and gave me this feeling I couldn't quite put into words but knew in my gut something was going on that well, you know, he had something in him that made him not all the way like a boy exactly. I couldn't even put it into words in my own head to think outright, much less say it, but there was something about looking at him that day that gave me the idea he was that way.

I've sometimes wondered if that's where my son went when he disappeared. Went off and left his family so he could be that way somewhere. Not that I ever got the same feeling with him as I did that day on the boat with Jimbo, but I was so uptight back then when I was raising Henry, worried about money and things that I can't say I would've noticed one way or another. I don't know. I can't say why he up and left his kids to fend for themselves with no momma—she had the cancer and passed a couple years before he took off. That's why I'm happy the world took a change about it all, so Jimbo won't have to go and disappear. All right out in the open these days.

And it's strange to admit, but for that one afternoon—that day on the boat, I could understand that feeling—had a feeling for him—Jimbo. I'm ashamed to say it, but it's true. I didn't do anything, that's not what I'm saying. I'm not that kind of man. There were just those few hours when something about the way he stood there, short and I'm telling you someway flirtatious, twinkle in his eye, the water lapping against the boat, the golden sunlight, there was some kind of line between us, some kind of tug like when a fish starts to nibble on your bait. I think he felt it, too. And then thank god he grew tall and gangly and I never felt that thing again.

So, here I am holding out my hand for a shake and Jimbo takes a breath, like, oh crap, now I'm going to have to talk, puts his little electronic machine in his pocket, and stands up. He gives me one of those half-ass hugs and says, "Hi, Pupa, this is my friend, Terry."

He points with his thumb at the kid and my head is kind of spinning cause my brain can't figure whether Terry is a boy or girl. It's just what the brain does, wants to know what it's looking at, so I'm staring at this kid and holding out my hand, and say, "Jim Jackson, how do you do?"

The light brown head of hair is short as mine in the army. The shirt and bow tie tell you one thing, but then I notice the long black skirt as Terry stands up and slides this small, smooth hand into mine, thin lips curling up a little. So I figure, well, Jimbo's got the beard and this one wears the skirt, so I'm guessing that's how it works and say, "Very nice to meet you, Terry. Glad to see Jimbo here is finally settling down."

The two of them look at each other with that sarcastic smile these kids always got. Jimbo says, "We're not dating or anything, Pupa. Terry's just a friend. I met them in school and when they moved to the city and needed a place to live, my roommate had just moved out, so they moved in."

I'm looking around for Terry's date or friend or what. "So how many you got living in that little apartment?" I look at Terry, "I saw the place couple years back. Hardly big enough for one person, let alone a whole group."

Terry's voice comes out awful lot like a girl's. "It's just the two of us. Jim has the bedroom, and I set up camp in what's supposed to be the living room. It's a little tight, but we're doing okay."

I'm confused. I look at Jimbo and say, "Oh. I thought you said…" I look back at Terry, "I'm just getting a little mixed up in my old age."

Jimbo gets that smart look on his face, glances at Terry and then back at me. "'They' is Terry's PPPN, preferred personal pronoun. Terry is gender neutral."

I know I'm an old fart, but I figure that means hermaphrodite. I put my hand on Terry's shoulder and say, "Hey, you can't help with what you're born with. Lots of famous people in history got both sets of equipment. No reason to let it hold you back."

Terry shakes her head a little and says real casual, like we were talking about the weather, "It's okay, Mr. Jackson. My grandparents are pretty weirded out by the whole thing, too, but the transgender movement is really helping more of us come forward—those of us in the middle of the gender spectrum. I was born biologically female, I just don't necessarily identify that way, though I don't identify necessarily as male either."

Jim looks like he's going to laugh. I'm pretty sure at me. I say, "Well, it sure is nice meeting you. I think I'm going to try and get a cold drink before the ceremony gets underway."

Terry says it's nice meeting me, too, and I'm still trying to figure out how one person can be a "they."

I trek back up the aisle and through the yard and take the backdoor into the house where I meet the cool air inside with a big sigh of relief and cozy on up to the bar where a man in a tuxedo shirt and vest is already setting up.

"Could I trouble you for a glass of ice water, sir?"

He looks busy and bothered but then takes a gander at me and decides to have mercy on the sweaty old man.

"Sure thing. Hot out there, huh?" He scoops ice with a metal tool, slides the frozen cubes into a pint glass, and fills it to the brim with H2O. Then he goes back to pulling bottles of champagne out of boxes to chill. He looks like a pretty regular guy, in his thirties or so, with the bald spot coming. Guy could stand to lose a few pounds, but who am I to talk—I've been carrying this truck tire around my waist for years. But what I'm wondering is, how do you know what anybody is any more?

Guy says, "Know the happy couple?"

I press the cool glass against my cheek. "Sure do. Giving away my grand-daughter today."

He gives me a look in the eye, real solid like. "Nice." And holds out a hand for me to shake.

I like this guy. I say, "Tell me something."

"Okay."

"You ever heard of being gender neutral?"

The guy laughs. "Didn't expect that would be the question."

"No?"

He shakes his head and sets a case of beer on the bar—then starts sticking bottles into a bucket of ice. "I guess that's one of these transsexuals?"

"I don't know if it's exactly the same. It's like they're not one or the other. In my mind it's like a hermaphrodite, but then, no, it's more like instead of having both, they've got neither—but I couldn't really say. I'm too old to get what these kids are telling me. All seems like a big joke on me."

The guy kind of chuckles and says, "Hey, you want a beer or something?"

I tell him I'd better hold off and ask for the men's room, and he points me in the right direction.

This old house has got good bones, windows with thick wood molding, wide plank floors, brass doorknobs, likely from the 1890s—bet they had an outhouse back in the day and had to retrofit indoor plumbing. Seen some jobs like that in my day.

Finally get around to a bathroom they've got tucked under the front stairwell, only to find some lady in there filling up little vases of flowers. I ask her where another men's room is, and she ignores me—probably don't speak English.

I go hunting for another, down some other stairs that lead to the basement—strike out in one direction, then head back in the other, turn a corner and just about urinate my pants. There's Barb in her white dress, kissing some fellow, a white man, not her fiancé, who's got one hand on the back of her head and one wrapped around her waist. And I mean a real kiss. French. I stand, petrified. They don't know I'm there. My jaw is hanging so low you could stick a fist in my mouth, and come to think of it, feels like someone's punched me, but more like in the gut than the kisser.

I know I should say something. Something like, "What the hell do you think you're doing?" But nothing comes out. I'm cowed. Confused. And I still need to pee. I back up, put it in reverse, slip back around the corner and creep up the stairs like a kid who's just spied on his parents.

Back on the main floor I see the flower lady's gone off somewhere, so I go in and have a seat, even though nature doesn't call that way. My sweat has turned cold in the AC, and I feel a little sick and disloyal, but I figure I've got to tell Leroy. He's got a right to know about this before he ties the knot. Or do I speak to Barb first? This is not the chat I expected to have today of all days.

I finish my business and wash up. I go back through the house and see the bartender. He says, "Find everything all right?"

I don't know how to answer. I just say, "You know where the groom's party is?"

His lips turn down. "Can't say for sure, but I think they're all upstairs getting dressed."

"Thank you kindly."

I go to the front of the house to take the stairs to the second floor, all polished carved dark-wood railing and a strip of oriental-style rug running down the middle. Look up and see the back of that white dress disappear around the corner. I pull myself up and up and when I get to the top I peer down a hallway. I'd think the groomsmen would be in a separate area, but in this day and age, they could all be sharing one room for all I know. I come to a door and try to hear what's going on inside. I hear women's laughter when the door flies opens to the look of surprise on some short middle-aged woman's face.

"Can I help you?" Real sassy and rude like I've just wondered in homeless off the street.

"Excuse me, ma'am, I'm looking for the bride and groom."

I see Barb at a mirror fixing her hair, and all I can think about is how it got mussed by that fellow in the basement. She can hear it's me and yells, "Pupa, the boys are down the hall, but what do you need? We've got to get started in about two minutes."

I can see I'm not getting a private moment with her until we walk down the aisle. "I, uh, thought I should have a little chat with Leroy. Man to man."

"Please make it quick."

The lady says, "Real quick," and shuts the door right in my face.

I shuffle on down the hall till I hear men's voices and go through a door. I'm determined and don't even knock. There's Leroy, wiry and tall as a bean stalk, with his best man and two other fellows, one of whom is the guy from the basement, all standing in a circle and holding out glasses for a toast. They all look over at me.

"Mr. Jackson!" Leroy says with all the warmth in the world, just about cracking my heart into two or three pieces, "Come over here and grab a glass."

"No. No, there's no time."

"Sure there is. Come on, now."

His best man goes over to a bureau and pours some whiskey into a glass and holds it out for me. What can I do but oblige? The fellow from the basement smiles at me with these beady blue eyes that just about make me sick to my stomach. He says, "To Leroy and Barb." I can't believe he calls her Barb. We all clink glasses and drink up, and then I tap Leroy and say, "Can I have a word?"

"Sure thing, Mr. J." he says.

I walk to one corner of the room and he follows. I turn my back to the others and put a hand on Leroy's shoulder and pull him close so no one else will hear. I say, "That fellow over there. The white one."

"Steven?"

"Okay, Steven. I think I should tell you something about him. This ain't easy for me to say."

Leroy looks down at me with his brow all wrinkled with concern, but more like for me than for himself.

There's a knock at the door and that short woman pops her head in. "It's go time. Groomsmen make a beeline for the altar. Mr. Jackson, you come with me."

I look at Leroy, his eyes gone wide and excited—giddy as a kid on Christmas morning.

I say, "Hold on just one minute."

That bulldog of a woman shouts, "Not one second more. I mean it. Groomsmen downstairs and out back this instant."

Leroy puts a hand on my back. "Can it wait until the reception? I want to hear what you have to say, but I don't want to get on this one's bad list." He gestures toward the lady with his head, and one of the other fellows appears out of nowhere with a camera and snaps a shot of me and the happy groom. Then Leroy pats my back and strides off clacking his shoes across the wood floor before I have a chance to protest. They all file out while that woman stands with her arms akimbo, staring me down. "Let's go, Jackson."

The planner, they call her. She's better than some of the sergeants I had in the army. Usually I would appreciate her running a tight ship, but everything's moving too fast for me to put a stop to it. She takes me by the arm and walks me down the hall, and I say as we pass the bridal room, "Can't I have a word with my granddaughter?"

She tugs me along to the stairs. "Not at the moment. She's got her final touches to make while I get you situated." Like I'm a child.

"But it'll just take a minute."

"You don't have another minute. Keep walking. One foot after the other."

We make our way outside the house and approach the back row of chairs. Music's coming through speakers connected to a keyboard played by a guy standing off to one side in a white tux. The groomsmen are making their way down the aisle, each one paired up with bridesmaid in pink. The lady's got me perched at the back and tells me to stay put. Leroy's down front with a minister of some kind holding a Bible. The congregation is all standing up, and once the wedding party's set in place, they all turn back to look at me, a bead of sweat sliding down the side of my ruddy skinned head.

Barb shows up quick and takes my arm with a grateful smile. She likely thinks my troubled expression is emotion due to the supposedly auspicious occasion. I look her in the eye and see no remorse, no complication. I tell her, straight, "I saw you with that fellow in the basement, Barb. Why the hell are you getting married if you're involved with another man?"

The blood drains out of her cheeks behind that grin, which she manages to hold in place, knowing all eyes are on her. She pulls me in close and talks fast. "I really don't want to have this conversation right now, Pupa. I'm sorry you had to see that, but Leroy knows all about it. He and I are completely honest about everything. That's what's so great about our friendship and why we're a few seconds away from *getting married.*" She pulls away a little and smiles big and hollow, showing her teeth for the crowd.

My head is swirling. Leroy knows? I lean down to keep it quiet. "Friendship? You call what you've got with your husband *a friendship*, and you've got the same kind of so-called friendship with other men?"

Folks are starting to get antsy. The planner lady is behind us shout-whispering, "Go, go, go!"

"It's not the same, and Leroy and I *are* best friends. Isn't that best for the long haul? And can we please start walking now?"

Barb and I take a step together and then another and I whisper into her ear, "And you both let the other run around?"

She raises her eyebrows and nods like a sweet little girl, like she was admitting to having an extra piece of cake. She squeezes my arm and makes eyes toward Leroy down by the altar.

I says, "Thank God Sheila didn't live to see this day."

Barb looks down, so sad.

I can't help myself. I stop in my tracks. I says, "I just thought we raised you better than that."

Barb looks up at me, and a tear drops onto her cheek. She gets on her tiptoes and says into my ear, "You raised me to be honest, and that's what I like about Leroy. He's honest, too. We're completely honest with one another."

People's smiles are starting to melt. I see some wringing hands. Leroy's squinting and biting his upper lip with concern. Barb looks at me, real determined, and takes a step forward. Part of me doesn't want to budge, but that tear's softened my outrage. I follow in kind, leaning down to speak into her ear as we make our way.

"Why don't you marry the other one, if he's the one you want?"

She kind of chuckles and says, "It would never work." A little girl waves at Barb, and she waves back with one hand as she whispers, "We're great for a few hours but then things blow up. It's a small-dose kind of thing."

I'm feeling more than a little sick to my stomach, but we're about halfway down the aisle, and I've got to get this straight before the nuptials take place, despite the fact that a few people are giving us funny looks. I whisper back, "Passion is a good thing. Not the easiest, but if you feel that way—well, nothing great comes easy." I hope people in the crowd assume I'm sharing some precious reminiscence. If they only knew.

Barb beams down the aisle at her fiancé and says, "Trust me. Leroy and I are much better suited for marriage."

We take a few steps in silence. She says, "I understand if you don't get it, but I wish you could still be happy for us."

We're almost at the front. I want to tell her I am, but I can't get the words out.

She stops, stretches her neck, and stands on her tippy-toes again to kiss me on the cheek. I let her arm go, and she steps up to the altar.

I turn back to go to my seat. I'm sure all the folks in the crowd are thinking how sweet it is that the old man has tears in his eyes—crying at his granddaughter's wedding. But it's not what they think. I'm crying for this generation. Crying for me. Crying for a world I don't understand. Don't fit into. Crying from confusion, disgust. Disorientation. Crying to think about what Sheila would've thought and grateful she doesn't have to know about it.

I find my seat there on the front row, and Leroy's mother pats my thigh. They're nice people, and I wonder how much they know about this free-for-all marriage. Leroy's father leans forward and gives me a grinning nod. I feel pretty woozy and realize I forgot to take my insulin shot, and my sugar's probably spiked up like the price of gasoline.

There's Leroy up there vowing and Barb up there vowing and all the while another man standing up there is sleeping with the bride who has the audacity to be in a white dress and they all know it and think it's perfectly fine. Who knows? Maybe Leroy's got something going with one of the bridesmaids—or a groomsman for all I know in this day and age.

I can't recall most of the ceremony—could be due to my sugar or to my state of mind, but somehow we get to the end of the show and Leroy kisses Barb and everyone hoots and hollers, and all I can think is, well, that's a farce if there ever was one—as if this is the first kiss that's ever been exchanged between these two, not to mention the rest of the wedding party. I'm sweating buckets and instead of waiting to take the long slow walk back up the aisle with all the helloes that'll be required, I explain to Mr. and Mrs. Winn that I've got to get to my medicine and make my way around the outside edge of the seats.

Inside the blast of air-conditioning is like jumping into an icy pond. I make a beeline for that bathroom and lock up tight so I can inject myself. My hyperglycemia crashes down, and I'm sweating fresh and feeling faint, now from low blood sugar. I sit there taking a breather and hear through the door the place start filling up with talk and the clank of glasses. Somebody knocks. "Just a minute," I say. I hear my voice come out weary and broken, and I wonder how I'm going to face this crowd with a smile on my face. I pull myself up off the toilet and wash my face with cool water. I pat myself dry with paper towels. I steady myself with the thought of a gin and tonic and open the door, resolved to not make Barb feel any worse that I've done already, even if I can't understand what she's about.

The bartender recognizes me and asks what I want even though a few others were there before me. I order, and he pours from a bottle and shoots from the soda gun all at once, pops a lime sliver onto the side of the glass, and hands it right over.

I says, "You're a life saver."

He says, "Any time, my friend."

I thank the Lord for small mercies.

I find Jimbo and pull him aside. Of all people, he's the last one I can expect to have any sympathy for my view—ain't nobody as righteous and judgmental as one of these bohemians—but he's all I've got at this point. Barb's over by the door greeting everyone as they come in. She looks at me and waves, and I want to wave back, but I stand frozen like an idiot, and by the time I get my arm to move, her smile's already fallen and she's turned to speak to one of Leroy's relations.

I tug Jimbo's sleeve so he'll lean down a little and I can talk through his bushy beard into his ear. "Barb's seeing one of the groomsmen. And it turns out Leroy knows all about it and doesn't give a rat's behind."

"Which one?" He says and looks around for them.

"Is that all you care about?"

"I thought the whole poly thing was just in the queer community, but apparently straights are getting into it, too. I'm impressed with Barb—surprised. Good for them." He takes a sip from his wine glass, like someone's just proposed him a toast.

I inquire, "Poly thing?"

"The idea that there isn't this one true love in life. It doesn't make sense. We're attracted to lots of people. Why should anyone be constrained to just one? It isn't realistic." He says it like he's having to explain how to tie a shoe to a moron.

"I can tell you from experience there's a lot to intimacy with just one person," I says, trying not to sound too high on my horse. "It's a deeper relationship. It just is."

He says right out loud, so just about anybody can hear, "But why can't you just be honest about being attracted to other people, even if you love someone and live with them and have a life together?"

I say, low enough to keep it private, "There's no law says you gotta fulfill every single urge you ever get."

"But why not? As long as everything is between consenting adults, no one has to have their feelings hurt."

"But it comes between people. I'm telling you, it just does." I look around wondering who can hear us and see that Steven fellow talking to a petite woman and a blond freckled boy around eight years old across the room. I lean into Jimbo. "That's him."

"Where?"

"Over by the window with that woman and child."

"Oh, Steven Brady. That's his wife Joyce and their son, I forget his name."

"He's married, too? Good Lord." I take a sip of my drink and still feel a little light-headed.

Jimbo swats his long bangs back. "Didn't you have those wife-swapping key parties in the seventies? It's the same thing."

"No, I did not, thank you very much."

"And you never slept with anyone other than granny?"

Like it's unbelievable, and I can't believe the words "granny" and "slept with" are uttered in the same breath.

"Not while we were married. No."

"Wow." He sort of smirks, and I'd sort of like to smack him. Then his friend appears with beer bottle in hand.

"Pupa and I were just having a conversation about poly-sexual relationships. He and my grandmother were totally monogamous."

Terry nods and says, "Sandy and I are monogamous."

I say, "Is that right?" I'm enjoying the look on Jimbo's face, like his friend just passed gas, and I shake my head at my own bewilderment that my ally turns out to be the skirt and bow-tie phenomenon.

They says, "It's just so much simpler. And she's all I have time for, anyhow, with grad school. And we both want it that way, so…"

I pat they on the shoulder. "Well, good for you two, Terry. That sounds real nice. And this Sandy of yours is a, uh, a neuter, neutral…"

Terry smiles matter-of-fact friendly, like a newscaster. "Sandy is a woman and identifies female. I'm generally attracted to feminine energy."

Though I was feeling a little relief, this last remark's got me reeling again. That combined with my cold sweat and the meds, the look on my face must be something like a ten-car pile-up on the highway.

Terry's kind enough to tap my arm and say, "It's okay, Mr. Jackson, if it's all kind of overwhelming. The truth is we're all a little confused, but maybe that's a good place to grow from. We're all just trying to figure out what it is that makes us happy."

I nod, absently, grateful for the warm allowances but a bit weary on my feet. I manage to hold up my glass and say, "Think I'm going to get another one of these. Thank you, both, for the enlightening conversation."

Jimbo rolls his eyes, and Terry smiles at me a little sweeter, now like a kindergarten teacher.

My bartender friend sees me coming and just about has the drink ready by the time I get up to the bar.

"You're swell," I tell him, and put a few bills in the tip bowl.

"Just doing my job. How's it going out there?"

"It's been a strange day, tell you the truth."

"How so?"

I look at his hand and note the gold wedding band. "Tell me something, if it's not too personal." I lean across the bar—they've taken away the stools to make it easier for folks to get right up to it. "You and your wife…in a one-on-one relationship?"

His eyes get real big. "We'd better be."

"It's just I hear all kinds of stories from my grandkids. They have all these ideas about sleeping around with their friends and strangers and all I can think is no wonder people catch all kinds of diseases. But hey, I'm an old fart." I take a sip of my fresh drink and feel the icy booze roll down my throat.

Bartender laughs and says, "Hey, I'm with you, pal." He opens a beer with a bottle opener screwed into the wall and sets it on the bar for one of the guests. "Say, you all right? You're looking a little worn out, if you don't mind me saying."

Now I'm leaning on the bar so that it's a wonder I don't push it over. "Tell you the truth, I could use a sit down. Seems like this place is packed to the gills, though, not much chance of finding a quiet spot, huh?"

"If you're not too picky, I can get you exclusive access to the walk-in pantry suite." He pulls a single key out from his shirt pocket and places it on the red rubber mat next to a couple empties. "No one but boxes of cranberry juice cocktail to bother you in there."

"You're a real friend. Maybe just for a few minutes or so."

"Just go through those swinging doors and take a right before you get to the kitchen."

I make my way like he tells me and find the small room with shelves on either side full of bottles and cans of this and that and a ratty old two-seater couch against the back wall. It smells like cardboard boxes and that's just fine with me. I plunk down on that little couch—the upholstery ripped here and there and foam popping out. I take a sip of G&T, set the glass on the floor, and let my eyes drift shut.

I think about how I don't get tripped up by my feelings too much, never did. Not that I don't have an urge now and then—some blonde at the hardware store, a waitress working her tip money, customer's kid hanging around, some flirt at a stoplight gives you the eye and gets the old engine revving. But I don't feel the need to pump every gas tank I pass on the highway. I mean, these kids talk like it'd be some kind of tragedy if they don't go wring out the juice of every little feeling they ever had. Not saying I'm some kind of stoic, but you don't have to eat every dessert on the menu just because they all sound good and the fact of the matter is you'll probably feel a hell of a lot better in the long run if you don't.

I wonder what the world's coming to, and then decide to try and not think about it. I don't want to think. I just want to rest. But my mind moves over pictures in my head: Barb and that Steven character, Leroy, the skirt and bow tie, Jimbo's stinking beard. I picture my son Henry and wonder if he ran off so he could find what makes him happy. I think about Sheila and our forty-five years together before she passed.

And then I'm shaking, and I don't know where it comes from. I got tears springing out of my eyes. I'm sitting there with my head in my hands bawling like a baby, and I think, what the hell am I doing in the pantry crying my head off on my granddaughter's wedding day?

And then I hear a little voice. "Hey, mister."

I look up and see that Steven character's boy standing in the doorway. Got a way about him, looks kinda like Jimbo at that age.

"Where's your momma, boy?"

The kid shrugs and pulls the door shut. Says, "I like to hide, too. I used to play at hiding places with my grandpa." He comes over and sits on the couch next to me. Puts a hand on my arm. "Don't be sad, mister." He looks at me, all twinkle-eyed and coy-like. Do kids know what the hell they're doing sometimes?

I think, maybe they're right. Maybe you just do what makes you happy. "Be in the moment" and all that. I turn my head to look at him. "What's your name, kid?"

"Patrick."

"They call me Pupa."

"That's a funny name." He puts his head on my shoulder.

Consenting adults. That's not what he is. He's just a kid for Christ's sake. And what does he want? What do I want? I let my eyes shut again and rest my head against the back of the couch. I feel his little body leaning into mine as he lets his hand fall onto my thigh.

Whatever makes you happy? I'm just not that kind of man.

# Border Guards

## HENRY ALLEY

The sun was rising on a park which we call "Amazon" here. There was a
pooling of mist over the hills, a part of that juncture where the Cas-
cade mountains meet the Coastals. I think they give the park that name
because of the green slough that runs along the wood-chip bike path. The
water is rich with willows and the sound of frogs. Wearing my "Pride" cap
and t-shirt, I had just come over our Iron Butte, through the patterned
shadows from the maples, past the Stone Face, where the shirtless climb-
ers with their magnificent deltoids test their moves. Today one electrician
(I know because his truck was parked right there by the stone) was inch-
ing his way up, with the sun just touching his naked shoulder blades. After
I had plummeted down the hill at a full run, reluctantly leaving him behind me, I entered a Sunday city with the morning light spangled all over
the streets. I saw three bronze spiderwebs in three separate gardens—one
had interstitched three crimson hollyhocks at once.

I was finishing my long run, which was at the start of every week, my
shirt all soaked. The route I chose was truly all over the map, but one I
had clocked several times in my car. I felt very strong—even at sixty-five
years old—a retired judge with part-time literary ambitions—and I knew
that I could have added another five miles if I had wanted, but I was ta-
pering down for the Gay Games ahead—a 10K in Vancouver, B.C. The
park before me, this multi-shaded Amazon, was like a reward for a com-
ing-out process that had taken most of my adult life. First the reward of
the water fountain just under the eaves of the white-stone, green-roofed

public restrooms, and then a quick chance to pee inside. With the sun like a full flower in the sky now, and the temperature rising to seventy degrees, I took my shirt off and wrung it out, just as a gray police car pulled up, with two men inside—and I mean in the front seat. At first I thought they would get on my case for splattering the sidewalk with sweat. One of them took me in—looking at my chest and back in a way that I had learned—and not too long ago—was a "cruise." Now even if I do say so myself, my torso looks good. All of my life (and it has been an unmarried one) I have been blessed with a physique which reminds you of the shirtless man on a pulp fiction cover.

I don't mind being admired, especially with all the memories I have of being hated by some of the people I've sentenced. "I'll get your ass, I'll get your ass," one of them said in court not too long ago, just before I retired. And I'll have to admit that I wouldn't have minded getting my ass "gotten" by a vagrant, this attractive man who belonged to "rough trade," who said that. But right now, visited by troubling thoughts, I felt spooked by these lingering policemen—two of them—in the car (we have the partner system in this town), and ducked into the bathroom, leaving my wet t-shirt on top of my car.

I'd scarcely finished at the urinal and was starting to wash my hands (no soap, as usual) when one of the policemen came in and went to the back booth, even though he had nothing more to do than stand and pee. Despite all the tension that exists between men in this situation, I was moved to washing my hands slowly and taking my time with the paper towels.

"That Pride cap," he said. "I need information." He stood waiting for the basin with the same intent expression. "Can you give me something fast? My partner is waiting."

Outside I could hear the police car still going. It sounded restless.

"What would you like to know?" I asked.

"Is there a place in town besides the bar where I can be proud?"

I observed him, returned the cruise. He was lean and in his late twenties. He looked familiar. "Plenty of places," I answered, "although I haven't checked them all out myself. I'm new to this business as well."

My heart misgave me a little. The moment I realized how attractive, actually beautiful, he was, instantly I went to the suspicion that he wanted an encounter with me now—even with his partner waiting with the car running!

He answered, "Just give me one quick example now."

I said, by way of penitence for even having a doubt, "We have a small LGBT running group just across the street at the shelter by the running trail. Every Saturday morning, nine AM. You can call me for information if you like. I'm—"

"I know who you are—Judge Behn. I've seen you in the paper. Heard about you on the Force."

"And I know you." It occurred to me. I'd seen him in the paper, too. You're—"

"Jimmy Melbourne. Pole vaulter."

But he seemed familiar beyond that.

"Although sometime pole vaulter," he added. "Present-day policeman."

We shook hands. "Sometime judge for me," I said, smiling.

He moved gracefully away. There wouldn't be any doubt in his capacity to run a few miles. Part of his story was that his career had been ruined by a broken foot, but there seemed no trace of that now. He was six foot two, in emphatic black, and he moved the way accomplished swimmers move, although there seemed to be catch to his shoulders.

"I'll get in touch with you," he said.

"You can get my email address off my website—I have one now for my poetry. Herbert Behn."

"A judge writing poetry," he observed. "How does that work?"

"Pretty well."

That night I tried writing a poem about how he looked, but I found him impossible to capture.

Jimmy did email me, and eventually we did talk over the phone. He finally decided against the Frontrunner training runs, out of fear of being found out on the police force as well as by his athletic dynasty of a family here in Carleton Park. I knew all about that, recollecting. Instead he joined me for one of my Sunday long runs, saying that just because I was wearing a Gay Pride cap, people didn't have to conclude he was gay, too. I took him on my Hilton Street route, one that, unusually, crosses the entire city.

Approaching our biggest hill toward the end—and in the eighty-degree heat—he said, "That whole thing is underhandedly devastating, man. I mean, to look at." At that moment, I was grateful to him for defining what I had been feeling for years when I arrived at the foot of this last hill. At this point, it seemed as if we had to run through a great bar of sun, across the railroad tracks, through the district of old houses and the Keystone Café (funky, overpriced, and featuring poached eggs), and up to the top of a mountain pass which promised a mirage or an oasis of green trees and much shade. The Iron Butte Climbing Columns (where we shared our admiration of the nearly naked young athletes, who were wet and tanned against the stone, again) were now behind us. And in this context, once he had heard about my plans to go to the Gay Games, he seemed intent on joining me.

"But what about you being found out there?" I asked, toweling off—we were back at Amazon Park by the time I got wind enough to say all this.

"Who's going to know in Canada?" he said. "Seems like the perfect opportunity to find out about Gay Pride, since I've chickened out on all the places here and in Portland. Isn't there a parade along with a sports festival—in a safe zone? The only thing is—would you be willing to share your car and your hotel room with me?"

"That's not a problem," I answered. "I wasn't able to find a roommate in the first place, and I'd be glad to split the cost. What with the retirement and limited income. But do you think you can get the time off?"

"I have a week coming to me," he said. "That's what it would take to do Vancouver."

He was right. Five hundred miles did not seem far off, but if you were going to take in a chunk of the sports festival besides your own event, and allow for arrival and exit, that's what it would take, for sure.

So a few weeks later, we launched out. The drive up there was smooth and sunny, after an unusual intervention of early August rain. We spent a night in Seattle, where I took him to Golden Gardens—the beach, sacred to me, where I had scattered the ashes of my father, just a year before. The huge and dignified cirrus clouds in their glowing burnt orange, and the assemblage of sailboats on the perfect blue below formed a kind of heraldry for the remembrance of my dad, who, although living in Carleton Park, had made a special request to be cast among the atoms which had been my mother; she was in the very veins of the yellow trees which grew at the base of the cliffs, because her ashes had been scattered there as well.

The meditativeness, brought on by this visit, followed us the next morning as we neared the border into Canada. Jimmy was wearing a tank top at the time, and he blushed as the flattened roofs and the chain-link fence of the holding station came into view.

"Already, already," he said, "I have pulled many people over as a police officer, and found they didn't have their driver's licenses with them. I feel as though my karma may be coming up now. This woman will find something, I'm sure."

He took his passport from the pocket of his jeans. I had mine out as well. The Canadian agent who leaned into our window looked Jamaican. "And what are your reasons for going into Canada?" she asked.

"We're doing a sports festival," I said.

"Ah, congratulations," she answered. "The Gay Games. We're very proud of you here."

With the sound of "congratulations," Jimmy's hand shook holding the passport.

"You're Jimmy Melbourne?" she went on, leaning in further. "The famous pole vaulter? Do they have a pole vault event? I wasn't aware of that."

"No," he told her. "We're just running."

His face had broken out into sweat, and she smiled again. "Have a good time. See you in a week."

We were silent for a mile or two into Canada. "By God, that woman was informal," he said.

"That's the gay part," I told him. "No doubt she's one of us."

"I've never been to Canada before," he said. "Although I've been in meets all over the world, never in Canada. Somehow I thought I might be able to slip in without any association with the gay thing."

"I don't know what you might be expecting, really."

"I could have told them we were going to the Butchart Gardens in Victoria," he said. "As a kid, I had the Viewmaster slides of them."

I had seen those myself. English boxwood and the Star Pond. The Quarry Fountain seventy feet high. Endless burning red and yellow begonias beneath geraniums in a green house.

When we arrived in Vancouver an hour later, we found, in the courtyard below our rooms, a garden of similar flowers, accenting a swimming pool. The Gay Games 10K was the next day.

"I have the strongest desire," he said, unpacking his underwear, "just to jump ship now, and take a slow boat to Victoria. 'I'd Love to Get Ya on a Slow Boat to Victoria.' Get hidden behind the ferns, and then have an exit reason for being in Canada once we go back into the U.S. Five will get you ten the American agent wouldn't say he's proud of us if we told him."

"And who cares?" I asked.

I was setting up my toiletries in the bathroom. I was calling to him over my shoulder. I could see him in the mirror. Through with his unpacking, he was taking off his sweaty pink tank. Although, because of our running together, I had seen him wear far less, the intimacy of the situation caused my chest to tighten. He had remarkable blonde-reddish hair and a kind of perfectly formed abdominal cage which was no doubt one of the past secrets to his success as a pole vaulter, all of which had, still, come to crash. I had the presence of mind to add, "Are you afraid the media's going to get a hold of your name up here, or see you in the parade?"

"No. I'm known," he answered. "But not that known."

"Well, then, what, then?"

He stripped off his underpants and slacks. "It's what I said about karma," he told me. "Ten years ago, at eighteen, I gaybashed a drag queen. It was just outside what was then called Pedro's, the one gay bar we had in town. The man was known as the Young Divine. Really very handsome, really very pretty. He came on to me, and I was drunk. I hauled off and punched him in the face. My case would have been sent to your court, but the D.A. dragged his feet so much in bringing everything to trial, it was cold by the time additional evidence arrived—a woman had seen me punch the queen on the street, and she had been slow to come forward. Also my parents had just the right pull. They knew which attorney to hire. My name as a brilliant athlete even then helped me. Later I won the decathlon. It was set right."

I came out of the bathroom. I remembered reviewing the case. Now. He was right—it had been plain as day it would have gone into my court. My relief back then had been extraordinary. I knew there was no way in hell I could have sentenced this near teenager (two years past the incident now made him twenty) without overcompensating and throwing the book at him. Being closeted myself, I had everything to prove to the world and to myself that I was sympathetic to gays and to all the political groups that had rallied behind the "Young Divine." It was at that time I began to feel I was walking around with a time-bomb ticking inside myself. Or I could think of myself as doing pole vaulting and being just on the verge of falling down on my face.

I came out of the bathroom, took out my running gear and put it in the one drawer below the television that was still free. Jimmy had gone naked to the window and stood behind the filmy white curtains. My refusal to respond immediately was raising a tension altogether different from the one we had first known in Amazon Park.

"I wish you had something to say," he told me.

"Your story isn't altogether surprising," I answered at last. "At eighteen, you were just a walking mass of hormones anyway."

"I'm in A.A.," he went on. "In A. A. now. He's one of the amends I'm going to have to make in order to stay sober, hormones or no hormones. His charges were right, but I was told by my attorney to deny them."

Again, I waited to answer. His nakedness, both emotional and physical, was so strong, I felt nearly ready to pass out. I had known this was on the horizon for some time. At sixty-five years old, I was new to sex (some flings with women and a few men, but all out of town and all ephemeral and under stress), and the prospect of making love with a man friend in his late twenties in a protected room nearly frightened me out of my wits—and even my desire to make up for the past.

"You're rather well known," he said, "for lecturing convicted criminals in court about their offenses. All this time I've been imagining what you would say to me once I told you."

"I would want to tell you to go and sin no more—that is, come out and live an open life, then you wouldn't have to go backwards into violence and booze as cover-ups, but how could I do that, when I couldn't come out myself?"

Relieved, he came over and put his hands on my shoulders. Then I took off my sweaty shirt and undershirt, and stepped out of my trousers and pants. He put on a lubed condom and I draped myself across the white bedspread of the appropriately queen-sized bed. He entered me and then came up against my back, pressing his thin but heavily muscled chest into my body. I went straight over the crest and emptied myself while he continued thrusting. At last he reached his peak, widened himself inside me, and then we turned and came down into an embrace. Lying there, I noticed the thickness of my chest, my arms, as well as his. I felt muscular from my hips to my ass, because everything was for him, and was him, moving straight at me. It was as if, in the Greek myths, I had been visited by Athena, who enhanced men's bodies, to make them more beautiful for the beloved.

"I have another confession to make," he said, as we lay together, spent and under the covers this time. "I informally tracked your movements—as a runner—throughout town. I knew you'd probably be in that bathroom on Sunday morning the way you always are when you're done. I work Sunday mornings so it took some ingenuity to figure out a way of 'running into you.'"

"Did you want me that much?" I asked.

"I wanted you," he answered tactfully. "But I wanted even more the pride you had on your cap. How was I to get that when I've been ashamed all my life?"

"You'll see tomorrow how to get it," I said. I was stroking his hair, his chest. He sat up and kissed me on the neck.

"I never imagined this would be something to be proud of, too," he observed. "But it is."

The next morning we ran the 10K in Stanley Park, right along the stone sea wall. The sun came up, a blinding torch above the water—so blinding I wanted to keep my head turned while I was running. Jimmy, in a yellow tank top, was gone and away from me in the first minute, and finished in overall second place. He was given a medal and had his picture taken.

I finished third in my age division (there were only three of us), but I thought it was part of my humility to take the medal anyway. Next morning, we marched with all the gay athletes in the vanguard of the enormous Vancouver Gay Pride parade, and I could see that Jimmy was moving past his reluctance to be known while still resting in the assurance that no one on the endless streets of the city would know who Jimmy Melbourne was. Besides, along with the balloons, drag queens, topless men, and nonstop disco floats, there were contingents of gay firefighters, gay policemen, gay doctors. I suppose I should have looked for one for gay judges. It was a thrill to wave our multicolored Gay Games flags, and clank our medals with the rest of them.

Back at the hotel room, we made love again. We drew and drew at each other as though trying to restore ourselves for our return. I could feel there was everything to face once we got back to Carleton Park. This time through, we would not be stopping in Seattle. I had already paid my respects to my mother and father. In many ways, I wished that we could do the same with Jimmy's parents, since they, perhaps, formed the most formidable obstacle, should he and I think of going on together. They were alive.

We had the border nearing us again the next morning, when Jimmy, who was driving, said, "You have no idea what it's like having a line of athletic champions in your family history. If you were to look at my family tree, you would see a line of discus throwers like a row of flying saucers. And then my father the revered decathloner who didn't win in Mexico in '68 but certainly distinguished himself. What would they say if they knew about me?"

"They'd have to say you were in line with the Greek tradition," I answered. "All athlete and all gay."

"Unfortunately," he said, his face falling as the line of stopped cars came into view—we were at the checkpoint—"we're not living then but in the present day where the men in the locker room—at least at the police station—put a towel around them even when they're pulling on their shorts."

A kind of freeze came over us now, not just because we were about to be checked but also because we were nearly back to our own original lives.

Our agent was a skeptical man—damn!—and wasn't thrilled to hear we had been at the Gay Games. He was dark and mustached—a man in his thirties whose eyes suggested cunning. He handed our passports back. Good, I thought, good. At least we're past stage one.

However, many things had been stacked in the back seat, including some pillows which Jimmy had brought for his back when he was sleeping. They covered our clothes underneath.

The man asked, "And are you two the only ones in the car?"

Jimmy and I looked at each other.

"The only ones?" I asked.

"Is there anyone else in the vehicle—hiding?"

"No," Jimmy told him. And started to sweat.

Seeing that, the agent asked Jimmy and me to get out of the car while the back seat was searched. Finding nothing, the man then asked for the key to the trunk. "Always good to have a look," he said, slamming it after a glance. "You can go on now."

Instinctively I knew Jimmy was too shaken to drive off, and so in a kind of dance that might have belonged to an aged couple, I simply got out and took the wheel while Jimmy sat in my place and slammed the door.

Looking straight ahead, we were silent a mile or two upon entering into a new country and what was to be a new life.

"What the hell do you think he was looking for?" Jimmy asked, and put his hand on my shoulder.

In the future, I would always think there had been a couple of bodies— our own—under those pillows—the old invisible selves we had brought back for burial.

# Contributors

**Henry Alley** is a Professor Emeritus of Literature in the Honors College at the University of Oregon. He has four novels, *Through Glass, The Lattice, Umbrella of Glass,* and *Precincts of Light,* which explores the Measure Nine crisis in Oregon, when gay and lesbian people were threatened with being made silent. His stories have appeared in journals over the past forty years.

**M. Arbon** lives and writes in Toronto. They are a regular contributor to the online gay fiction webzine *Shousetsu Bang\*Bang* under the name Hyakunichisou 13.

*Fun with Dick and James* is **Rich Barnett'**s first collection of published stories. As evident by his writing, he not only enjoys romance but comedy as well. He's an expert on gay life in Rehoboth Beach, Delaware.

**Matt Caprioli** attends the MFA program at Hunter College. He was a freelance reporter in Alaska for three years, and works as an English tutor. His phone is full of peculiar stories.

**Jonathan Corcoran** is the author of the story collection *The Rope Swing,* published in April 2016 by Vandalia Press, the creative imprint of West Virginia University Press. His work has been named a finalist for the Flannery O'Connor Award in Short Fiction and a semi-finalist for the St.

Lawrence Book Award and is forthcoming in the anthology *Eyes Glowing at the Edge of the Woods: Fiction and Poetry from West Virginia*. He received a BA in Literary Arts from Brown University and an MFA in Fiction Writing from Rutgers University-Newark. He was born and raised in a small town in West Virginia and currently resides in Brooklyn, NY.

**Lou Dellaguzzo**'s stories have appeared in *Hot Metal Bridge, ImageOut-Write, Hinchas De Poesia, Best Gay Stories 2014* and *2016, Jonathan, Glitterwolf, Chroma, HGMLQ*, and two editions of *Best Gay Love Stories* and *Best Gay Romance*. His chapbook *The Hex Artist* won first place in the Treehouse Press (London) Fiction Contest.

**Mike Dressel** is a writer and teacher living in New York City. He has been published in *Litbreak, OCHO: A Journal of Queer Arts, The James Franco Review*, and *Vol. 1 Brooklyn*, among other places.

**Edgar Gomez** is an MFA candidate at the University of California, Riverside, with a focus in nonfiction. Sure, he would love a chill pill. You can find him on Twitter, Tumblr, and Youtube @ edgarsucks.

**Carlson Heath** is a professor, artist, and horse trainer currently living in rural western Nebraska.

**Troy Ernest Hill** has written fiction, plays, and poems, including the novel *Myzocene* and the short fiction collection *Whatever Makes You Happy*. His work has appeared in *Sobotka Literary Magazine, Underground Voices Magazine*, and *The Circus Book*. Originally from Atlanta, Georgia, he is a graduate of Washington and Lee University and lives in New York City and the Catskill region of New York State. Learn more at troyernesthill. com.

**Thomas Kearnes** grew up in an East Texas county infamous for its teen pregnancy rate. His small hometown bordered Tyler, world famous for its roses and being bereft of an interstate. His maiden short-story effort sold to a long-defunct horror venue. His then-boyfriend boasted to the local patrons of the gay bar, boasting he fucks an actual author. Kearnes realized then being an author might get him laid. To date, he's published roughly 120 short stories, flash stories and essays His collection, *Steers and Queers*, is forthcoming from Lethe Press

**Mark William Lindberg** is a queer author, theater-maker, and educator, living with a man and a dog in Queens, NY. His novels *81 Nightmares*, *Forest Station*, and *Queer On A Bench* are available on Amazon. You can find him on Facebook and Twitter, posting tiny poems on Ello and fiction fragments on Tumblr, and interviewing other humans who write things at markwilliamlindberg.com.

**David Barclay Moore** is a writer and filmmaker, focusing on Black cultures. He was born and raised in Missouri where he read too many novels and comic books as a child. His own debut novel, *The Stars Beneath Our Feet*, will be published by Knopf in September of 2017. A Yaddo Fellow, David has received grants from the Ford Foundation, the Jerome Foundation and the Wellspring Foundation. He now lives and works in Brooklyn and is constantly trying to see the world differently. Follow him online at DavidBarclayMoore.com, on Twitter at @dbarclaymoore and on Instagram at dbarclaymoore.

**David James Parr** is a playwright and author. David's full-length play *Slap & Tickle* has been produced all over the U.S. David lives and works in New York City.

**Jerry Portwood** is currently the Editorial Director of RollingStone.com. Previously he was the Executive Editor at *Out* magazine and the Editor in Chief of *New York Press* and the founding editor of CityArts. His work has recently been published in the *New York Times*, the *Atlanta Journal Constitution*, *Backstage*, and *DuJour* magazine. He teaches an arts writing course at the New School in New York City. Jerry and Patricio were legally married in January 2015 in New York City.

**Val Prozorova** is an erotica and science fiction writer based in New Zealand, who dreams of traveling out of the country as often as possible. She was lucky enough to be a speaker at Eroticon in London earlier in 2017, and hopes to get more people appreciating the intricacies of the genre through her work. Val has been published by Less Than Three Press, Sexy Little Pages, #Trans, Polychrome Ink, and others, and you can find more information about her and her work on Val's website: valprozorovawriter. space

**Martin Pousson** was born and raised in Acadiana, in the Cajun French bayou land of Louisiana. He is the author of *Black Sheep Boy*, winner of a National Endowment for the Arts Fellowship; *Sugar*, a finalist for the Lambda Literary Award; and *No Place, Louisiana*, a finalist for the John Gardner Fiction Book Award. His writing has been featured in *The Advocate, Antioch Review, Epoch, Five Points, Los Angeles Review of Books*, NPR's The Reading Life, *The Rumpus, StoryQuarterly, TriQuarterly*, and elsewhere. He now lives in downtown Los Angeles and teaches at California State University Northridge in Los Angeles.

An introvert but dedicated reader and author, **George Seaton** lives in Colorado. He admires horses, dogs, and honest men. His newest novel, *Listening to the Dead*, is a paranormal mystery.

While **Brett Stevens** has been an avid reader his whole life, he started writing fiction about four years ago. He joined a writing group online, Gayauthors.org, and has been promoted to Signature Author and is now on the author promotion team. He has written four novels published online and two novellas as well as several short stories. His story "Jager" won the Secret Admirer contest under the pen name, Cole Matthews. Stevens lives in Minneapolis with his husband Randy and collects antique cookbooks, goes on biking vacations, and is writing a new novella based on childhood events.

This is **Stefen Styrsky**'s third appearance in *Best Gay Stories*. "The National Gallery" in this year's volume is part of an unpublished linked story collection. His work can also be found online at *Great Jones Street* and *Litbreak*. He holds an MA in Fiction from the Johns Hopkins University and is on the staff of the *Tahoma Literary Review*. He lives in Washington, DC.

Raised in London, **Dave Wakely** has worked as a musician, university administrator, poetry librarian, and editor. Currently a freelance copywriter after completing a Creative Writing MA, he lives in Buckinghamshire with his civil partner and too many guitars. His stories have been published by *The Mechanics' Institute Review, Ambit, Holdfast, Chelsea Station, Shooter, Prole, Token, MIROnline* and *Glitterwolf,* and he has recently been short-listed for the Retreat West First Chapter Competition. He blogs at theverbalist.wordpress.com.

# Editor

**Joe Okonkwo**'s debut novel *Jazz Moon*, set against the backdrop of the Harlem Renaissance and glittering Jazz Age Paris, was published by Kensington Books. It won the Publishing Triangle's Edmund White Debut Fiction Award and was a finalist for Lambda Literary Foundation's Best Gay Fiction Award. His stories have been published in *Love Stories from Africa, Shotgun Honey, Best Gay Stories 2015, Chelsea Station, Cooper Street*, and *Storychord*. Upcoming work will appear in *The New Engagement*. Joe serves as Prose Editor for Newtown Literary. He lives in Queens, New York.

# Publication Credits

CPSIA information can be obtained
at www.ICGtesting.com
Printed in the USA
LVOW07s1358110118
562704LV00003B/123/P

9 781590 217030